Western Swing

AND OTHER STORIES

by John Thomas Baker

Cover Design: Michael Hale, Artist (A.F.G.F.)
Book Design: Marsha Slomowitz
Cover Photo: Courtesy of Paul Yoo

ISBN: 978-0-9890336-1-92
First Edition

Library of Congress Control Number: 2019916516

Lost Wages Publishing Company LLC
PO Box 1051
Port Townsend, Washington
98368

lostwagespub@olympus.net

In memory of Bill 'Willie' Kush,
David 'Jaws' Haupert,
Thomas (Tommy) Nice, and the three Irish girls,
Mary, Connie, and Helen.

CONTENTS

FAILURE
TO
FILE

FAILURE TO FILE

Robert Hendricks gazed dully out the window of his second-floor accounting office, a cup of coffee in hand. The November morning draped cold and gray. Down on the street below, several cars silently passed. They pulled up to the blinking red stop light, pausing momentarily before moving on. Robert's practice was slow this time of year. His first order of business would be to figure what he might do today. Perhaps he would study some tax research, perform several client file reviews, or other duties that would keep him occupied until something came up.

A battered Ford van slid into a vacant parking spot across the street. For several moments the driver appeared to stare through the windshield, his hands on the wheel as if lost in thought. When the door of the van finally broke open, it revealed a husky man with black hair wearing a worn cowboy hat. Robert took a sip off his coffee, continuing to peer below. The man was dressed in a loose flannel shirt, covered by a sleeveless denim vest. He held a manila folder in his right hand. Robert watched as the man stuck the folder between his teeth, before wrenching up the door of the van to force it shut. Turning back to face the street, he tucked the flannel shirt into his pants. Taking the folder from his mouth, he checked both ways before crossing the pavement toward Robert's building, finally disappearing from sight.

For Robert, there was nothing particularly unusual about this scene. During the last five years the state unemployment office had been renting the first floor of Robert's building. It was just another day of glimpsing a desperate American without a job, another wallet thinned by life's circumstances, searching for some help. Robert stepped away from the window, returning to his desk.

Sitting down, Robert placed the coffee cup aside, beginning to shuffle through a small stack of yesterday's mail. Shortly thereafter, he heard the door of the reception room open and close, followed by the sound of muzzled voices. The intercom cracked into Robert's office, the voice of his receptionist, Judy, coming through the speaker.

"There is a man here," she began, "a Mister Armstrong. He apparently has some delinquent tax issues and would like to speak with you. Should I make an appointment for him, or would you like to discuss?" Robert paused briefly before deciding. "No, Judy. Go ahead and send him in. I have some time this morning."

Putting up the mail, Robert simultaneously heard the phone ring in the reception room. Standing up, he took another quick sip of coffee before the office door began to open. To his genuine surprise the person who entered was the very same man he had just witnessed down on the street. Robert made his customary introduction, holding out his hand in greeting. Although responding with a firm grip, the man turned his head away, choosing not to make eye contact. Robert motioned for him to take a seat in one of the client chairs. As the man slowly settled into the seat, the intercom once again sounded into the office.

"It's Mary calling", Judy reported. "I've got her on hold. Would you like to speak with her before you begin?"

Robert turned and rounded toward his desk. Staring at the intercom, he unconsciously shook his head. "No, Judy. Please tell her I'm with a client and we've gotten underway. Tell her I'll call back as soon as I can."

Upon Robert's response, the man tried to interject. "You can take the call if you want," he volunteered. "There's no big hurry here."

Robert watched as the man spoke. There was a slight drawl to his speech. His face remained downward, his eyes still aimed deferentially toward the floor. Judy held in silence at her end of the line. "No, that's all right," Robert responded. "Just tell her I'll call her back." The receptionist acknowledged his remark, the intercom clicking off.

Robert settled down at his desk. It was easy for him to sense the man's discomfort in his surroundings. He was hefty in stature, the client chair hardly seeming to fit him. His hair was mostly a shiny jet-black, although graying at the temples. The denim vest was frayed and worn, the black cotton pants paling white with wear, the boots aged and rough. Sitting back in the chair, his dark eyes met Robert's attention. The nose and cheeks appeared a veined and puffy red. The man did not look particularly healthy. A battle with the bottle was the silent impression that crossed Robert's mind. He had seen that look before. Yes, the bottle, and all the possible consequences that might come with such a circumstance. The man had yet to introduce himself, so Robert made the inquiry.

"Mason," the man responded, "Mason Armstrong".

From Robert Hendrick's years of experience, Mason Armstrong seemed like a man that likely had some tax problems. And more often than not, problems whose eventual outcome would not be favorable.

"So you have some issues with your tax situation?" Robert questioned. As Mason Armstrong shuffled in his seat, Robert strangely remembered that the man didn't have his cowboy hat. He must have left it on a hook in the reception room. The manila folder lightly wavered in his hands.

"Yeah, I guess the Feds are starting to catch up with me," Mason Armstrong began. "You know, the boys at the IRS. They must have found me at my current address. Last week or so,

I saw your nameplate downstairs when I checked in with the unemployment. I reckon I need to find out how bad things might be, maybe what it would take to make things right." Then the man began to lean forward, his forearms resting on his thighs, a tight grimace crossing his lips before continuing. "But hell, it's sort of hard to get blood from a stone, don't you think?"

Robert sat silent for a moment, before gently nodding at the man's remark. "Yeah," he agreed, "hard to get blood from a stone."

And so the story began. In Robert's particular line of work there was often a confession that needed to be told. Robert had listened to plenty of them over his nearly twenty seasons in the tax trade.

Apparently, since Mason Armstrong's divorce, he had been living on the road for most of three years, moving here and there throughout King County and much of the Peninsula. He had two children from the former marriage. His daughter was now fifteen, his younger son, twelve. Mason had continued to send his ex-wife money whenever he could. But the money was always in cash so they wouldn't get kicked off state assistance, or perhaps lose the health insurance for the kids. Mason had continued to spend time with the children as often as possible, but it was usually at his sister's home in Shelton. Nevertheless, the state remained after him for the court-ordered child support. They had eventually filed a lien against him, the amount growing month after month over the years.

Robert leaned back in his leather office chair. Normally, if this man had entered the office during the tax season, Robert would have quickly cut him off at the pass. During tax season individual tales of woe never made a busy accountant a goddamn dime. For during the tax season time was always of the essence. But today, on this somber November morning, with little of import before him, he let the story continue. For soon enough, whenever this appointment was over, Robert would have to call his own ex-wife back on the phone. Thus, for the time being, it would be just as easy to let the man's probable act of penance take its course.

Mason Armstrong was a carpet installer working for a number of big furnishing stores throughout the region. He got paid by the square-yard on a contract basis. Most of the time he lived regularly in a myriad of cheap motels that rented by the week, at other times camping in his van. In between those jobs, he would check the employment offices to see if short-time work might be available. Armstrong had a brother who lived nearby, and he would visit and stay over with him from time to time. Other than these sporadic occasions at his brother or sister's place, Mason Armstrong was generally on the move. He had lately been busy with work throughout the summer and early fall. But now, with an early winter underway, and the holidays coming soon, things had begun to slow. Some months ago, he had foolishly decided to get a post office box where his mail could be received, one his brother could check on. Possibly, that's how the IRS had tracked him down.

During the man's story, Robert had cast a quick glance at the carpeting on his office floor. Although beginning to wear a bit, it was far too early for any serious thoughts of replacement. Putting this somewhat charitable concern aside, Robert reminded himself that everyone had their own personal problems. They would always be singular problems of course, but still problems nonetheless. When Mason Armstrong had finished his confession, Robert asked him to pass over the manila folder. The man struggled a bit getting out of the client chair. Robert easily noticed the difficulty, thinking to himself that carpet installation was definitely a young man's occupation. And Mason Armstrong indeed was no longer young. He was most likely nearing fifty, appearing prematurely aged by the nature of his work and life on the road. And maybe, just maybe, Robert surmised, by something else in life that he knew too well.

Upon his inspection of the contents of the folder, Robert's yet unspoken professional suspicions rang silently true. Enclosed were about a half-dozen 1099 information forms, all from the furnishing stores for whom Mason Armstrong had worked. These particular forms meant that the outlets were treating Mason as a subcontractor, without a single dollar of taxes having been paid over to the IRS. Included were forms for each of the last three years of unfiled taxes. As Robert pretty much expected, things did not look good, did not look good at all.

Robert was very familiar with this scenario. Over the many years of his tax practice, how many self-employed contractors, commercial fishermen, and other freelancers had blown off filing returns when they found out what the tax consequences might be? And predictably, more often than not, all the money had been spent. Meanwhile, blowing things off was an easy path to take, because the Internal Revenue Service never immediately came knocking at one's door. If only such self-denials could be the end of things. But they never ever were.

And so Robert Hendricks began the obligatory routine that came with his profession. He asked Mason Armstrong if these were all the 1099 forms that Mason had received. Did the man have any records of expense for any of the years in question? Did he perhaps keep a mileage log of all his auto travel from job to job? Did he have receipts for tools or lodging, or any other costs related to his work? And finally, where was the correspondence letter that Mason had recently received from the IRS?

Robert Hendricks got the answers he silently predicted. There were no records of anything spent from job to job. And Mason Armstrong could not be certain of any additional reported forms, he had moved so many times. There also were no records of any expenses from one job to the next. And then came a more reluctant admission. A few weeks ago at the Post Office, Armstrong had balled-up the letter from IRS, before tossing it into a trash can upon its receipt.

Once again, Robert Hendricks leaned back in his chair. He unconsciously raised his arms, clasping his hands behind the back of his head. With his eyes drifting toward the ceiling he exhaled a quiet breath of concern. He tried to consider where the hell to go with this circumstance. Not surprisingly, people like Mason Armstrong were taxpayers that fellow practitioners in Robert's profession kindly referred to as a 'difficult client'. In fact, they were the kind of taxpayer that none of them wanted to see. These clients generally required more time and effort than they honestly deserved. And they usually had little money to pay for the accounting services, and most certainly not the U.S. government.

Robert absently wished he had not consented to see the man this morning. If he had known what to expect, he definitely would have instructed Judy to make the appointment for another time. For more often than not, with this type of taxpayer, very shortly after their shallow moments of resolve had passed away, most never returned. But just as Robert began to consider his response, he once again heard the phone in the reception room begin to ring.

Mason Armstrong must have sensed the measure of his situation. He lazily shook his head, shifting his large torso in the chair.

"Yeah, I figure this deal is pretty screwed up," he started. "Like I said before, I just wanted to find out from somebody where things might stand, just how bad it might be. Perhaps see if I could start to get things straight." There was a moment of uncomfortable pause before the man continued.

"You know, sir, I mean to say......, I mean have you ever had any regrets in life that you wish you could fix?"

There was another silent pause in the room, as if there just might be some heavenly answer hanging in the air. "Now, don't get me wrong," the man continued, "I'm not trying to make excuses here. And hell, I'm still not really sure why I even came here today. I suppose I just needed to find out, you know, one damn way or another, just where I need to go with all this stuff."

Robert could feel the mood changing in the room. Sadly, he'd been here often enough before. Yet the curse of confronting personal financial troubles in peoples' lives simply came with the turf. How many times over the years had discussions in this office really not been about income taxes, not about the Internal Revenue Service, or the consequences of the same? The real things were more about the other circumstances in one's life, things like divorce or death, injury and health, difficulties with family or children, and on and on. Nevertheless, at the end of the day there would always be the one single thing that was ever constant in this business. And that one thing was money. The almighty dollar. And nine times out of ten, the lack of its possession.

And so upon this November morning, Robert Hendricks could not help but give something of an impatient response. "Are you kidding? Who in this world doesn't have regrets? You're not alone on that one my friend."

"Yeah, I reckon not," Mason drawled. "But sometimes I'll tell you, I sure feel like I've had more than my share. And lately, for some damn reason, I can't seem to get these pressures out of my head. Not that I can ever really do anything about them. But I do have these days when I would like to try." Then the man shrugged his shoulders and gently laughed to himself. "Well, at least until I can find an excuse to forget them for awhile. I guess I've gotten pretty darn swell at finding ways to forget."

Robert sat coldly silent, escaping any eye contact with the man, staring at the forms in his hands, thinking to himself. He supposed he could easily follow this expected line of conversation that now had been thrust before him. He certainly knew that he could give it the sympathy it deserved, perhaps delve deeper into all it could engender. But this would not be the place or time.

Maybe in earlier years, whenever these stories did find their way across his desk, Robert would often let them flow for awhile, allow the client to make an attempt at finding their way. But over time, he had also come to know that eventually all he really could give such troubles was a practical resolution. For practical resolutions were the only truths he was honestly capable of delivering. And so, Robert needed to return Mason Armstrong's concerns back where they needed to be. It wasn't that he didn't understand or care. No, he understood and cared all too well. He just knew it wouldn't make any difference in the end.

And so Robert kept to the matters at hand. Mason Armstrong would be requested to go home and attempt to reconstruct his working life the past three years. Where did he work, how many miles did he go? What did he generally pay for the motels while working on the road, what tools and work clothing might he have purchased, anything and everything that Mason might recall in terms of legitimate expense?

It would undoubtedly be difficult, Robert advised. However, the performance of this chore would significantly reduce Mason's tax bill. As Robert spoke, he began jotting down a list of the things he mentioned. Whenever Mason Armstrong was able to return with this summarized information, Robert would then request from IRS what income had been reported for the three-year period. At that point, the delinquent tax returns could likely be prepared and filed.

Robert continued to be frank. There would no doubt be a tax liability. Also, there would be some significant penalties and interest for failure to file. Although the chances were slim, Robert could at least attempt to get some of the penalties waived. Regardless, he would certainly help Mason request a monthly installment payment with the IRS, for as small an amount as the Service might accept.

Robert went on to reassure this client that thousands upon thousands of taxpayers were in the same boat, that Mason Armstrong was definitely not alone. But if he was serious about trying to get his tax issues into compliance, this would be the way it would have to be done. For the time being, Robert would set up a client file. He would hold the information in the manila folder until Mason's return. Upon their next appointment, they would discuss the cost of the tax preparation, and if necessary, a plan for the payment of Robert's services. This is what it would take if Mason Armstrong wanted to get these matters into compliance.

As Robert delivered these directions, Mason Armstrong's eyes returned to looking at the floor, nodding his head in agreement. When Robert was finished speaking, he stood up from his desk, signaling the end of the consultation.

Mason Armstrong pushed himself up from his seat. He took the written list from Robert's outstretched hand, placing it into the chest pocket of his denim vest. Then, appearing uncertain, he raised his hand toward the top of his head, before searching down by the client chair.

"I think it's in the reception room," Robert suggested.

"What's that?"

"Your hat."

"Oh yeah, right."

Mason Armstrong thanked Robert for his time, promising he would get back to him as soon as he could. As the man turned toward the office door, Robert hit the switch on the intercom and spoke.

"Judy, no need for a billing today. Mr. Armstrong will be getting back to me. Also, don't let him forget his hat."

"Okay," Judy responded. "And Robert, Mary just called back again a second time. She says you definitely need to call her right away."

Reaching the office door, Mason Armstrong turned back toward Robert. He raised his eyebrows, something of a pursed smile shaping his lips, as if to acknowledge something of an understanding between the two men. Then he exited the office, the door closing behind him.

When the man had left the office, Robert Hendricks sat back down at his desk. He unconsciously reached over to the phone, placing his hand on the receiver. However, he did not pick up. He knew full-well that his ex-wife had every reason to be angry. He hadn't yet called her to say that he had forgotten to send the

child-support check. On this specific occasion he had no legitimate excuse, he'd simply lost track of the date. Still, he knew
that it wouldn't have mattered to Mary either way. These days,
no excuse would be acceptable to her, whatever the cause.

It wasn't that Robert didn't have the money to pay. That
circumstance, thankfully, wouldn't be the issue today. But it
was also true that the total amount of money they had once
shared together as husband and wife, was now far less than
before their divorce. Before his own troubled fall from grace.
And so, he let his hand slip from the receiver. It was funny to
think about, that there had once been a time when he had felt
a sense of familiarity and comfort when hearing Mary's voice.
But such reassuring moments had long ago faded into the past.

Robert got up from his desk. Back at the office window
he could see Mason Armstrong crossing the street to his van.
Mason walked around to the passenger door before climbing
inside. Robert watched as the man struggled to push his large
frame between the seats over to the driver's side. And once
again, similar to Mason's earlier arrival, Robert witnessed the
man sitting behind the wheel for an extended length of time.
Perhaps, Robert wondered, as if he was trying to decide where
to go next. Then the old weathered vehicle flared to a start, a
puff of white smoke forcing its way out the exhaust. The van
made a right turn at the streetlight before motoring out of sight.

The coming afternoon passed slowly. The November sky
remained low, static, cold. Since it was a Friday and not another phone call had rung, Robert let Judy go home shortly after
lunch. No matter. She would surely begin making up for lost
time once the new-year arrived, with another tax season ahead.

A short time later, Robert bucked himself up and made
the phone call to Mary. He felt obvious relief upon getting her
answering machine, being able to explain his forgetfulness
without rebuke. He wrote the support check and placed it in an
envelope. It would be ready for tomorrow when he would pick
up his own son and daughter. He spent the rest of the afternoon

trying to read some recent changes in the tax code. But with all the time left to himself his mind began to drift.

It was certainly odd to think about, how a tax law, or any law for that matter, was some kind of societal attempt to put a period on the sentence of human behavior. There was little doubt why even the briefest summary of the federal tax code was several inches thick. As the years had passed, Robert had come to believe that all these legal constructs were nothing more than a continual struggle to make order out of chaos. Nothing more than a constant moral battle to thwart and codify the human drama of every man for himself, in a world where there was only so much to go around.

With the experience of passing time, Robert had come to believe that human beings are not really created equal, despite all the symbolic gestures that governments and men of faith were constantly devising in order to make that wish be true. Instead, there were circumstances in life that could not be overcome. This was a singular truth, as unavoidable as the hours of a day. And yet, within the context of that truth, the complicated reality of 'free will' continued to have its reign. Where decisions are made, or not made. Where actions are taken, or willingly avoided, whenever crucial moments might demand. And later, when things had run their course, one looks back at those choices made, and simply wonders how different it might all have been. Those sentinel places and moments, where either fortune or regret had taken their turn.

Not long ago, Robert had started to think a lot about how much he enjoyed going to sleep at night. He had begun to convince himself that this present state of nocturnal comfort might be a product of his daily beleaguered reality. How the stale regularity of his life had become consistently redundant in so many ways. During sleep, his nightly dreams had begun to sustain him. They might be a good dream or a bad one, although it didn't really matter which. And despite the fact that the effects of these dreams were so often unfulfilling, he seemed to treasure their sensation. They were always so wildly different from what his real life had become.

Darkness came early, and with it a harsh chilly rain. Robert waited until five p.m. to close the office and turn out the lights. As he pulled on his winter coat, a familiar but conflicted remembrance came to mind.

It had not been so very long ago when the closing of his office on a Friday night was just the beginning of his day. It would be filled with the careless anticipation of an evening ahead. There would have been the smooth bite of a blended whiskey, of loud and raucous conversation, and later, the attractive scent of a woman amidst the sound of a razor blade chopping on a hand mirror.

But on this night, on this present Friday evening, Robert remained uncertain. Could it be that these particular recollections were something of a cherished memory, or perhaps an unfortunate regret? Once again, it really didn't matter anymore. For at least on this night, his mind would be clear enough to tell one from the other.

Starting up the car, Robert turned on the windshield wipers. Although there were several different routes to arrive at his next destination, there was one particular road out of town that directly passed by the Patrona Bar and Grill. Sometimes on a Friday evening Robert would force himself to take this direction. It had become something of a test of sorts, a personal challenge for Robert to overcome. Old friends and associates would still be present at the Patrona tonight. But they were the kind of friends who remained steadily capable of managing their lives, as Robert Hendricks needed now to manage his own.

Sometimes on the more difficult occasions, Robert had to force himself to look straight ahead while passing by the Patrona. But tonight he took a gander, easily spotting several very familiar vehicles parked outside. It was then, at that very moment, that he saw the battered van sitting alone on the edge of the parking lot. There was no doubt about it. It was the same worn-out vehicle of a man named Mason Armstrong, who earlier today had hoped to change his ways. Robert was not necessarily surprised by the sighting, for he had come to understand something that once upon a time had previously escaped him.

It was simply this. Those two desperate emotions, one of guilt and the other of shame, would forever remain like eternal lovers. Each and every day they would seek to walk together hand in hand. And yet later, as another dissonant evening began to fade, they would each retreat to their solitary corners, preferring at the last, to drink quietly alone. Robert Hendricks continued onward towards his five-thirty meeting, feeling that tonight he might have a story to tell the group. But instead, his thoughts preferred to wander back towards a man seated at the Patrona Bar and Grill. If only to simply remind him, that to make order out of chaos is never an easy task.

TABLE
SIX

TABLE SIX

Sonny Floyd rumbled his pick-up truck toward the town of Port Swan. The morning was early, just past five. Burdened with a hangover from the previous night, Sonny had no legitimate reason to complain. There was only one direction he could point the finger of any intent or guilt for his present condition. Although hangovers sometimes have extenuating circumstances, claims of innocence are rarely given credence for those who seek excuse.

Reaching the crest of Monastery Hill, Sonny looked out upon Harrington Bay and the Straits of Juan de Fuca. In the middle of its wide expanse a heavy fog bank rested silently on the swell, partially obscuring the Cascade Mountains further beyond. Below the hill, within the harbor of the Haven Marina, the slender masts of sailboats rose like toothpicks towards the sky. Further on, the old brick buildings of the business district lined the shoreline. And perched high on a bluff above the downtown corridor, the homes of the town's populace rested in early morning silence, marked by the red-bricked County Courthouse, its rising clock-tower soaring above.

Sonny figured there was little chance that the fogbank would challenge the land mass today. The heavy mist would likely burn off right where it lay, securing another warm summer day ahead. Warm at least until the late afternoon, whereupon the coastal barometric could frequently change. During most days of a Port Swan summer, as evening approached, a cold marine breeze would often sweep through city, chilling in its wake. This was the price paid for living by the sea. Comfortable summer evenings in towns like Port Swan were rarely in the cards.

However, during the precious month of August, sometimes a different story could be told. In fact, yesterday's weather had been one of those special summer days. The familiar winds had failed to blow, the resulting daylight hours remaining pleasant with the heat. In Port Swan, on evenings such as these, it became a tee-shirt night calling all to play. Teen-agers and tourists roamed the downtown streets. Backyard barbeques smoked into the sky, the residents of Port Swan happy to be living outside their homes instead of in.

Unfortunately for Sonny, this sentient pattern of summer weather had been the cause of yesterday's mistake. After completing his Monday shift at the Evergreen Café, he had chosen to have a quick-one at the Sand and Surf Lounge before heading home. The downtown watering hole had been busy, with good-spirited patrons enjoying the weather. Shortly after his arrival, Sonny had run into a couple of fun-loving guys vacationing from Canada. The two men were hungry for some local color, with money in their pockets ready to burn. Unexpectedly for Sonny, after several drinks into the occasion, there was no turning back.

It could be said that only vacationing tourists and hard-core alcoholics ever drank on a Monday. But occasionally, there were exceptions to the rule, especially upon the siren-song of a warm summer night. Thus became the moral of Sonny's story, and some hours later his midnight surprise. Although obviously unanticipated, he was now finding an early Tuesday price to pay.

Reaching the Evergreen, Sonny was the first to arrive. He unlocked the restaurant, turned on the lights, before setting up the juicer machine. With a paring knife in hand, he began slicing up oranges for the morning fresh-squeezed, the high-whine of the appliance pounding in his head. It became another hellish reminder of his foolish night before, of that something widely-known in America as having 'too much fun'. With the juicing chore complete, Sonny reached for an aspirin bottle in a nearby cupboard, gulping several down with a tall glass of water. He then started up the coffee machine, continuing with his daily preparations.

By about six-fifteen, Sonny was no longer alone. As he set up the cash register, the prep cooks, Maria and Shannon, now stood behind him. They diced up potatoes for the grill, chopped vegetables for the omelets soon to come. Meanwhile, Jimmy, the dishwasher, fumbled with his apron, before setting up his sinks. Freddy, the short-order cook, mixed up the pancake batter, before stacking dozens of eggs for the early morning rush. Sherry, the second wait-person, would not arrive until shortly before seven. That's when the Evergreen Café would officially open its doors to the world at-large.

With the till counted and verified, Sonny began measuring coffee into filters for the brewing machine. Once things got underway, the coffee brewer would run non-stop until late in the morning. The Evergreen had a reputation for the finest fresh-roasted coffee in all of Port Swan, and word on the streets was definitely out. With the aspirin and a first cup of coffee starting to kick-in, Sonny drank down another glass of water. Not long ago, Sherry had instructed him that too much alcohol created dehydration in the body, which she believed was the primary cause of a hangover.

Sonny had been a little embarrassed by Sherry's practical recommendation. Imagine that. Here he was, over thirty-years into his life, and only now had he learned this little tidbit of important information. Sonny wondered why in public school he had not been advised of such a significant piece of precaution. One would have thought that such a reminder would have been eagerly bestowed during a high school health class. But then again, maybe not, for in doing so his teachers would have had to admit an obvious truth about alcohol use and teen-age recreation. But who could blame them? What adult teacher in the world would seek to lose their livelihood upon delivering such a simple prescription? Drinking alcohol in high school? No, never heard of it.

It sure was odd, Sonny thought to himself, the level of outright denial most of the world was still capable of deceiving itself. Yet, these days, on that particular count, he wasn't totally in the dark. He'd been around long enough now to realize that what one sees, and what one gets, don't necessarily walk around arm in arm. Nevertheless, if adequate hydration was an important key to alcoholic recovery, then he would certainly add such advice to his personal repertoire. Better late than never as they say.

The Evergreen Café had opened its doors several years before. And during that time it had become the hip place to 'meet and greet' in the town of Port Swan. That's not to say that the Evergreen was making any serious money. Sadly, in the group's questionable hippie wisdom, along with a bad case of ideological fervor, the Evergreen's owners, Sonny included, had decided to become a democratic cooperative enterprise.

For those who might not understand such an economic formulation, this decision meant that everyone who worked at the café would equally share in both the profits as well as the administration of the Evergreen's business affairs. At the time, the concept had sounded quite egalitarian and progressive. The owners had adopted a business model where the eventual capital surplus from everyone's labor would not simply ascend into the hands of a few. Unfortunately, as a result, there was only one problem. And that problem was that three years later the eventual capital surplus of the cooperative remained just that, 'eventual'.

Take for example, when it takes almost two hours out of a three-hour company board meeting just to decide what colors the curtains will be in the café windows. Well, any serious neutral investor might start to get the picture.

At the outset, Sonny had willingly gone along with this intended macro-economic reality, although it had sometimes challenged his own personal experience. Having grown up in the urban streets of a tough Chicago neighborhood, the rules he learned had usually been 'every man for himself'. But lately, after three years of this so-called 'cooperation', he had begun to have an ideological re-conversion. As far as democratic worker representation was concerned, he was now leaning heavily toward a more pyramidal model of authority, a capitalistic theory of total private ownership and control. And despite the fact that this particular model had historically resulted in either monopoly or some form of economic tyranny, or perhaps both, Sonny figured he might as well apply for the job.

But whenever Sonny might have considered offering such an organizational change to the rest of the cooperative, he was also keenly aware of the expected outcome. Most likely, upon finishing his presentation, he could envision himself standing alone on the sidewalk in front of the restaurant. The café door would be shut and locked behind him. And most likely, he would have looked pretty lame standing out there on the street, still dressed in his waiter's apron, without a supportive friend in town and nowhere else to turn. So, for the time being, it was best to let things pass, to try and keep his mouth shut, and just live another day.

Meanwhile, he kept to the tasks at hand, placing cream-ers on the tables, while checking the condiments to see if they were full. And a few minutes later, when Sherry came walking through the back door of the Evergreen, Sonny was once again reminded why he would never want to leave this place behind.

Yep, here she was, 'Miss Sherry the Divine', in all her winsome beauty. Not even Sonny's rugged morning hangover could halt that little skip-skip in his heart. He watched secretly as the woman hung up her summer coat, before bending down to stuff her carry-bag under the register. Rising up, she offered him a cheery smile of good morning. But just as Sonny began to acknowledge her welcome salutation, he could already see that she was looking toward him strangely. Her head was slightly askance, her lovely lips pursed with concern. "You know Sonny, you look a little peaked this morning. Are you a little under the weather today?"

"Yeah, a little peaked, I guess," Sonny admitted. "I sort of had an unfortunate detour last night."

"An unfortunate detour", Sherry questioned? Then, suddenly shaking her head with a grin, she turned and engaged the rest of the Evergreen staff. "An unfortunate detour," she repeated sarcastically! "That's a pretty unusual way to describe things, don't you think?" Everyone in the kitchen laughed and agreed. Then turning back to face him, Sherry continued. "We're all very sorry to hear that, Sonny. Now, have you been drinking your water like I told you?"

"Not as sorry as I am," Sonny confessed. "But yes, Sherry, I have been drinking my water. Like maybe a gallon so far morning, just as you instructed."

"That's good," Sherry laughed. "You're learning. That's very good. I'm impressed. But remember, you need to drink it little bits at time, not all at once."

With her remarks, Sherry wore this devil-may-care look on her face. She was certainly enjoying rubbing things in just for some fun. As for himself, Sonny secretly wanted to just walk up to this woman, before planting a giant kiss on her lips. But he knew damn well that such an act of volition would not be happening today, and most likely any other day for that matter. Not now, not anywhere, at least for the time being. But such an understanding didn't make his wanting any less. So instead, he just turned toward the restaurant door, knowing it was time to open things up for business. Once again, it was time to get this morning breakfast trip underway, another day of serving coffee and breakfast to those faithful customers in need.

At the Evergreen Café, there were two separate sections of the restaurant needing to be covered. Whenever Sonny worked a shift, he almost always worked the front section. Sherry and others primarily worked the back. The back section was called the Solarium. It was a sun room or atrium of sorts, an all-glass structure attached to the back of the building. The Solarium was actually a very pleasant place to have a nice breakfast or lunch. But Sonny preferred not to work in the Solarium unless it was absolutely necessary. And most everyone at the Evergreen agreed with his decision.

The patrons who chose the Solarium generally expected a little higher level of a dining experience. And as a result of that desire, they expected a little higher level of attention and respect. Sonny didn't argue with such an obvious expectation, just as long as they left a hefty tip. But he had never been able to fit such a required and gracious service profile, and that was just fine with him. Consequently, his regular turf was the front section of Evergreen. This area was where most of the working locals preferred to gather, as well as the steady regulars who liked to smoke. The front section area of the Evergreen was far better suited to Sonny's style of service.

Unfortunately, in the recent weeks, Sonny was silently aware that certain circumstances in his working life were about to change. And definitely not be for the better as far as he was concerned. Other members of the cooperative would certainly argue differently, and perhaps they were right. The problem was that a new restaurant edict was about to come down, and to-morrow the initial announcement would be made. As for Sonny, there was little doubt that the new rule was about to upset his current status quo, and without question send certain steady customers reeling in its wake.

Meanwhile, the ordinary breakfast routine at the Evergreen had gotten underway. The early regulars had begun straggling through the door. Mostly male in gender, they were the working stiffs in the marine or construction trades here in the town of Port Swan. Whenever these young men happened to come in as a group, they usually took either the two or four-seat tables in the front room of the restaurant. Normally, they would order the basic two-egg breakfast, or perhaps a bowl of heated oat meal, or maybe a stack of pancakes with maple syrup and butter. But always, despite their hunger for food, they would surely need that first cup of 'joe' right from the jump.

But whenever one of these early customers might enter the restaurant alone, they would most likely grab an open chair at Table Number Six. Ever since the very first days of the café, Table Six had been the center of the Evergreen's daily universe. It was a large oval table in the front room that could seat about eight in number. From its earliest beginnings, Table Six had quickly become the community nexus of information and local exchange amongst the youthful counterculture of the town.

By its circular design and size, Table Six had consistently promoted a unique kind of human interaction between its patrons. In its own way, Sonny had come to believe that Table Six served this larger societal purpose more effectively than any traditional lunch counter in America. In Sonny's view, whenever anyone entered the world of Table Six, they had to make the personal choice to engage in something beyond their private selves. By their presence, they would usually be called upon to share the elements of their own individual personality and character with others; to give of themselves and perhaps receive something in return. Sure, maybe sometimes they just needed a place to sit and eat. But it was rare that Sonny didn't see a customer at some point either engage a discussion or at least lend it an ear.

And most mornings of the working week, both the servant as well as the master of ceremonies of this Table Six dominion was Sonny Floyd himself. Since its inception, Sonny had become something of Table Six's circus ringleader. And over time, he had also become its corporate CEO, its judicial arbiter, the minister of its church, and whenever necessary its bad-ass cop. And by virtue of this unusual reality, Table Six had strangely become Sonny's own little kingdom. It was his beat, his baby, his journalistic unnamed source. And indeed, ever so slowly, during his current three-year reign, Sonny knew deeply that Table Six had unconsciously become the source of his own personal identity. And he knew deep down, it was an identity blessed with some undefined elements of spiritual inspiration, the very heart and soul of his sometimes disorganized life.

But now, with this new rule only two days away from becoming the law of the land, Sonny was certain it would forever change this special world that he affectionately believed was his own. For only two days from this very morning, the Evergreen Café would officially become a totally 'smoke free' restaurant.

The expectation of such a reality had been coming secretly for several weeks. Even though the Solarium room of the Evergreen Café had always been a non-smoking zone since the restaurant's beginnings, the cooperative had continued to allow such habitual behavior in and around Table Six. But the pressure for a complete smoking ban in restaurants and other locales had been mounting both state and nationwide. And so, on this coming Thursday morning, the Evergreen's singular prohibition would finally arrive. Sadly, Sonny knew that upon this final admonition an eternal dye would be forever cast.

As for Sonny himself, when it came to smoking tobacco, he didn't really have any direct skin in the game. He had never been an everyday smoker. Sure, there had been times with friends over a shot of whiskey or a line of cocaine that he might have chosen to light up. But those moments were rare. As well, he understood that the evidence appeared clear. Smoking tobacco, and even secondary smoke inhalation, was medically bad for your health. Nonetheless, it bummed Sonny that he would likely lose many of his regular Table Six customers. They were mostly customers who either needed a cigarette with their morning cup of coffee, or enjoyed lighting up promptly after a satisfying meal.

And so it angered him that this one specific form of non-violent behavior might cause such a tumult. All his soon-to-be-affected customers were good people. They were otherwise normal law-abiding American citizens, living or working here in the town of Port Swan. Well, maybe they weren't exactly 'normal', or even particularly 'law-abiding' in the traditional sense of those words. But living and breathing citizens they were for sure.

Sonny didn't necessarily begrudge the best notions of a society trying to protect people who seemed incapable of protecting themselves. There were certainly plenty of those folks about, in all sorts of troubled circumstances. Folks even like Sonny himself, who at one time or another could easily become their own worst enemy. Take last night for example.

But on the other hand, how many in this world absolutely knew how long their mortal life would last? None, that's how many! It wasn't like one could simply choose the time and circumstance of their eventual demise. Well, unless of course a person might be choosing an act of suicide. But otherwise, it seemed pretty clear that either God or fate had their own unquestioned prerogatives when it came to one's eventual mortality.

Even as Sonny continued to dish out the early morning's coffee and food, inside his head certain personal judgments kept running through his mind. Consider Mount St Helens, which was just down the road apiece about five years back. Suppose that a person decided to take a little week-end camping trip down that way. And on that beautiful Sunday morning in May, that person awakens and climbs out of their tent. They languidly stretch their torso, breathing in some fresh mountain air. They brew themselves a hot pot of coffee over the campfire. Maybe they even light up a cigarette, or maybe they don't. Then suddenly, without a hint of warning, Mount St Helens decides to blow her ever-loving top. She buries that person and everything in sight for miles and miles. End of story, right?

So, here's the question. Whenever that horrific fateful moment had arrived for them, how much of a consequence had it been that they decided to have a morning smoke. Or perhaps they didn't, because they were a non-smoker. Either way, upon their fateful end, absolutely no distinction had been made.

Sonny knew full-well that someone could take his reckless argument here, and they could bend it any number of ways. It wasn't like he believed one should offer a cigarette to a five-year-old boy. But all in all, it just bugged Sonny from time to time, how some people were always getting into other people's lives, whether for good or ill, or sometimes just to command their own personal views of the world.

But honestly, if Sonny had to reluctantly confess, deeper down he was just pissed-off because he damn well knew the outcome. And that outcome was this. By the end of this very week, all his smoking customers at Table Six would be slowly trudging down to Mom's Diner, which was just a couple blocks down the street. That was going to be the goddamn impact, no doubt about it. And from that point forward, his current world at Table Six would never be the same.

But hell, no matter, for time was of the essence. Sonny Floyd needed to stay on track. To keep dealing with the early arrivals, taking their orders and delivering their food, while keeping the coffee cups full.

As he continued his morning rounds, Sonny could overhear people discussing the latest news on the streets of Port Swan. The boatyard boys were chatting about diesel engines, or re-frigeration problems, maybe bottom paint or mast rigging. The sporting fans were talking Mariner baseball, or the Seahawk football season soon to come. The construction guys were going on about hip roofs, cement pours, or lumber prices. By the end of Sonny's first hour or so, they all would be paying their checks, while reaching for a small gratuity before heading out the door.

A number of these early customers were definitely smokers. And in a couple of days they would be the first ones to get the big surprise. Somewhat ironic, Sonny mused to himself, was that whenever the boat boys left the restaurant, more often than not, drifting behind them was that familiar noxious odor of marine diesel in the room. And although that aroma was downright unappealing for just about everybody, apparently it had not yet reached the current Evergreen Café hit list.

During the early morning rush, Sherry had been helping cover some of the tables in the front section of the restaurant to help Sonny out. Sherry was definitely a keeper in more ways than one. And in Sonny's wistful private world, he would surely love to be doing the keeping. But there was little time for such reflection. Because right on schedule, as the hands on the dial turned toward the nine-o'clock hour, the Solarium section had begun to fill, and Sherry would be busier than a bee in spring. Not to be outdone, Sonny would be back on the hustle as well, as his next group of front-room regulars sauntered lazily into the Evergreen.

Outside the restaurant, the sun had climbed higher in the morning sky, bathing the café in its warm summer light. There was absolutely no chance any fog bank would be pushing its way in today. When the weather was right, August and September were the best months of the year in the Great Northwest. And no doubt about it, it was a season that everyone who lived here richly deserved.

Before his own arrival to Port Swan some years back, Sonny had lived in Mendocino, deep in the interior of the coastal range, high above the fog line of the Pacific Ocean. Most people probably would have called him a hippie, but he never thought of himself that way. He had met his ex-old lady down in Mendocino, and things had been good for awhile. Hidden way back in the hills, he and Carla had lived off the land, even growing a little weed for both sustenance and profit, much like everybody else. But as time went by, things had begun to erode.

Ever since those California days, whenever Sonny looked back at what happened between him and Carla, he couldn't help but view it in two separate ways. When he felt rough about the bad times, he sort of took from a lyric by Lowell George and the band 'Little Feat'. "She was just one more bad habit I was too blind to see." Then, on the other hand, when a certain sense of sadness and regret might strike deeper toward his heart, another understanding would take hold. "Everything comes to pass, and nothing comes to stay." Sonny still wasn't sure who might have been the first to leave at the end of their time together. Last he had heard, Carla was down in the Bay Area going back to school. And as much as he preferred not to think about that final day, it was he, Sonny Floyd, who had closed and locked the cabin door.

Sometime after, Sonny had stumbled into Port Swan, much the same way a lot of other people had arrived in recent years, more by word of mouth than any form of dedicated volition. At that time, Port Swan had become a dying little mill and timber town. It was a place pretty much on life support. As a result, rents were cheap and work was non-existent, which was a perfect formula for Sonny and others. And so here they all were, a disparate band of youthful wanderers, happily living together while trying to make ends meet. And much to this little town's own civic credit, Port Swan was decidedly different from so many other places in America. First, the town was a down-right beautiful place. Second, and particularly unusual, was that the locals appeared pretty damn neutral when it came to the hippies rolling into their neighborhood.

Sure, a few of the Port Swan homeboys had a stick up their ass from time to time. But for the most part, there seemed to be a kind of 'live-and-let-live' attitude in the town. Although the Native Americans in this part of the world had gotten a short-shrift when the initial white invasion arrived, even in their own earlier Northwest history, they had often lived fairly peaceful and respectful among their own. In addition, Port Swan had

always been a seaport town, a rough and tumble place for sure.
And so, with so many unique and diverse kinds of people passing through, chances were probably good that Port Swan had
just become blind to the differences. As a result, even though
the hippies might not have been particularly welcomed, there
seemed to be no militant resistance towards their arrival.

What had sealed it for Sonny was a story his old buddy,
Louie, had to tell. Sonny had known Louie down in Mendocino.
In fact, it had been Louie who had been Sonny's calling card
north to Port Swan after his break-up with Carla. Apparently,
one night in the middle of winter, a surprise snowstorm had
motored off the Pacific, barreling down the Straits toward
Seattle. Louie had run out of firewood at his home, so he had
taken some shelter downtown at the Sand and Surf Lounge.
Hours later, when he stumbled out onto Water Street at closing
time, Louie had failed to get very far. Having reached the middle
of the street, he ended up sprawled in the fresh-white powder
of the storm. According to his later account, he must have appeared like a stricken snow-angel that had fallen from the sky.

Some hours later, when Louie finally regained conscious-
ness, he found himself staring at a pair of tire tracks that had
been aimed directly at his makeshift bedroom. But instead of
being Louie-No-More, the tire tracks had simply circled around
his exposed position, before continuing down the street. For
some odd reason, this particular image had always stuck in
Sonny's memory. And maybe it had sealed for him a certain
understanding that Port Swan might be a place where he could
comfortably be himself. It always seemed, at least in his mind,
the veritable text-book definition of 'live and let live'.

With the Tuesday morning having reached nine-fifteen, most
of Sonny's next batch of regulars had taken their familiar positions at Table Six. Standing at the coffee maker, Sonny took

a silent reflective moment to view his predictable ensemble. He figured that tomorrow might be the last time he would see them all together, once the non-smoking edict went into effect. Only then, did he realize that someone was missing. But it would not be for long.

Outside the café window, Sonny could see the man rolling up to the restaurant on his run-down bicycle. And just like every day before, the man was dressed in a worn-out jacket and tie. His khaki pants were slightly soiled, his hair askew, a pair of sunglasses masking his eyes. Draped over the rear fender of his bike were two side-pouches, one surely containing his traveling briefcase of worldly destruction. Pulling the weathered case from its pouch, he would soon make his appearance. Although it was very likely that this man had a registered legal name, including a known address and social security number, at the Evergreen Café, and particularly at Table Six, there was only one moniker that identified him. He was simply known as 'Doctor Doom'.

As the good doctor entered the café, Sonny placed an infuser of green tea into a glass cup, filling it with hot water. He also reached down for a second jar of honey from the shelf below. The Doctor rarely ordered breakfast at the Evergreen, unless a jar of honey could be defined as a legitimate source of food. Sonny set down the cup of tea, along with a spoon and napkin, as Doctor Doom took his seat at the table. He placed the extra jar of honey nearby, knowing full-well that the Doctor would likely drain the current jar before his daily session at the table would adjourn.

Doctor Doom was Port Swan's local nihilist philosopher, or transcendentalist, or some kind of 'ist', Sonny wasn't sure. Within the Doctor's eccentric mind, he had become something of an iconic religious figure. Each day, he would pull papers and notes out of the briefcase, waiting and hoping that someone at Table Six would engage him on issues regarding the fate of mankind. Whenever they did, the Doctor would regale them with his latest orthodoxies on the tragic state of the universe.

Whenever they didn't, his studious note-taking and shuffling would continue, waiting for a chance. Word had it that Doctor Doom lived with his mother in Port Swan. Due to his odd eccentricities, Sonny figured that the Doctor was likely a pretty lonely guy. And perhaps, most days at Table Six gave him a chance to have an audience, a spiritual following of sorts, or at least some company for part of his day.

Sonny and the rest of the regulars at Table Six were just fine with this genuine necessity. For the Doctor, in some abstract way, fit like a glove into this peculiar menagerie of the human experience. At Table Six there seemed to be an unspoken understanding, one that each and everyone shared. For if any individual member might have been forced to speak truthfully about themselves, each one of them would have had to admit to their own particular unknowns, their own resident afflictions, afflictions that they preferred to keep secret from the rest of the world. Thus, over time, Table Six had slowly become an odd family of sorts. And like most families, there was certainly no fear about picking on each other from day to day. But whenever it came to the hidden truths in each of their lives, nary a stone would be cast.

And Sonny, in his rather unique position as leader of this domain, he slowly became aware of his important role in the drama before him. And with this understanding, he had begun to feel a sworn responsibility to each of them. Because if Sonny was honest with himself, he knew there were similar unrevealed truths in his own life that he felt inclined to safely hide as well.

Across the table, Brownie lit up a second cigarette, the ash from the previous one hardly extinguished. A soft-pack of Pall Malls lay next to his black cup of coffee, always black. Sonny was forced to empty Brownie's ashtray at least once each morning. He knew for sure that Brownie would be one of the folks long gone on Thursday, the first day the non-smoking edict would be put into effect. Down the street at Mom's Diner would likely be Brownie's new morning home, along with many of the others. In fact, Mom's Diner would surely be the last smokers' holdout, along with the Sand and Surf. Those owners would hold out right up to the very last minute, whenever a proposed state-wide ban might be passed and put into law.

Brownie was in his fifties, wearing that rugged urban look that Sonny knew too well. If Brownie hadn't spent the bulk of his adult life at some thoroughbred race track on the East Coast, then Sonny figured he was losing his touch. Brownie was probably from the Big Apple. One could tell by the accent, he was a 'Fuckin-A' sort of guy. Brownie currently lived in one of the small apartments at the subsidized housing units in the center of town. He appeared to have no realistic connection to the locality of Port Swan.

Jimmy, the Evergreen's dishwasher, firmly believed that Brownie was in the Federal Witness Protection Program. Sonny actually agreed, but they had kept this belief strictly to themselves, just to be safe. And wouldn't Port Swan be the perfect place for the Feds to stash a guy like Brownie away? About a year after Brownie's arrival at the Evergreen, Jimmy was bussing the table one morning. And while doing so, he began to crack wise, casually asking Brownie what he had done.

For Jimmy, this off-hand comment had been a big mistake. Brownie had given Jimmy a look to kill, an honest-to-god look to kill. Brownie never said a word, but a clear message was being sent. Sonny happened to be nearby, and when he went to fill Brownie's coffee cup, Brownie mumbled a few words that only Sonny could hear. "You tell that boy to watch his back, if he knows what's good for him." Sonny quietly nodded in response. Ever since the remark, Jimmy had kept his distance, and mum was definitely the word. Still, Sonny and Jimmy couldn't figure out whether Brownie might be a real-life killer, or maybe a big-time snitch. But they both agreed it was probably better not to know.

The mid-morning rush was now underway. Sonny kept the front room going, the earlier aspirin having taken their effect.

Sherry remained busy in the back. The whole breakfast crew was going strong. Together, hands down, they were one of the best service tandems at the Evergreen. No one ever had to wait for long when they were hitting their stride, and each would cover for the other whenever they could. With the warm summer sunshine shining outside in full display, people were out and about, looking for social contact, with the Evergreen Café a good place to engage.

Table Six was now fully in attendance. This included 'Jed the Head' and his father, Howard. Both father and son lived on their separate sailing vessels down at the Haven Marina. 'Jed the Head' was a professional 'dumpster diver', probably one of the best on all the Pacific Coast. 'Jed the Head' didn't need a bank account. He received and paid for everything in cash. That included his slip rent and utilities at the Marina, as well as his daily cups of coffee at the Evergreen Café. Everything else in Jed's daily consumer life was either scavenged or traded for, including food, clothing, furnishings, you name it. Each day Jed worked the dumpsters all over Port Swan, especially the restaurants or the Safeway store on the edge of town. Jed was intimate with the insides of every garbage container in the city, including solid-waste locations like the public dump, the paper mill, and other well-known illegal sites throughout the County.

Jed's father, Howard, was equally eccentric. With his working career as a chemical engineer now in retirement, Howard had bought a boat and sailed to Port Swan to be near his son. Recently, Howard had purchased a beater pick-up truck, working as Jed's driver. Each day, they would cruise their route through town, 'diving' for whatever Jed could find, then sell and deliver the foraged goods throughout the community. No checks or credit cards were accepted, only cash at the point of sale.

Although the average citizen might have looked disdainfully at such an unseemly occupation, Sonny had figured otherwise. Whenever one thought about it, the United States of America was the single largest producer of unwanted waste in the history of mankind. America was a throwaway society that couldn't be matched. So in one sense, Jed and Howard were sitting on a gold mine of continuing available resources, a veritable treasure-trove of constant opportunity, day-in and day-out. And just like those day-traders down on Wall Street, they were simply looking to buy cheap and sell high.

In exchange, all Jed and Howard had to do was personally renounce any concerns about community social stigmatization, as they plowed inside dumpsters all over Port Swan. Their only overhead was the cost of some necessary gasoline, and plenty of quarters for a daily cleansing at the Haven Marina shower-room. And more often than not, their friendly customers usually ended up winners as well. In fact, Sonny had a perfectly good lawn mower back at home, all for the easily affordable price of ten US dollars. Perhaps the pull cord was a little tricky at times, but it ran like a champ.

But to say that Jed and Howard were dedicated skin-flints would be no minor understatement. At the Evergreen, Jed would order a cup of coffee, then attempt to see how many refills he could obtain before Sonny would call his bluff. And there was little doubt the family apple never fell far from the tree. Howard was even more of a cheapskate than his industrious son. On some mornings, Sonny would have to chase Howard out the restaurant door, before shaking him down for a meager cup of coffee. That's when Howard would begin his practiced routine of how much his memory had begun to fail him in his later years. Sonny would simply answer by ripping a dollar out of Howard's reluctant hands, before asking Howard that if his memory had gotten so bad, how come he never forgot to show up at the restaurant each morning. In other words, case closed.

The remaining regulars of this daily Table Six contingent might be more courteously described as 'artists', at least in Sonny's mind. Although this particular label was perhaps a perverse descriptive in terms of definition, there was little doubt that a multitude of so-called 'artists' were currently existing in the local demographic of Port Swan proper. Whenever a person didn't happen to have a job in Port Swan, they could simply declare they were an 'artist', and all would be forgiven. However, Sonny's definition of 'artist' was a little more direct. In other words, they were folks who had truly perfected the art of having time on their hands. And there was no better place to practice such a dutiful pursuit on an everyday basis than Table Number Six at the Evergreen Café.

They were a steady bunch, these 'artists', especially Gloria and Virginia. Each morning, like clockwork, Gloria and Virginia would arrive with their pencils and erasers in tow. One might have the Seattle Post newspaper under her arm, the other the Seattle Times. Neither of the women was there to read any breaking news per se, but rather to work the crossword puzzles. Suffused with their coffee and cigarettes, and perhaps a blueberry muffin, they were prepared for the task at hand. As a result, doing the crossword puzzles allowed no time for Gloria and Virginia, and maybe others at Table Six, to perchance reflect on their employment inadequacies. For at any particular moment, each person sitting at the table might be called upon to assist in the cause.

What had become curiously strange, was how acutely adept Sonny had become at this challenging literary exercise. For some reason, his newly acquired skill must have occurred through some form of daily osmosis rather than any kind of studied behavior. Over these recent years of serving and supervising Table Six, somehow his personal command of both linguistic definition and culture had improved immensely, simply by being in earshot of Gloria and Virginia's daily routine.

For instance, what's a five-letter word for 'a bowl game'? Well 'Super' of course, Sonny would blurt out, followed by a thank-you from either Gloria or Virginia. Although such an exercise might seem trivial to some, such little moments of personal success often make a person feel pretty sharp, and Sonny was no exception. The feeling was like suddenly getting the right answer in class back in your school days. And when everyone sitting at Table Six got to participate, it became a shared positive experience. Moreover, at least for Sonny, this daily crossword activity seemed to make the day go by a whole lot faster. Sometimes, before he knew it, the clock was pushing toward the lunch hour and eventually the end of his work day.

But on this morning, such a pleasant rumination for Sonny was tinged with an unspoken well of anger and regret. For the facts were certain, both Gloria and Virginia were tobacco smokers. And more likely than not, in less than forty-eight hours, a regular Table Six tradition would be heading towards a tragic but predictable exit.

However, there was little chance to grieve. The breakfast rush continued along, the normal Tuesday clientele coming and going without much fanfare. Things were pretty much under control. However, right about the ten-thirty hour, Sonny suddenly realized that another key regular had not shown up at the café this morning. And today, the fact that Jerry Bancroft was missing was of particular concern.

Jerry Bancroft was the Evergreen's resident autistic savant. Perhaps a more careless human being might have called Jerry a 'simpleton' or 'retarded'. For Jerry Bancroft's disability was easily apparent, and had been since his early days of childhood. Sonny and Sherry, as well as the other members of the Evergreen cooperative, had always taken a special care and liking for Jerry, always making sure he was comfortably fed, as well as engaging with him whenever time might permit. Jerry's special genius was for old movies from the forties and fifties.

A person simply had to name a movie title from that period, and Jerry would be able to name all the major actors who starred in the film, as well as most of the plot or action, frame by frame. Jerry's extraordinary skills of recall on this subject were something to encounter.

Most days, Sonny would place Jerry at a two-seater nearby Table Six. To place Jerry at Table Six, well, it was a little over Jerry's pay grade. And yet, from time to time it had to be done. Still, everyone present understood the circumstances, and tried to include Jerry in any way possible, hopefully without upsetting him.

Obviously aware of Jerry's amazing sense of cinematic recall, one particular morning Sonny decided to show off Jerry's special Hollywood talent. With Ronald Reagan currently wandering through his latest performance as President of the United States, Sonny asked Jerry for his rendition of "Bedtime For Bonzo", a film which appropriately starred Reagan, and was released in 1951. By the time Jerry had completed his memorable review, everyone at Table Six was wiping their eyes with tears of laughter.

But just yesterday, something of a traumatic event had occurred for Jerry Bancroft. His arrival had begun innocently enough, with Sonny seating Jerry at an open two-seater in the front room of the café. Per the usual, he then brought Jerry his coffee in the Evergreen's standard glass cup. Terribly, that's when disaster struck. Very infrequently, such glassware had a penchant for cracking upon its filling with heated liquid. When Sonny had put down the cup for Jerry, there began a little pinging sound. This was quickly followed by a loud pop, the cup expanding from the change in temperature. Thankfully, the flawed glassware doesn't shatter all over the room, it simply cracks in place. But the mishap can be quite startling for anyone, whenever it might occur. However, in Jerry's sometimes difficult world, the incident was more than he could endure, and a commotion ensued.

It took about five minutes to calm Jerry down. Sonny did what he could, but it was Sherry who was able to soothe Jerry's fears with her gentle words and a woman's comforting touch. Things eventually got under control, but Jerry had been noticeably shaken. Now worriedly, on this following Tuesday morning, Jerry was nowhere to be seen. For the moment, Sonny was left to wonder, but he made a note to himself to check on Jerry after his shift.

Sonny kept up the hustle as the breakfast hours turned. Although his physical discomfort from the previous evening had seemingly passed, there remained a certain level of disenchantment roiling inside him. He was certain that the imminent 'no-smoking' edict was bothering him, as he began to realize the disastrous impact it would have on his familiar daily routine. He tried to convince himself that this circumstance was why he had felt so compelled to have more than a few drinks on an otherwise ordinary Monday. It was a pretty lame excuse, but what the hell could he do? The cooperative at the Evergreen had made their decision despite his tepid objections. And it was an issue he knew he couldn't win. What was done was done. Nevertheless, his emotional feelings of dispute remained front and center.

One such feeling was a simmering distaste that he felt towards some of the customers in the Solarium section of the restaurant. Without reason, he wanted to blame them for the ban that was soon to come, that it was their complaints about second-hand smoke that had engineered these new rules for the Evergreen. He whined to himself that the town of Port Swan was soon to become their world view, a cleaner and more correct reality, one that the Evergreen Café would now be forced to accept.

In Sonny's opinion, certain types of changes had been on their way. Newly arrived downtown merchants were seeking to make

Port Swan into a theme park, a kind of a seaport Disneyland, one that would have boatloads of tourists wandering the streets every week-end, and all summer long. And down at City Hall, a new urban planning department had been recently installed, it's purpose to create the appearances necessary to effect that singular vision. This new image would be of a perfect Sunset Magazine community, decorated with all the trimmings. And right behind them, there would be 'Bullshit Bob' Beavers and those of his ilk, all looking to get rich at every opportunity.

Bullshit Bob was a card-carrying Christian real-estate broker. And Port Swan had now become his very own mission from god. Bullshit Bob was buying up properties from many of the economically-troubled long-time locals, all for nothing more than a song and a dance. He was placing them on his Monopoly board for later sale. One might contend that the word 'trust' had been conveniently deleted from Bullshit Bob's vocabulary. Instead, the word 'avarice' had a much truer ring.

In Sonny's opinion the color 'green' was Bob's favorite shade, the 'dollar-sign' his preferred numerical symbol. Bullshit Bob's hands were soft to the shake, his hair greased to the slick, his patent leather shoes as pointed as a devil's trident. Whenever he entered the Evergreen with one of his fellow sycophants, Bob had a smile that made Sonny reach for his wallet before racing home to take a long hot shower. As the old homeboys back in Chicago might have described him, 'Bullshit Bob' was the kind of 'flamer' that would put ketchup on a hot dog. He was a damn carpetbagger through and through.

And right behind Bullshit Bob were a host of new 'woo woo' types, or 'new agers' as they liked to describe themselves. Each blessed with their totally pure temples of the body, as well as their medically undiagnosed anxiety issues. Many of them were 'trust-fund' babies who didn't have to work for a living, didn't have a rent or mortgage payment to make, and therefore had plenty of time to complain about how the other-half lived. One by one, these newcomers had begun to make the Solarium room of the Evergreen Café their morning place to gather, to congratulate themselves on their new stations in life, while re-writing the rules of the game in the town that Sonny Floyd now called home.

Meanwhile, the old guard, the longtime good-old-boys of Port Swan, didn't have a clue. Those boys never ate or drank at the Evergreen. Their daily haunt was the Sand and Surf Lounge back down the street. Every weekday morning, they would meet promptly at ten o'clock sharp. These boys had been making their own private deals about the future of Port Swan for a very long time.

In fact, some of the local folks said that not a single divorce case had ever been settled in a court of law for years and years. Instead, the house, the car, the kids, and of course the bank account, had all been divvied up over some bitter cups of Maxwell House at the Sand and Surf. Not to mention all the permits and land deals that had been traded during their late-night poker games at the local Elks Club.

As far as the good-ole-boys were concerned, the Evergreen Café was just that no-count hippie place, frequented by customers that probably needed a bath with a fire hose, or maybe another unannounced visit from the health department. In fact, it had never crossed their minds that any customers who frequented the Evergreen would ever be a threat to their private little game.

But Sonny believed he knew better than the rest. Just like in California, there would soon to be a new regime in town. And many of those folks were presently making their headquarters at the Evergreen Café. If any of these good-old-boys had ever thought to ask him, he would have happily given them the low-down for a few shots of Jack at the Sand and Surf. But these good-old-boys were totally in the dark. They were missing all the signs. Pretty soon, Table Six wouldn't be the only thing to fall.

Sonny continued his shift, all the while trying like hell to get these negative thoughts out of his mind. Weirdly, as he made a pass by Table Six, Gloria questioned the rest of the group. "What's a seven-letter word for 'underhanded'," she queried? Sonny didn't miss a beat. "Devious," he quickly replied. And sure enough, Gloria promptly penciled the word into her puzzle before nodding at Sonny approvingly. Sonny could only shake his head and smile. No doubt, practice made perfect. Yet, on this particular morning, little did Gloria know how perfectly timed her question had come.

By eleven-thirty, the breakfast rush had begun to temper. As his familiar Table Six contingent began to straggle out of the Evergreen, Sonny knew that tomorrow would be the last pure day he would have with them in their present configuration. Yep, tomorrow he would have the unwanted duty to announce the change in policy, already knowing the impact it would have. The following morning, Gloria and Virginia would be up and gone, along with a number of other regulars who liked to smoke with their coffee or breakfast in the morning. Perhaps even Doctor Doom would follow them, for this banished group might be the only family with whom the good Doctor really felt like he belonged.

As for 'Jed the Head' and his father, Howard, they would probably remain, as smoking was not their thing. But for Brownie, there would never be any doubt. Moments later, when Brownie casually picked up his smokes and prepared to leave, Sonny quickly followed him out the door. The two men stood outside on the sidewalk in the morning sun, speaking together for several minutes before Sonny returned inside.

Yes, tomorrow would be the final day. Tomorrow, the Table Six smoking crew would awaken in the morning as if nothing had changed in their lives. They would head for the Evergreen before taking their designated seats. They would begin their normal patterns of behavior, the interior surroundings familiar and thoughtlessly the same. All would seem right with their world. Then suddenly, everything would get turned on its ear. And later that same morning, Sonny would watch as a funeral procession of outcasts shuffled out the door. The ultimate consequence would be this: that an off-beat and unique collection of human engagement had reached its final act.

Sonny worked the lunch hours, going through the motions, a silent sense of discomfort still gripping him within. However, he had to be honest with himself. He knew damn well that on Thursday morning the world would not come crashing to a halt. The smokers would simply wake up, gather their cigarettes and their collective bearings, before moving on down to either Mom's Diner or the Sand and Surf, or any other place wherever smoking might still be in play. Everyone would eventually adapt to their new surroundings. They would create a new reality, and their lives would go on. And Table Six at the Evergreen Café would promptly do the same.

And so the lunch hour came and went, Sonny and Sherry working the rest of the day together. Sherry helped him in the front room, and despite his hysteric distaste for the Solarium crowd, Sonny courteously worked the back. There was no way he would ever let Sherry go it alone.

The prep cooks, Maria and Shannon, by virtue of their unique position between the kitchen and the customers, as well as their constant opportunity to both labor and gossip all day long, each always seemed to know the latest news in town. And not long ago, word had it that Sherry was going through a separation. Although she wasn't legally married, Sherry and her partner had built a house together, which for some odd consequence often led to complications.

Sonny certainly understood that reality. And just as certainly, he had never figured out the reasons why. He and Carla had done the same when they built the cabin in Mendocino. But it seemed like the very moment the house was complete, their relationship had begun to tear apart. Perhaps there was something about this process that led to the truth about themselves becoming known. Whatever it might have been, Sonny still didn't have an answer.

At two o'clock, Sonny flipped over the 'Closed' sign at the restaurant. Another working day at the Evergreen neared its end. Sherry put on her recent favorite cassette of Chrissie Hynde and the Pretenders, while everyone cleaned and prepped for the following day. Sherry leaned over one of the tables setting the condiments in place. Her long brown hair, tied in a pony tail, flowed gently down her back. Sonny silently mimed the lyrics to the song that played, "Don't get me wrong if I'm looking kind of dazzled. I see neon lights whenever you walk by."

Finishing their shift, Sonny and Sherry walked out the back door together, carrying bags of trash towards the dumpster in the lot. As they tossed the bags inside, Sherry turned to him and spoke.

"Sonny, I know you are kind of hurt and sad about Thursday. But it will be okay. You know, everyone will make the best of it, they will find their own way. And you really shouldn't take it so hard. Sometimes things are just the way they are. And often, something new and different arrives to take its place."

Sonny nodded his head quietly. "Yeah, I know, I know. I understand."

A short moment of silence ensued. Then Sonny's head perked up quickly. "Hey, but listen to this, Sherry. I finally got to ask him today about what he did. I figured I had to ask him before he went away."

"Who did what," Sherry questioned, looking confused?

"Brownie! You know, how he ended up in Port Swan of all places. I mean, I always figured he ratted on the mob or something, but it wasn't like that at all. It was just a big arson and insurance scam back in New York City. When Brownie agreed to testify, he told the Feds that somebody threatened his life during the investigation. So they were forced to put him into the program when he agreed to sing. I got to tell you, that scenario never crossed my mind."

Sherry took a step back, staring at Sonny with an utterly perplexed expression. Then she started to laugh convulsively, her hands reaching up to cup her mouth. "Brownie," she tried to ask?

"Yes, Brownie! He's on the lam. Jimmy and I figured it out, but we couldn't tell anybody."

Sherry steadily shook her head. "You boys, I just can't believe you sometimes."

Needing to change the subject, Sonny continued, "Listen, would you come up with me to see how Jerry is doing? I'm a little worried about him. He didn't show up today. It wouldn't take us too long. And I'll buy you an ice cream after we see him. Would you do that for me?"

Sonny knew that Sherry couldn't refuse. Jerry Bancroft was the Evergreen's pet customer of sorts, and Sherry really cared about him. Together, they walked the few blocks up to the center of town. It was a beautiful afternoon, pleasantly warm in the bright sunshine, a perfect Port Swan day. Sonny silently thought back to similar afternoons in Chicago, when he and the gang would often take in a Cubbies' game up in the bleachers at Wrigley, before heading over to Gene and Jude's for a hot dog after the game. It was the sort of bright summer memory that he knew would never leave him.

They checked on Jerry Bancroft and found him okay. They promised him a porcelain coffee cup whenever Jerry returned to the Evergreen. There would certainly be no more glass. Sherry's comforting presence obviously sealed the deal. They left, both believing that Jerry Bancroft would feel safe to return.

After purchasing two ice-cream cones, Sonny and Sherry sat on a park bench at the intersection in the center of town. From their position, they could watch the automobile traffic come and go at the only red light in the county, yet they still had an open view of the calm expanse of Harrington Bay. Side by side, they watched as small groups of tourists wandered on by. They snickered about how these visitors always looked somewhat confused and lost. In between, the locals of Port Swan headed with purpose toward some daily destination. Sonny knew better than to probe Sherry's present personal circumstances, even though he wished he could. But today, he was happy enough to just have her beside him. Feeling relaxed, an unusual admission came forth.

"Sometimes I wonder about myself," Sonny began to confess. "Why the concept of 'change' seems to so often bother me. I sometimes think that the use of that word, 'change', is one of the most prostituted notions in the human language. What is it about the emotion of that word, that in one moment can feel so dramatically fearful and defensive, and in the next so inspiring and seductive?" There was a momentary pause. "I suppose it's true, that nothing in life ever really lasts forever. That the seasons come and the seasons go, and there isn't much left to say."

Sherry sat quietly, licking on her cone, her expression focused in the distance, as if lost in thought. "I'm not sure sometimes," she began. "I guess one really never knows what changes in your life tomorrow might bring. I suppose no one ever really knows. But I do hope that one thing is true. That when the bad changes come, I hope I can survive them. And that whenever the good ones come along, that I will always make the best of them." She turned her head to look at Sonny, as if to seek some confirmation.

Sonny nodded slowly in response, silently wishing to himself that maybe one of those 'good' ones was sitting right here beside him.

"Me, too," he agreed. "Yeah, the good ones. I just hope I don't blow it whenever they might come."

Finishing their ice cream, they stood up and began to walk together down the street, bathing in the summer glow of a Northwest afternoon.

WEDDING
OF THE
WEEK

WEDDING
OF THE WEEK

Birth and childhood are not something that one can choose.
They are only delivered for what they're worth.
As a child, years of time and circumstance must pass
before freedom of choice is granted. And yet,
once such choice is offered, fate may have already
worn a path that cannot be altered, a presence and outcome
that cannot be avoided. Under certain circumstances,
one might choose to never look behind, to never seek a return.
But such a conscious decision can never erase the trail.

DANNY

The Saturday morning flight from Denver had taken several hours. Danny Stone sat in the car rental lot, getting acquainted with the various buttons and dials in the new vehicle. He checked the lights, the wipers, the heater, the radio. A map would not be necessary today. Danny knew the way. It wasn't his first time traveling this route before him, and likely not his last. The path leading 'home' would always remain familiar.

Finding the interstate north, Danny settled in for the journey, retracing the way towards his past. Like so many others, Danny was a member of that greater multitude of sons and daughters that either by desire, or love, or familial obligation had chosen to return. Although it sometimes felt more like obligation, he knew it would always be more than that. By this time in his life more than forty years had passed. Forty years where thoughts of home rarely crossed his mind unless dictated by reflection or request.

The late October afternoon was sky-blue and sunny, the temperature nipped with the presence of autumn. The leaves of the trees were turning with color, the chilling nights of fall prompting the change. As he cruised along the highway, old memories of his childhood began to come to mind.

Slipping back, Danny could feel the roar of a Saturday afternoon football game. He could see the coaches on the sideline, their voices booming across the field. He could hear the static in the loudspeaker announcing the contest. He could see the frosted breath of his teammates while standing in the huddle, see the blue and white bunting billowing on the breeze, the leg kicks of the cheerleaders rising toward the sky.

He recalled a moment during one of those games. While waiting on the field during a stoppage of play, he caught sight of his little brother, Ronnie, crawling with his friends under the chain link fence at the far end of the stadium. Danny laughed to himself as he sped further down the interstate, for it was the same spot that Danny and his friends had used several years before. And just like themselves, Ronnie and his pals had carried along a football, before choosing to play their own game behind the bleachers as the high school game played on.

Now, decades later, Ronnie was living in Florida, working for a firm that contracted with NASA, and living near Cape Canaveral along the Atlantic Ocean. Although the two brothers had not seen each other since their father's death fifteen years before, they did speak occasionally, usually around a birthday or holiday. In between, they kept tabs on each other through their mother, who would pass on any current news or updates.

It seemed that Ronnie and his wife were generally happy with their lives, enjoying their work, family and friends. And Danny figured he could pretty much say the same. But it was odd to think about, how quickly their childhoods had suddenly turned into an adult life, each finding their different paths. Luckily, things had worked well enough for he and Ronnie, as their bond remained strong without the necessity of discussion. Sadly however, it had not been the same for their other brother, Billy. Shortly after his childhood years, Billy Stone had left his family far behind.

It was always hard to think about Billy, for a sense of guilt would always make its play. Billy had never made this trip back home. Danny understood that every family endured their own troubled facts of life. But to lose a brother would never be an easy thing to accept. His parents couldn't help but blame themselves for this terrible outcome. And over the years, even though the family's loss silently became accepted, the reasons would remain forever certain.

Billy was their middle brother, the quiet one from the very start. And even though he may have escaped the worst of the crossfire between their mother and father, he had likely become the most affected. For as soon as Billy was able to break the familial bonds and venture out on his own, he was gone, headed for California.

The destination made perfect sense. In high school, Billy had taken up surfing, driving with his friends for the Atlantic beaches every chance he could find. The choice was one way of taking flight from the family tumult, to find some peace away from the conflict. Eventually, California was something of a no-brainer decision for a kid that loved to surf. At the time, Danny had been finishing college in Denver, and Billy had visited while passing through. Danny could never have imagined it would be the last time he would see his younger brother.

But all these years later, that remained the reality. Along the beaches of Southern California, Billy had met an Australian girl. Within a year, he had crossed the Pacific Ocean, leaving his past ever further behind. In the many years hence, there were always Christmas cards to the family, wishing a happy holiday. There was a wife and two children, a job as a long-distance truck driver. There was a home on the Mornington Peninsula south of Melbourne, with surfing beaches nearby. But there was never a single visit back to the states. Although it would always remain a hard thing to accept, Danny couldn't really blame his brother. Billy had found his own way out and that was enough.

The interstate traffic was light as Danny made his way toward his destination. Saturday afternoons were often a good time to travel. He was about an hour away from the site of his week-long mission ahead. His sister needed a break from the extra load she had been carrying each and every day. Upon his arrival, both Kelli and her husband, Jack, would be packed and ready to go the very next day. They would be heading to South Carolina for a week's vacation. Danny would stay at their home, spending the time to visit and look after their mother. With her full-time job, as well as her constant care responsibilities on behalf of their mom, Kelli was getting worn to the bone. And so Danny had made arrangements to come and offer some relief.

Over the past several years, their mother had begun a pre-dictable fall. Shortly after the death of their father, the family home had been sold. Jean Stone had been moved to a small townhouse only several miles from Kelli and her family. Jean had managed to live independently for quite some time. But one day, Jean's neighbors had called, expressing concern about her driving. Things had become unsafe. Soon, something would have to be done, the car taken away and options explored. But before any decisions could be made, a fait accompli had occurred. Their mother suffered a broken hip while simply walking through her kitchen. Hospitalization and replacement surgery ensued, followed by two months of rehabilitation in a nearby care facility.

And so a die had been cast. The townhouse was put up for sale. From his home in Colorado, Danny dealt with the realtors, gauging the market and the offers, while Kelli searched for an assisted-living facility that might be close and affordable. In the meantime, their mother had lived for a time with Kelli and family, until the townhouse could be sold and the money received.

Finally, an opening presented itself at a place called Windsor Hill. But assisted-living facilities were by no means cheap. The cost would be far more than Jean's pension and social security, by as much as two thousand dollars a month. Danny had calculated the financial projections. They would have maybe three years on the outside before all the savings were drained. There would be no inheritance to split. In fact, it would be just the opposite should their mother continue to live. And Windsor Hill would make no guarantees that Jean could stay in the facility. It had only a small number of Medicaid rooms available at any one time. Danny figured their mother's funds were now down to eighteen months and counting.

Throughout all these arrangements their mother had been kept in the dark. Just dealing with her declining health and loss of independence were enough of a burden. Danny knew that the family was probably luckier than most. At least they had bought some time before more difficult choices would have to be made. Still, the clock was ticking. And even now, according to Kelli, Windsor Hill itself was no piece of cake. Despite the money spent, the care was sometimes questionable.

As Jean's only family advocate, Kelli had to be tough and resilient on both ends of the situation, trying to deal with her mother's emotional needs, as well as the facility's level of care. While meeting these constant pressures, his sister would break down from time to time. And being seventeen hundred miles away, Danny could do little but console her from afar. All he could do was to let her vent, then try to buck her up.

Nevertheless, there had been at least one silver lining throughout the difficult transition. For their mother would now be barred from her long-time addiction. Jean Stone could no longer access the one thing that had cut through the life of their family like no other blade. In Jean's case it had been the curse of alcohol. But in these days and times a family could take its pick.

However, according to Kelli, the prior hospitalization, as well as the six months living in her home appeared to have done the trick. And even before, their mother had often been able to go long stretches without her favored crutch. Still, Kelli had been surprised there had been such little physical impact. So, at least for the foreseeable future, their mother's troubled abuse of drink would not be an issue with which they had to contend.

The drive was now less than thirty minutes away. The world outside the car continued to become increasingly familiar, filled with further thoughts and childhood remembrance. Danny felt excited to soon be seeing his sister. And even better, tonight he would be seeing the mother he loved, not the other woman whose erratic behavior had so often disturbed their emotional lives.

JEAN

Jean Stone slid her bottom uncomfortably within her recliner chair, trying to ease the ever-present soreness, seeking another position to relieve the constant daily discomfort of sitting for hours at a time. Finding a moment of relief, she reached for her can of Boost, drawing a shallow sip from the straw. A short distance away, the television screen flickered before her. The remote control rested across the bend in her waist, the volume raised loud enough to hear. It was a Saturday afternoon, and like every Saturday this time of year, Notre Dame was playing a football game. The announcers became her only company to keep for several hours of time. She watched the college kids so joyful and exuberant in the stands, the players in uniform jumping wildly upon each other whenever they scored a touchdown. Intermittently, her eyes closed, nodding off to rest, flickering back whenever an audible change in sound might cause her to awaken.

When the game was over, Notre Dame had lost. In recent years, the Irish were not as good anymore as they used to be. There had been a time when they were always the best. But those times had somehow gone wanting over the years. Turning her head to look out the window of her room, Jean could see that darkness was beginning to fall. The afternoons were now getting shorter every day. Still, she felt an anxious excitement, hopeful and expectant that her eldest son would soon be getting close.

All day long it had been difficult watching the clock pass so slowly. If she had been at her own home, she would have had Danny's dinner ready to prepare. The spare bedroom would have been arranged and cleaned. All the family favorites would have been stocked inside the kitchen cupboard. She would have welcomed her son's company for as long as he could stay. But today, as the afternoon waned, Jean could only wishfully await her son's arrival. She had instructed her daughter to immediately call upon Danny's arrival, if only to know that he was safe.

Then suddenly, she felt a movement in her bowels. Reaching over towards the nightstand, she fumbled for the call button. The aides were always so slow on the week-ends. Earlier this morning she had directed an aide to dress her well, and now she was frightened to have an accident. For a singular moment she felt the urge to weep, for every day in her life had become so terribly hard. Pushing the button with her thumb, she leaned back in her chair, holding firm while closing her eyes.

KELLI

Kelli Stone stood by her bedside at the family home, folding clothes out of a laundry basket. On the bed, two suitcases lay open, partially packed. In the morning she and her husband, Jack, would get up early. They would have their coffee before loading the SUV, then driving south for a week's vacation in Myrtle Beach. Once there, they would meet their old friends,

Bill and Marie Murphy. The particular destination wasn't new. Myrtle Beach had been a trip the two families often shared during the springtime breaks from school. In the more recent years, they had continued the time together, but without the children along.

The kids were mostly grown and out of the house by now, either in college, or living and working on their own. So on this trip things would be less hectic and busy. Jack and Bill would get a chance to play golf every morning. Kelli and Marie would walk the beaches and shop the boardwalk, or simply sleep in late and read a book. As little as possible would be fine with Kelli. Just to be away from her job and the daily care of her mom would be pleasure enough.

Kelli placed some items of clothing into the suitcases, before sliding them off the bed and onto the floor. She placed the rest of the laundry in the drawers nearby, except for a pile of clothing that belonged to her son. Harry was the youngest of her three children. He was twenty now, yet still living at home. He had dropped out of school and was working steady. He had a girlfriend and was often never around the house. Her son was certainly old enough to do his own laundry, but some motherly routines were hard to let go.

The late Saturday afternoon had begun to grow dark. In the neighborhood outside, the streetlamps had begun to light. Her brother had just called from his car, saying he was about a half hour away. Kelli was anxious with anticipation. She hadn't seen her big brother in a couple of years. Although it had taken some effort to make all the arrangements for his trip, now it was finally here.

Kelli had already made a long list of things for Danny to be aware. The list included their mother's daily routine, the best times to visit each day, things for him to look out for, as well as specific members of the facility staff he should seek to engage. Kelli had learned that for elderly residents like her mom, keeping a normal routine and eliciting social engagement were very important. These things helped to keep their mother's depression at bay, especially when so much of her independence had been lost forever. Kelli wanted her brother to at least have some basic guide for keeping things regular during the week ahead.

Returning downstairs, Jack was laying back in his recliner chair in front of the television, having fallen off to sleep. He had already run the pre-trip errands, before washing and prepping the car for their journey. Sandwich fixings rested on the kitchen counter-top, a pot of soup simmering on the stove, ready to serve. Except for some last-minute packing in the morning, things were pretty much ready to go. A moment later a flash of headlights shone through the windows and hallway. Her brother had arrived.

DANNY

Around seven o'clock that evening, Danny Stone turned the rental car off the highway into the Windsor Hill facility. Exiting the vehicle, he and his sister walked toward the entrance together. The building complex was well-lit on the outside, with tall white columns out in front, as if entering a Southern mansion. Kelli reached in her purse. She handed him a small card to put in his wallet, the code necessary to get through the security doors. Entering the initial set of glass doors, they both halted before a second set of the same. Kelli punched several numbers into a keypad. The doors unlocked and they pushed inside.

The lobby of the Windsor Hill facility was rather large. Throughout the spacious room a myriad of aging faces had stirred. It seemed like everyone turned at once upon their entry, each with expressions of either curiosity or concern. Some of the faces seemed genuinely worried by the disruption, as if fearful of their presence. Others appeared as if searching for something familiar, as if wishing it might come true. Most of the residents were seated on sofas or cushioned furniture, their walkers at their reach. Others sat in wheelchairs, hands and forearms resting on the rails. Danny was struck by this initial introduction, uncertain of response.

In contrast, Kelli seemed completely unaffected. Instead, she immediately became a member of the crowd, grabbing a woman's hand warmly, expressing her salutation. With this simple act of acknowledgement, the woman became a momentary center of attention. As well, the rest of the room appeared to relax immediately, returning to their distractions as if nothing had occurred. Danny was introduced to a woman named Lucy, he himself as Jean's oldest son. After making some small talk, Kelli led on.

Danny quickly realized that something strange and alien was stretching before him. So this was the place his mother had come. And possibly, the place she might never leave. When their father, Tom, had died in a nursing home, Danny had been unable to return in time. There had been no last words to say, no chance for a final good-bye. It still remained an unavoidable regret he carried inside. His father had lasted only a few short days after his final hospitalization, his remains lying in a funeral home before Danny could arrive.

Danny followed his sister's lead. Kelli nodded to a woman in a white nursing outfit seated behind a reception desk, acting as if nothing was amiss. Reaching the elevator, she pushed the button for the second floor. As they waited together, Danny continued to look around. Not far from him, an old man sat slumped in a wheelchair. The man's head was rolled over to one side. He seemed unresponsive towards the lighted activity within the lobby, his eyes open, though staring at the floor. He was a large man, still appearing healthy of muscle and skin, with huge meaty hands gripped upon the side rails. They looked like a mason's hands, Danny thought to himself, or maybe a steelworker's grip. They were definitely the hands of a man in the builder's trade. But tonight, the hands appeared as if worn with a history that could no longer speak to the hundreds of stories that such hands might tell. Danny stared at the hands, wondering for a moment where they had so firmly traveled for so long a time. Then looking back up, he met his sister's eyes as the elevator doors began to open. As they stepped inside, Kelli grimly shook her head before whispering with one-word effect. "Stroke". Danny slowly nodded in response.

It had been most of two years since Danny Stone had seen his mother. Kelli had sought to prepare him, mentioning how the impact of the hip surgery had further slowed and aged her. But he was unprepared for what he was about to encounter.

Upon entering the studio-sized apartment, he saw an elderly woman resting in her chair. Struck by the physical changes before him, his mother appeared narrow and crooked in stature, her skin sagging off a bony exterior. He was stunned for the quickest of moments, the first sight of her almost halting his advance. But he managed to step quickly forward, before gently corralling his arms about her. Delicately, he tried not to exert too much pressure as he kissed her upon the cheek. Then stepping back, he held her withered hands before release. Surprisingly, the hair on her head remained full, much as the last time he had seen her. Jean Stone had always had the most beautiful hair. It now was an even brighter white, far from the luxurious blonde she had worn for so many years.

Despite the stark infirmity of her appearance, his mom expressed her delight and happiness at the sight of her eldest son. Danny pulled up a chair to be close to her, his mother seeking his arm to restore intimate contact. They engaged in conversation about his trip, including news of her two grandsons, as well as his ex-wife.

As Kelli listened or occasionally joined in the exchange, she roamed about the apartment, unloading a bag of provisions and toiletries she had brought along. But soon enough, she got down to the business of her mother's care. Had Jean gone down to dinner? Did she need to go to the bath room? Had the nurse come by with her evening medication? Within this interrogation, a longstanding mother-daughter confab began to ensue. Danny leaned back in his chair, listening to a familiar exchange.

Just like it had always been, this constant banter between his mother and sister remained just short of argument in the manner delivered. And per the usual, the subjects were mostly about something, or perhaps someone, that either had or hadn't gone wrong or right. For Danny, it continued to be a funny two-way communication between mother and daughter, one that the rest of the planet would never need to share. Danny couldn't help but be reminded of the past. Yes, he was home again, that was definitely for sure.

As the evening discussion continued, Danny surveyed the domicile that now was his mother's new address. Kelli had furnished and decorated the apartment with knick-knacks and wall hangings that had previously graced the family home, as well as the townhouse for so many years. His sister's efforts were obviously a genuine attempt to bring a semblance of continuity to his mother's new world, an honest endeavor to sustain a sense of home. In a way, the presence of these objects seemed to create a comforting sensibility, lessening the overall strangeness of this new location to which his mother had come.

Sometime later, there was a light knock at the frame of the open apartment door, a slender young black woman entering the room. It was time for his mother to change into a nightgown and get ready for bed. Danny stood up, pulling his chair aside. Kelli introduced the aide as Sharice, and the sweet sound of the woman's accent spoke of Jamaica immediately. Her long black hair was braided in dreadlocks, shining in the overhead light. His mother happily reached over to Sharice, holding her arm under the table lamp.

"Doesn't Sharice have the most beautiful skin you have ever seen?"

Shining under the light, the young woman's skin color was indeed beautiful, a soft golden-brown. Sharice tried to deflect her embarrassment, smiling deferentially as she gently pulled away. Danny looked over at Kelli, both of them smiling in silence. Danny said a temporary farewell before leaving the room.

Once outside the apartment, Danny took a seat near the nurse's station. He exchanged a wave at a woman in uniform, who sat at a desk behind a large glass window. The wide-carpeted hallway was empty of residents or visitors, the facility appearing to settle down for the evening. Stretching his legs, he rubbed a hand over the back of his neck. As he gazed about, he began mulling over the current institutional reality of which he now was a part, quietly considering the questions they had begun to raise.

What does a person do when this is the end of the line? What does one feel when there is no longer anything ahead, when there exists no future to perhaps dream upon or ponder, when most everything in one's life appears to have been left behind? Certainly such questions were difficult to consider, or much less answer when burdened with the malaise of a final understanding one is required to accept.

Sitting alone, Danny could feel a determinate outcome had begun. An outcome that was colored with those natural fears of the unknown. But within this moment of recognition, Danny knew that it was not necessarily a fear for his mother that concerned him, for she now unfortunately had come to this place. Rather, he felt an elemental fear for himself, a future outcome that he might one day be helpless to avoid.

JEAN

Later that evening, within the darkness of her room, Jean Stone lay in her bed at Windsor Hill, her body exhausted from an eventful day. Yet her thoughts were still awake, anxious from seeing her son after so long a time. She could feel the heaviness in her ankles and feet, the soreness in her gums, the scratchiness in her bottom from the nightly diaper taped about her. Whenever such sleeplessness was upon her, every little discomfort seemed to prompt a restlessness she could not escape. On nights like this, trying to turn one way or the other gave her no relief, no relief until her fatigue might finally let her drift towards sleep.

Danny had been her first-born, the light of her life so many years ago. His birth had become the beginning of her duties as a wife and mother. It was a time when she was young and beautiful, a time when the marriage to her husband was the happiest it would ever be. Danny's birth would always feel this way. Everyone was alive, the future so bright. The war was over. People were working and making new starts. Friends would gather together whenever they could. Looking back, it would always seem to have been the best of times of her life, with never a question that things might change.

But tonight, such memories were little more than wistful reflections. It was hard for her to imagine that she had once experienced such contented anticipations, that she had actually possessed them so long ago. Danny's first years would forever recall those feelings, that the true happiness of love could be something very real. Her oldest son would always be a link to those moments in time. But the passage of time has its fault lines. The happiness of certain moments can sometimes be a prelude to a fall, the other side of the coin.

Jean's weary body stiffened upon this reminder. For her youthful expectations had never come to pass, had not flowered in the manner she had so wishfully believed. With time and circumstance, her life, her husband's life, and the lives of friends and others, had begun to take their turns. There had come no heaven on earth, no eternal bowl of peaches and cream. Instead, mistakes and misery were also part of God's magnificent plan. And most everyone who lived long enough would be delivered their share. And so, upon this special night, lying here alone, her body further withering with the winter ahead, she tried again to slip back to the warmth of that happier period in her life, and finally into rest.

DANNY

Returning home from Windsor Hill, Kelli made cups of tea with coffee cake. Danny sat with her and Jack, catching up on family information, things like kids, jobs, sports, people from their past. During the conversation, Kelli and Jack's youngest son, Harry, came through the door. He hugged his uncle and briefly answered a few obligatory questions. Then, grabbing some food and drink in the kitchen, he dodged upstairs. Harry had become the only child left at home. He was twenty, a dropout, was working for a moving company, and had a girlfriend where he spent much of his time. It was doubtful that Danny would see much of Harry in the week ahead. More than likely, any free time not shared with his mother would mostly be spent with a dog, a cat, and a television set. With the evening snack complete, everyone hugged and said good-night.

Lying in bed, Danny rested his hands behind his head. Although he felt physically tired, he remained wired from the day's travel, as well as the succeeding events that had consumed his arrival. So this would be his life in the week to come. He would do whatever he could to help the cause. Although he was pleased that his mother appeared stable and safe in her new world, it was still tough to accept that the final chapter of her life was likely upon her. At this place called Windsor Hill, she would be engaged upon a daily road of basic survival, perhaps until her mortal end would come.

So, for the week ahead, comfort and understanding would be his single purpose at hand. No longer would the emotions of past behavior need to be addressed. The prior events that had shaped the family angst over so many years now seemed trivial in perspective. Although such unintended consequences must play a part of any life experience, they would no longer be important. They were now nothing more than what they had become, the scars of a destiny that only fate had shown the power to command. Tonight, the Stone's family history felt as if sculpted into bronze. Why would there ever be something more that needed to be reconciled. As Harrison had sung, "all things must pass...... all things must pass away".

When morning came, Danny got up to see Kelli and Jack off on their week's vacation. As usual, his sister had added a few last minute instructions. There could be little argument that Kelli had clearly inherited the daily concerns and worries that their mother had always engaged. Both mother and daughter were worry-warts of a sort, always attempting to avoid the troubling whims of possible forgetfulness or error. It had become something of a family trait no doubt, one that even Danny was not immune. So there was no need to argue to the contrary. With coffee cup in hand, he simply nodded his assent.

After Kelli and Jack had driven away, Danny stood in the kitchen of a seemingly empty house. As expected, it would now be just himself, a dog and a cat, and perhaps his youngest nephew upstairs. As directed by his sister, he would wait until later in the morning before driving over to Windsor Hill. The Sunday paper lay unread on the kitchen counter. He poured more coffee, before sitting down to read.

KELLI

As her husband drove the interstate highway heading south, Kelli nestled deeper into the passenger seat next to him, trying to relax. She could again feel that familiar tingle throughout her upper torso. It was like an electric hum that greeted her whenever things might reach a heightened level of activity. But it could also come even in moments when she might have a chance to unwind. She knew it was some form of sporadic and unwanted anxiety, a feeling she was unable to control. Although she had somehow become accustomed to living with this buzz, she hoped and prayed that one day it would cease. In the interim, she continued her methods of keeping it at bay. There were the steady walks in the neighborhood when available, quiet deep breaths during the daytime, as well as hot baths in the evenings before bed. When nothing else worked, there were the little pills of Xanax that the doctor had prescribed.

This uncomfortable condition had owned her now for a number of months. It had begun not long after her mother's fall and hospitalization, followed quickly by the sale of the townhouse and the move to Windsor Hill. Along with the daily duties of her employment, her marriage and children, there was the constant necessity of her mother's emotions and advocacy. Consequently, there was little time for any peace, little time for just being her regular self. She hoped the week ahead might grant her some relief, or at least some distraction from the current burdens of her recent daily life.

Still, she knew better than to think that her nervous condition would simply peel away, that her patterns of worry and solution would easily melt with the miles ahead.

No, that reality would take more time than a one-week vacation could offer. This trip, this little break of sorts, would be nothing more than some hopeful days of diversion. It would be a chance to catch her breath, before returning to the continuing circumstances for which she must attend. Nevertheless, the eventual alternative was even less inviting. For the kind of relief that she might one day be seeking, would only be delivered with a tragic loss, a loss she could not bring herself to imagine.

Outside the car window, the countryside was colored with the beauty of autumn. Her thoughts drifted to her children. They were all young adults now, each of them making their own way. Certainly, there would always be a cause of worry for their safety. But that kind of worry was a given, an elemental concern shared by all parents who cared for their own. As for her mom, thanks to Danny, Jean would at least be safe in her surroundings should some emergency occur.

It had been so good to see her older brother in the flesh, to feel his calmness and support. Danny's presence would make her absence this week pass quickly. There was a good chance she would hardly be missed. She just hoped that she could manage to enjoy herself, perhaps calm these feelings inside her. Let things go for a bit, and once again be a happy wife and friend.

Still, with the long drive ahead, Danny's arrival couldn't help but bring to mind their shared family history. For herself and her brothers, their childhood had been full of complication, periods of enduring love and safety, peppered with incredible hours of fear and distress. Certainly not intended, her older brother's arrival seemed to be cracking open a closet door. Obviously, there was the happiness of his coming. But it now seemed accompanied by the memories of more difficult air to breathe.

Their common childhood story appeared on the outside to be reflective of a normal suburban life. But within its interior, it was also a story interrupted by sudden tempests of stress and disruption that had injured them all. These infrequent yet regular dramas had begun with their father.

On the night of their father's funeral fifteen years ago, Kelli and her older brother had reminisced upon his passing. For the first time, Danny shared a belief that their father may have been a victim of an undiagnosed medical condition throughout his adult life, a condition that only since the end of the Vietnam War now had a name. Post Traumatic Stress Disorder, or PTSD. During the world war in which their father had fought, the diagnosis was commonly referred to as 'battle fatigue'. And although its impact had been quietly acknowledged at the time, it was a condition that had received only nominal recognition, and very minimal treatment or support.

Thinking back to her childhood years, Kelli remembered that her father had always been a fidgety man, a constant smoker who never seemed capable of being fully relaxed. Upon his return from Europe, Tom Stone, along with the many thousands of men that joined him, were simply expected to start all over again. Despite the trauma of the past, there should be no complaint. To have returned alive was more than enough fortune in one's life. To do so held no quarter in the company of men. The emotional consequences of any soldier's service were small potatoes when measured against the ultimate sacrifices that other men had paid. A combat veteran was expected to move on, to return to work, to meet a girl, to get married, to have children, to somehow resume an optimistic normal life. Any unseen scars were given little credence and never discussed.

But as time passed, other pressures in life had found their way. The pressures and stress of full-time employment, a marital relationship that was expected to last forever, as well as the rearing of children that required constant monetary support in a place called 'home'. Danny believed that something haunting had remained inside their father, maybe the fraying of a nervous system that periodically was unable to cope. Whatever the spark, the family began to learn, and learn all too well, that from time to time there came a break. A break fueled by alcohol, and then suddenly unleashed without any opportunity to either prepare or escape.

These troubling events of chaos would sometimes continue for days, full of disturbance and silent terror, especially from their mother, who was always the initial victim of their father's pointed anger and derision. As a child, Kelli had no clear recollection of when she first became aware of these terrible incidences. But today, upon these memories, she could still feel their emotional effects inside.

And then, just as suddenly, her father's drinking binges would come to a halt. Upon some silent unspoken morning, or perhaps on a late afternoon when their 'real' father would return from work at a normal time, the drama would end. At that point everyone's life would quickly return as before, as if nothing troubling had ever occurred. Still, a worried fear always remained locked within, lying dormant until the next bout would come.

Kelli felt that she and her youngest brother, Ronnie, had gotten off the easiest of the children, at least in the harshest years of her father's verbal abuse and disarray. As Tom Stone's only daughter, for some reason her father never seemed to challenge her whenever he was at his worst. It was only when her mother began to take up the alcoholic cause that Kelli had been forced to contend.

As for Danny, he had taken the hardest hit. As the oldest boy, it was Danny's necessity to become the protector, whether against a father filled with bodily threat, or sometime later a mother filled with alcoholic nonsense. It didn't matter which or when. Danny was the one who always chose to ride with his mother whenever their father's binges would occur. And once becoming sixteen, he would often drive alone to pick up his father at the Seventh Heaven Lounge or the Elks Club, watering holes where Tom Stone would be drinking with his buddies from either work or the war. Once back at home, their father would begin the usual tirade against their mother, whereupon Danny would try and deflect the assault, thereby taking the brunt of his abuse.

Finally, some years later, there was the night when Danny was home from college. Kelli's father had always seemed to challenge Danny, to try and make him change his ways, to try and put him in his place. But Danny was old enough by then, strong enough to hold his ground. On that night, again inebriated, Tom Stone mistakenly needed to show that he remained the man-in-charge. But in a flashing moment, Danny knocked his father flat to the floor. Then, holding him down, pressing himself face to face, Danny shouted. If his father ever abused any member of the family ever again, Danny would knock him senseless forever. Kelli could still remember the look in her father's eyes. It was an aging shock of recognition, as if something in Tom Stone's world had suddenly changed.

Although this lone incident of family physical violence was never repeated, their father's pattern of sudden alcoholic behavior continued into the years ahead. In between, there was the smoking, the nervousness, the inability to discuss his emotional troubles in any productive way. There was only the booze to give them their dark expression and release.

It was a tale of Jekyll and Hyde. For whenever their father was sober, which actually was most of the time, Tom Stone was a truly quiet and generous man, a dedicated and loving father, who never asked much for himself. Still, this strange contrast of behaviors loomed constantly over the family's daily reality, as if waiting for another shoe to drop. And drop it did, when their mother found a similar medication to kill her own anger and pain.

As the drive south continued, Kelli and her husband made small talk about their own family's affairs, as well as the vacation ahead. But between these distractions, Kelli fell back into this reverie of her childhood. Sometimes, as the years passed, whenever she had discussed these admissions with a trusted lover or friend, it was always easy for them to say, "Hey, relax. Forget about it. You have to let things go. The past is the past, there's nothing you can do to change things. It's best to move on."

But for Kelli, those responses were just too easy to say. Sure, she understood that they were just trying to be helpful and nice because they cared. But really, it was so much talk. For the truth was evident, such hurtful memories in life never really leave you. They are always a part of you, waiting for their moment of return. The present tense only allows them to be forgotten for a time.

She also knew that to forever dwell on such past emotional dramas made little sense, and could only bring one down. But to act like they don't exist, that they could easily be forgotten or erased was so much crap. Those friends didn't have a missing brother who had pretty much disappeared from the family all these many years. So what does one do, just pretend like Billy died many years ago, and just say that life is life? What does any person say to a family that has lost a child to violence? That perhaps one day time might ease the pain? Who in this world would ever say such a thing, or ever believe it could be true?

Billy had pretty much left after high school. But in a way, he had checked out long before that marker in time. As a child, her brother had grown more solitary in his activities, often saying little and keeping to himself. Whenever their father's binge streaks would occur, Billy would disappear into the closet of his bedroom, or hide somewhere in the basement of the home until the tumults would cease. And yet, despite the impacts, he became a good student, a voracious reader, and quietly found a group of friends who shared the same. And later, as a teenager, when their mother had eventually become captured by her own addiction to alcohol, acting so foolish in her talk at the dinner table, Billy would again remain silent, eating quickly before escaping to some solitary fortress away from the family.

After his high school graduation, Billy agreed to college, but didn't stay long. As a surfer, he found his way to California, working different jobs. He became a camper and a hiker in the mountains. He would occasionally write postcards or notes addressed to the family, saying he was well, but he never came home for holidays. Then, somewhere in his twenties came a postcard from Southern Australia. He had become a long-distance truck driver, and was soon to be married. In the years that followed, there would be brief annual letters of Christmas greeting. There would be pictures of a wife and two children. The letters would always state that things were good. But never ever was there a return address. All the while, a sad unspoken reality was clear. Billy Stone had left his birth family behind.

And so, on certain nights of alcoholic disturbance in their later years, the blame would be passed back and forth between mother and father. In between, the loss was silently shared alone by all the family, hidden with its guilt. Billy's disappearance was to this day the single family tragedy. There was just enough information to tell the outside world everything was fine, but never enough to absolve the truth. Kelli squirmed in her seat, the memory sparking an unconscious involuntary reaction. "Yes", she thought angrily to herself, "just tell someone they need to let it go. Just go ahead and you'll be looking for a fight."

As for little brother, Ronnie, he had carried the torch the longest, before finally leaving home. Initially, college was not for him. With his older siblings gone from the house, Ronnie went to work, staying behind longer than was needed. Kelli believed that deep down Ronnie felt a certain responsibility to be their parents' caretaker. But not long after, even Ronnie's endurance had reached its limits. And when an opportunity in Florida finally gave him an option, he decided to go back to school and was on his way.

In the end, it was only herself alone that was left with the patterns of the aftermath. Upon returning from school and other travels, she had met and married Jack, settling down close to home.

All the while, even though her parent's drinking continued, there was never a consideration of a breach in their marriage. Each soldiered on with the lifelong vows they had chosen to make. Having been raised as practicing Catholics, they acknowledged that divorce was a sin and thus never in the cards. And eventually over time, with the children gone and old age beginning its progressive descent, Tom and Jean Stone fell into a tired complacency. Thankfully, upon his retirement, their father's drinking bouts began to temper, his angry outbursts less intense. But as time went by, his worn-out body began to fail.

Through it all, Tom Stone had labored and provided, had given all that he could give. As he grew weary with his health, the better parts of his character remained. Perhaps he had fallen into a begrudging acceptance that things in his life had not become what he might have dreamed them to be. But instead of growing sullen, he chose to fawn over his grandchildren, perhaps trying to make up for the earlier failures he had been unable to reverse. He also quietly endured the persistent alcoholism of his wife, a circumstance that he had helped create by his own behavior. As well, there was the irreconcilable truth that as a father, Tom Stone eternally mourned the loss of a son, the boy who had chosen never to return. Nevertheless, upon his death, Tom Stone went to his grave without ever an admission or apology. It was simply not the way of his world.

As for their mother, once it had begun, her own addiction could not be overcome. From time to time, there were periods when she had made efforts to stop. Trying her best, she had gone to AA meetings off and on. But Jean Stone was never strong enough to finally beat the odds. While the objective evidence of her failure was hidden downstairs stashed in the basement laundry, its visible result was always clear. Her routine would always begin in the late afternoons, followed by angry or foolish talk during the dinner hours, before dissipating later at bedtime. Alcohol had become their mother's stubborn crutch, a familiar necessity for making it through the day. And despite her deeper wishes for strength and fortitude, her desire was never enough. She was left with only her shame, her only company to keep. Her husband's death had made no difference, her reliance was so complete.

It had only been the consequence of her recent hospitalizations and rehab, followed by her internment at Windsor Hill which had thankfully done the trick. And strangely surprising to Kelli, her mother had managed to recover from her addiction without much of a struggle. For everyone concerned, the circumstances of her mother's broken hip had come with an unexpected blessing, one that Kelli had never considered. As a daughter, she welcomed it with open arms. For once again, she would have the mother she loved, sober and back in her everyday life.

Upon reaching adulthood, Kelli had come to realize that the troubles of her own family's experience were not uncommon. There were many other families, even families that she might never have imagined, that carried within them similar burdens and consequences, similar truths that were hidden from sight. For the tragedy of alcohol and substance abuse was a fact of modern human life. In her years of teaching and work with children, Kelli had continued to witness its effects in all its inexplicable formations. But more than anything else in her life, she would be forever grateful that such incredible difficulties had not visited her second family, the one she could call her own.

Jack suddenly broke her wandering reverie, pulling off the interstate to take a break and get some gas. Kelli rubbed her eyes and sat up in her seat. It was funny how easy it was for a person to slip back into the past, to trouble oneself over things in life that one could not repair. She promised herself that it was time to be on vacation, time to leave the childhood troubles of her life alone, at least for awhile.

JEAN

Through the window of Jean's studio apartment the morning sky was covered in a light gray overcast. More and more often, she awoke from a night's sleep without being sure what day it was. The days of her life seemed always the same, even those before she had to leave her home and come to Windsor Hill. But here at Windsor, each day was like a broken record, the same song playing over and over again. In a way, it really didn't matter what day it was anymore. For Jean believed that she would never leave this place. She was now convinced that she would die here. It would just be a matter of time.

Nevertheless, Jean tried to hold onto a memory this morning, a memory which reminded her that her son was nearby and hopefully coming soon. This knowledge of her son's arrival raised her spirits. She was looking forward to the day ahead. Moments later, one of the aides arrived, helping her to get up and out of bed. Wrapped in her robe, Jean was assisted to the bathroom, her overnight diaper changed, before being dressed.

On a lot of mornings, whenever she felt weak and tired, Jean wished she could just stay in her nightgown as long as they would allow, hoping that everyone would simply leave her alone. But not today. Today, she would pick out something special. The morning aide, Charleen, was always gentle and nice. Charleen only worked the week-ends. She was a student at the local college, learning to be a nurse. Jean really liked her, being so unlike many of the regular girls during the week. Those girls were rougher and fast, always rushing to get things done. So it was very likely Sunday, although she still questioned Charleen just to confirm.

Ever since first coming to Windsor Hill, Jean had refused to go to breakfast. She had never been one for breakfast, even in her earlier life when she was working or raising the kids. Charleen helped Jean into her recliner chair. She made sure Jean's teeth were set securely, before placing the call button and television remote within easy reach. Jean's coffee would hopefully be coming soon.

Although Kelli was constantly reminding her that it cost more to have this special service, Jean could have cared less. She was too darn tired to face the day so early, to have to push the walker and go downstairs. And why would she worry about money when so little seemed to matter anymore? They could kick her out on the street for all she cared, at least when it came to breakfast. She would still make the regular trips for lunch and dinner, but that would be enough. She was fine with trying to do her part, but that was all she could do.

Thinking of Kelli, Jean remembered that her daughter would likely be gone on her trip. Such recognition always worried her a little, whenever Kelli was away. On the one hand, she was happy that Kelli and Jack would now be on vacation. And she knew that Kelli would call whenever she could. On the other hand, it did make her worry not to have her daughter nearby. She was so grateful that her oldest son had come back to help, because Kelli would have worried as well. Both of her sons had always tried to come whenever they could, even though they lived so far away.

She felt glad that Danny would be with her today, it made her happy to think about. But whenever she began to think of her children as a group, there was always that one painful remembrance which had never gone away. Although this pain had grown duller over the years, it remained a hurt in her heart that she would always be forced to endure. The deep sadness of a child lost from her, the guilt of a parents' behavior that no wish for forgiveness could ever absolve. Billy, her precious and quietly internal son, had never come home. It seemed like only yesterday that her husband had passed away, all the while still carrying this shared burden deep within him. For Tom, it had been a burden without a resolution. It seemed only fair that she must do the same.

Moments later, her coffee arrived. And with it, Charleen would always bring something solid on which she could nibble in the time before lunch. When Charleen asked if anything more was needed, Jean answered that everything was fine. On most days, this answer was usually a pretense that Jean had become expert at deceiving. All was fine, she usually evaded, all was fine. But today her response was a little closer to the truth. Oh yes, she smiled, one of her sons was coming to visit. Everything was good, thank you, better than any other day might be.

DANNY

After reading the Sunday paper, Danny Stone took a shower and dressed. He leashed the dog, Freddie, before stepping outside into the suburban neighborhood beyond. The morning weather was a cloudy gray, the temperature cool with a mildly autumn chill. The streets were quiet, normal for a Sunday. The neat suburban homes with their big yards rested sleepy and silent. Walking the paved streets for most of an hour, he returned to the house, feeding both Freddie and the cat before heading upstairs. Lightly tapping on his nephew's bedroom door, he pushed slowly inside. Harry rustled in the bed, rubbing his eyes. Danny apologized for checking, but he was now heading for Windsor Hill. Harry numbly acknowledged the information, sending his greetings to 'grandma' before rolling back over towards sleep. Walking away, Danny had to smile and shake his head. He had raised two boys of his own. Harry's response was a familiar reminder of his own sons' youthful lazy days.

Arriving at Windsor Hill, Danny parked in a side-lot near the back of the building. Walking toward the front entrance, he could see several young women, both black and white, dressed in their green scrubs. They stood smoking together out behind the facility, obviously catching a break from their duties inside. Reaching the front of the building, Danny passed through the first pair of glass doors. He pulled out the card that Kelli had given him, punching in the access code in order to enter the lobby.

Similar to the evening before, the room was crowded with faces seeking recognition. Danny gave a measured smile to no one in particular, as if wishing to alleviate any concerns. Walking toward the elevator, he passed by the service desk, raising his hand in salutation toward the woman who sat behind. With her ear to the phone she simply nodded in response. At the elevator, once again the man from the night before sat slumped in his wheelchair. His head was turned askew, devoid of any expression, his large rugged hands resting beside him. The elevator door slid open and Danny continued on.

At his mother's apartment the television audio was loud inside. Jean was lying back in her easy chair, her eyes closed. As he leaned down and whispered his arrival, her head rose abruptly. Smiling at his presence, she gently spoke his name. Danny kissed her on the head before reaching for the remote to lower the sound. Pulling up a chair, he sat as near as he could manage, raising his voice to be sure she could hear. Mother and son exchanged pleasantries regarding whatever came to mind.

When it was time for lunch, Danny planted the walker in front of the recliner, his mother rising up slowly. He stayed beside her as they made their way to the elevator and down to the dining room. Reaching her table, three elderly women were already present. Feeling a sense of pride, his mother introduced her son to Bernice and Lucy. Both women responded with normal greetings of clarity and interest. Danny helped his mother into her seat. As Jean settled in, Bernice leaned over to the third woman sitting numbly in her wheelchair. Speaking into the woman's ear, she announced Danny's presence. Janice was the woman's name. She slowly nodded as Danny spoke her name in salutation. It was clear that Janice was less able than the others.

The Windsor Hill dining room was rather large, with many round tables, and residents in varying states of condition. The servers moved briskly throughout, delivering plates of food, filling cups or glasses with coffee, tea, and colored juice. At several tables, aides sat beside the residents, helping to feed them. Scattered throughout were a number of other diners, mostly younger than the rest, sitting beside. Like Danny himself, they appeared to be family members paying a Sunday visit.

During the lunch, Jean was alert and talkative, as if energized by her son's attendance. Danny did his part as well, asking Bernice and Lucy about their families and personal histories. Bernice was obviously the most adept and consciously aware, the leader of the group. Lucy a little less so, but her mind was still active and verbally on point. Unfortunately, Janice was barely able to feed herself, Bernice assisting her whenever necessary. She was not necessarily able to engage.

When the meal was over, Danny and his mother returned to her apartment. Danny suggested they make a trip outside. Jean agreed. But first, Danny pushed the call button for some help with the bathroom. After some time, Charleen arrived, assisting his mother with her toiletry, before rushing to another call. Danny spread and secured the wheelchair, helping her into her coat. Once outside the facility, he pushed his mother along the cement-paved walkways that circled the grounds of Windsor Hill. The temperature remained brisk, the afternoon sun peaking through a broken sky. After circling the grounds, they sat together on the front portico of the facility until Jean began to chill.

Back at the apartment, Danny eased his mother into the recliner. He could tell she was beginning to tire. It was time to leave and let her rest. He arranged what she needed on the light-table beside her chair. He set the television on the news channel, adjusting the sound to her need. He would return in the early evening after dinner was complete. Walking to the car, Danny could feel his own fatigue. Back at the house, he made his way toward the couch in the den. Turning on the Sunday football game, he slipped into a nap, the dog Freddie curled comfortably beside.

KELLI

By early evening Kelli and her husband had reached their destination at Myrtle Beach. They unpacked, met their friends for dinner, making plans for the following day. Back at the condo unit, Kelli made a call to her mother at Windsor Hill. After a couple of rings, Jean answered the phone, sounding alert and in good spirits. Danny was back at the facility. He and their mother were paging through some old photograph albums that Kelli had brought from home. But her mother had some anxious news to tell her. An aide had taken Janice away at dinner. They had rolled her wheelchair over to another table in the dining room. Bernice had said that Janice would not be coming back. Soon, they would be having someone new sitting at their table. Within her mother's small world of Windsor Hill, Kelli knew this change would be something of a disruption. The situation with Janice had only been a matter of time. Kelli was relieved that Danny would be nearby, hoping that her mother would not dwell too long on the circumstances.

Expressing her sorrow about the incident, Kelli quickly changed the subject. She asked about the photos that Danny and her mom were viewing. The deflection worked. After listening for a time, she wished her mother good night, before requesting that she speak with Danny to do the same. When Danny came on the line, Kelli asked him to walk the hand-held receiver into the hall. Outside of earshot, Danny explained that Janice was having trouble feeding herself at lunch. And despite Bernice's attempts to help, someone must have made a decision. Kelli explained that she knew that things were imminent. Sadly for Janice, it was another step in the process.

Kelli also wanted to be sure that the night nurse had come with the evening medications. She asked her brother stay around until their mother had been changed for bed, just to be sure that the aides were aware of his presence. On most week-end evenings the care was often less than adequate, as fewer supervisory personnel were present at the facility. Danny said not to worry, that things seemed okay. Kelli continued with a reminder. Her mother had an appointment the next day to get her hair and nails done, and this was very important. Again, Danny tried to let her know that things were fine, to be sure to relax and have a good time. Kelli said that she would call again the following evening. With that, brother and sister said their farewells.

As Kelli turned off her phone, she could see her husband giving a gentle smirk and shake of the head. Jack was stretched out on the bed watching the television. Kelli didn't respond, but understood the message being sent.

No one, including her husband, really understood. And even if they did, it was just not the same. Affirmation and sympathy were easy to express. There would always be plenty of sympathy to go around. But sympathy doesn't make this phone call. Sympathy doesn't make the doctor appointments. Sympathy doesn't have to listen to an aging woman's worries or concerns, nor fill every necessity that might arise day after day.

One can't just let things ride and say everything is fine, or easily walk away and call it good for awhile. Someone's life just doesn't work like that. And why not? Well, because a person's physical needs don't stop until they are met. A fear isn't overcome until it's relieved. The care of an elderly human being doesn't stop until it's mortally undone. That's damn why.

Kelli wasn't angry at anyone. It wasn't that her husband, or her brother, or her compassionate friends didn't desire to do what they could. But it also wasn't they who were living at seventy-five miles an hour most of the time. No, it was only she herself who couldn't slow down. It was only she herself that sometimes needed a pill in the evening just to get some rest.

She wished she could be like her kids. They often seemed so comfortably oblivious to the world around them. Sure, they undoubtedly had their own youthful angst and concerns as young adults in this world. Surely they had their own insecurities about how they appeared to others, or what expectations of the future they might be required to attest.

Nevertheless, they sometimes appeared like zombies to her, waiting for the next party to attend, or the next phone or text message to distract them. That was what Kelli really craved sometimes, to be as outwardly unconcerned as her children were most of the time. Or perhaps even better, to end up like an Alzheimer victim of sorts, where she too could just wander down the halls of Windsor Hill without a care in the world. Or perhaps become like Janice, simply rolled over to another table, a napkin tucked under her neck, with a spoonful of baby food placed in her mouth. To spend some time emotionally unconscious, without a goddamned thing to worry about.

Dressing for bed, Kelli reminded herself that she would be okay. It was just that this caretaking thing with her mother seemed so constantly constant, and always so hard to let go. Her father had gone so fast in comparison. And during his final decline, it had been her mother who had been the stalwart caregiver most of the time. In native societies, this dying problem was nothing more than the ritual of life, where you dragged the ailing person quietly behind with teepee poles, before bundling them up in animal hide. Then, with their backs resting upon a rock, facing the sun, they would be left to the heavenly care of the spirits beyond. Kelli put on her nightgown, brushed her teeth, sneaking under the covers next to her husband, praying for some sleep.

DANNY

On Monday morning, Danny awoke in bed, unfortunately thinking about life and death. Upon his most recent birthday earlier in the summer, he had turned sixty-four years old. At the time, thoughts of mortality had caused him to have a reflective pause upon another year's passing. Thankfully, there had been little consideration since. But on this morning, after three trips to the Windsor Hill facility in the last two days, it was hard not to give it some continued rumination.

To witness his mother approaching the last stage of her life was difficult. Despite all the challenging circumstances and mixed emotions of their past, she was his only mother, and so much closer to death than ever before. She was now so very weak, and in such serious need at this point in her life. No longer would she be able to emotionally provoke him, as she had been so unwittingly capable for so many years.

Honestly, it had never really been more than her drinking that troubled him. But the consistent effects of her addiction had always created another woman with whom the family was forced to endure. Today, it appeared that this other woman was gone now, and would not be coming back. And gratefully left behind was the real mother that they had always known and loved.

And so here he was, closing in on the final chapters of his own life, while beginning to see first-hand the difficult path that his eventual debilitation might take. Being divorced and single these days, it was hard to imagine requiring his two sons to be tasked with his needs for care, for them to have to make time and decisions on his behalf, whenever his failings might come. And yet, such circumstances were really nothing one could easily make plans for, no scripted solution he might spare them down the stretch. Perhaps things would be quick when it came to his own sickness and death, not become some long drawn-out affair that the boys and their families would have to attend. But hell, such eventualities would always remain a mystery of fate, playing out however they must.

Still, the markers were certainly there, amidst the realization of a mortality that would someday come to pass. Danny had witnessed his father, as well as other family and friends suffer their leavings, including his business partner several years ago. As for Steve Holt, it had been a long and painful end. And although the exact causation could never be determined, a myriad of possibilities might offer their justification.

Steve Holt had been granted the luxuries of military service at a time when the same vaccination needles were used over and over again. Or perhaps it was the chemical realities of his days in Vietnam. Or maybe it started later, from his nights in San Francisco, when survival for Steve had carelessly been given no youthful concern. Eventually, Steve Holt had been able to pull out of those digressions, making something positive of his life, long before this lottery of death had held its final drawing.

Shortly before his death at home, Steve had requested that Danny deliver him his firearm. Danny had refused immediately, telling Steve that only his wife or children could answer such a request. Steve didn't argue further, but a knowing smile registered upon his face. A few weeks later, Steve's wife had called. Things were close. Upon Danny's final visit, Steve had slipped into an unconscious sleep, his breathing joined by a rattle that Danny had never heard before. The next morning Steve was gone.

Upon these thoughts, Danny wondered how he might face the inevitable whenever its approach. What might be his chosen response when faced with such a mortal imperative? Would he wage a fight to overcome, some mysterious survival gene kicking within him? Or would he simply accept the final declaration, knowing by then that his own time had finally arrived? Once again, he didn't have an answer, but felt certain he would never be prepared. No matter, it was certain that time would tell.

He did know a few things. He did know that the memories of his past were now more often upon him. He did know that he was slowly beginning to look back at his life more than he seemed to look forward. Any ambitions for the future were less and less important these days. With each consideration, he had begun to quietly measure what time might have left at hand. It was obviously true that his daily life had begun to slow. Outside of his work, the phone didn't ring as much anymore. And more often than not he felt reluctant to call out. He had begun to feel less and less part of any particular story in life.

Strangely, whenever he did drift into this thinking of his past, he had begun to focus more on his regrets in life, and less on any accomplishments for which he might feel proud. Instead, he had begun to look back at the more troubled moments of his own personal history, circumstances where he wished to make amends. And from time to time, he would think of certain people from his past from whom he might wish to ask forgiveness.

Glancing at the alarm clock, he shook himself free. Kicking off the covers, he rolled out of the bed. He still had a job to do. And right now, it was a job to please his mother with his presence, to help her in any way he could. To lay here and have a pity-party had little redeeming social value. As well, it was the kind of self-absorption that frankly never paid its debts. And honestly, there was one singular truth he needed to remember. In the end, who in the hell really cared? And even if they did, it would never be for long. Everyone else in the human race had their own concerns to address, their own moments to aspire. For now, it was time to hit the ground and get into the day.

JEAN

Jean Stone sat nervously in her recliner. Several feet away, the television screen rested dark before her. On the carpeted floor below, she could see the remote control lying nearby, easily out of reach. Jean had pushed the call button as soon as she had fumbled the remote away, but still no one had come to help. She waited a bit before pushing the button a second time, but again no help arrived. If she tried to retrieve it herself she knew the alarm would go off immediately. And although someone would likely answer in haste, they also would be angry with her, reminding her that she could have a serious fall and be required to go to the hospital.

These were the moments when she hated this place, hated the whole idea of living like this. But she also didn't want the aides being mad at her, to begin thinking of her as a problem resident. Jean had overheard the aides talking together at times, often complaining about some of the other residents always pushing the buttons and making trouble for them. She worried about being identified as one of those people, and what it might mean for her. Why was everything in her life so terribly hard anymore? Lying back in her chair, Jean closed her eyes and continued to wait.

Jean tried to remember if she had her hair appointment with Anthony today? And wasn't Danny coming soon to have lunch with her? She believed that these things were supposed to happen, but more and more she seemed to lose track, wondering if she might be wrong. It had become so frustrating never being sure anymore, as if always being lost in uncertainty, not knowing what was coming next. If only she could be back at her home again, doing the things she wanted to do. It was no longer important having to be alone in this world. She had gotten over that concern. And being alone was certainly better than being trapped all the time, trapped by this place, by these people, by this body and mind that seemed to be slipping away.

More and more, she just wanted to close her eyes and go to sleep. To go to sleep, then wake up and be in heaven, be with God. But despite her wishful intentions, only God could tell her when to come.

When Jean opened her eyes, the day nurse, Mrs. Conforto, was standing before her, whispering her name. The nurse held a plastic container of colored medications in her hands. Jean pointed to the television remote laying on the floor. The woman reached down and picked it up, placing it on the lamp table beside her. As Jean began drinking down each pill, one by one, the nurse inquired about her condition. But Jean's attention had become distracted, for her oldest son was standing just outside the apartment doorway, a vase of flowers in his hands.

DANNY

Danny had stopped at a flower shop on his way to Windsor Hill, picking up a bouquet and some soft chocolate candies. Entering the Windsor Hill facility, a now familiar response awaited him. Smiling again politely, he headed for the elevator. The man with the meaty hands sat slumped nearby, impervious to his world. As Danny stood waiting, it perversely occurred to him that someone could dress the man up as a Halloween display and he would have never known the difference. But just as quickly, he silently chided himself for this moment of dark humor, the obvious lack of respect it undoubtedly conferred. Still, it was hard not to feel like this place was like something out of a horror movie, a strange land of zombie characters remotely clogging about, slowly coming to get you with no chance of escape.

Sadly, Windsor Hill was not a fictional horror film, and certainly not deserving of an unkind human thought. Rather, it was a far-too-real reflection of the human circumstance at the end of a person's days on earth. And yet more important, by its very reality, places like Windsor Hill at least attested to man's genuine treatment of its own, its honor and attempted respect for human life. It mirrored the integrity of a species that aimed for the best in themselves. Even within the prison populations of America the sanctity of life was generally respected in its preservation, whereupon a wrongful person's last breath, their spirit was then consecrated with a respectful farewell to either the unknown or the believed.

And yet, as he scanned the lobby and patiently waited for the elevator, another strange conundrum crossed his mind. For when it came to death row inmates, man's respect for life was not so generous. As well, for most of the lesser beings on this planet, there would be little Christian dignity, unless perhaps one might be a beloved family pet. Nope, when one got down to it, some strictly hard lines needed to be drawn when it came to the sanctity of life. It might be safe to say that survival of the fittest still held the roost, despite any number of moral or religious proclamations written after the fact.

In addition, one could be certain there were a number of other concurrent realities at play on the so-called moral high-ground of the human endeavor. These realities might include CEOs and other corporate shareholders, all those folks purposely invested in the monetary profit of such a charitable and life-affirming enterprise as Windsor Hill. In other words, there was no reason to expect the sanctity of life to necessarily be a tuition-free experience, at least not in the current dominion of American capitalism.

So Danny wasn't going to beat himself up too much over his somewhat cynical take on the ways of the world. Unless of course, it might be his very own mother that someone thought it funny to dress up in a wheel-chair Halloween costume. In that case, his response might be a little more egregious in its impact.

Leaving the elevator, Danny moved onward to visit his mom. Being a week-day, the facility was far busier than his previous week-end visits. There were more administrative staff present, as well as nursing and aide assistants moving quickly about the hallways. As he approached the open doorway, flowers in hand, he could see a woman standing over his mother. She was dressed in a white smock and slacks. Outside the door, a metal cart rested on its wheels. The cart was stacked with numerous colored medications locked inside individual plastic boxes. Danny halted at the door, but the woman quickly motioned him into the apartment.

"Well, hello Danny Stone", the woman spoke with some delight. "You don't recognize me, I can tell." Danny searched across the woman's face, seeking some recognition. She did look somewhat familiar, but he was unable to recall.

"Donna", the woman said, "Donna Spencer". Although it's Donna Conforto now," casually pointing toward the name tag pinned to her chest.

"Oh, Donna, you're kidding," Danny responded. "Geez, I'm sorry. It's been so long."

Danny was surprised by this unexpected greeting. Strange, here was a person from his days in high school, someone he likely hadn't seen since his infrequent returns home during his college years. Both he and the woman stepped forward, engaging in a light embrace.

For several minutes they both made explanations to Jean about the school days they each had shared. Shortly after, Donna Spencer needed to move on with her work. However, it was arranged for Danny to meet Donna for a late lunch during the time when his mother would be with the hairdresser. Danny looked forward to having an old friend to visit and catch up with after all the time gone by.

Upon Donna's exit, Danny filled the flower vase with water. He placed the bouquet on top of the television set where his mother could see the arrangement. With lunch approaching, he helped his mother into her wheelchair, before rolling her downstairs. Upon joining Bernice and Lucy at the table, all three women began to mourn the unexpected loss of Janice being taken away. They worried about who might be next to come.

Bernice had gotten up early, baking a batch of cookies in a small kitchen reserved for the residents. She was without question the most capable of the three.

It pleased Danny that Bernice appeared to have some special liking for his mom. He was reminded of how Bernice had looked after Janice the day before. He was glad that Jean would have such a friendship. But then again, it came as no surprise. For his mother had always been a kind and caring person, and had made friends easily throughout her life.

Yet, Danny had always sensed that his mother's kindness toward others did not spring so much from a confident strength of character, as much as it did from a fear of how she might be perceived by those around her. Not that his mother's genuine concern for others lacked in authenticity, it was more like she often worried about her own acceptance amongst the outside world. There had always been a certain lack of self-esteem within his mom, something she seemed to make up for by the self-deprecation she displayed.

Over his adult years as her first-born son, Danny had come to feel that his mother's lack of self-confidence was a major contributor to her later addiction. He also believed that his father had clearly understood that particular weakness, often using it against her whenever his own frustrations with life had reached a breaking point. As the difficulties in their marriage began to spill out in front of their children, Jean Stone's own drinking problem began in defiant response. At first, it was simply done to give her unrepentant husband a dose of his own medicine after-the-fact. And silently burdened by the acknowledgement of his previous behavior, Tom Stone would weather each of these reactions without comment, and yet never with apology. And thus, these infrequent but regular battles became something of a stand-off between them, normally followed by a strange and silent détente. But steadily over the years, his mother's disease had grown until it could no longer be put aside. For Danny and his siblings, the consequence became a double-whammy that each of them would have to contend, the hidden personal impacts so multiple in their effect.

When the lunch hour was over, Danny rolled his mother back to the apartment. After helping her with a trip to the bathroom, Jean Stone took to her walker, pacing herself down the hall to the salon room where the visiting hairdresser made his bi-weekly visits. With that appointment met on time, Danny made his way back to the dining room, anxious to meet his old high school friend.

Donna Spencer sat alone at a table in the dining room, the lunch period for the residents at Windsor Hill having ended for the day. She welcomed Danny's arrival. As Donna ate her lunch, the two of them exchanged brief histories of their adult lives since their youthful school days so long ago. After nursing school, Donna Spencer had returned to her hometown. She had married her high school sweetheart, Richie Conforto, and like Danny had raised two children. Currently, she had been working at Windsor Hill for several years, mostly serving as its social services director, but intermittently performing nursing duties as schedule necessities required.

Donna Spencer had known that Jean Stone was Danny's mother, and that Kelli was his sister. Donna said that Jean was well-liked by the staff and aides, that his mother was extremely friendly and did not complain very often, certainly when compared to a number of the other residents. She also praised Kelli's faithful assistance and advocacy on behalf of her mom. This was such a special blessing Donna commended, as circumstances could be so wildly different and difficult when working with families.

Typically, Donna explained, there was often only a single family member who carried the weight of visiting and looking after a particular resident. Usually, it was an elderly husband or wife, but more often than not a single daughter or son. In fact, a number of the residents had little or no family nearby, and others for whom no family member felt any responsibility. As a result, many residents lived much of their time alone and without visitation, except for the occasional volunteer who might take them under their wing. And sometimes, it was just the aides and staff who became a resident's only human interaction and care. These variations within each family dynamic were unlimited in scope and circumstance. It could range from a wife who insisted on coming each day to shave her husband, or sadly to a man that had never had a single visitor, eventually dying alone. In her work in this profession, Donna Spencer had seen it all.

Windsor Hill was indeed an assisted-living circumstance, Donna continued, a pay-for facility with a level of care generally above the standard nursing home. However, Windsor was required to have only a limited number of Medicaid beds. These beds usually were a double to a room, and were generally occupied by current residents whose funds had been depleted. Although the purported aim of facilities like Windsor Hill was to allow its residents to 'age in place' as much as possible, corporate financial realities often prevented such an outcome. As a result, an eventual move to a less favorable or public facility might have to be arranged.

Danny listened with interest. No doubt Donna Spencer was indeed experienced in her professional career. And yet, within her working life on behalf of the aged and infirm, there were any number of challenges she could not control. These included the constant corporate pressures for monetary profit, the state-mandated regulations regarding standards of care and compliance, all the while trying to balance the very real needs of innocent human beings who were battling both the physical pain and emotional fears of a life that was slipping away. With each kernel of her expert knowledge being received, Danny was acquiring a new level of respect for those engaged upon such demanding daily tasks.

During their discussion, an afternoon bingo game was being held in the front lobby nearby. Donna laughed as she mentioned the appearance of an Elvis impersonator sometime the week before. His poor performance had been so hilariously comical. She went on to tell a humorous story of her time as an aide at a nursing home while studying for her degree in college. For several semesters, it became her job to provide each female resident their weekly shower at the facility. She jokingly recalled one elderly woman who had angrily complained that Donna had washed her down like a car in the driveway.

This had become Donna Spencer's career, a career spent amongst these everyday events of death and dying, including the sad reality of being present for the final chapters of so many human souls. And yet, despite her presence within this difficult world, Donna reminded Danny that all the normal activities of living remained. They were filled with similar events and circumstances of any younger generation that lived outside these walls. People made friends. Men chased women. There were even times when residents would fall in love. Every single day, there were human acts of either kindness or cruelty. But never be mistaken, Donna thoughtfully explained, there was one singular desire that almost all agreed. It was the one universal constant that each and every resident wished so hopefully might come true, but likely would never be granted. They all wished to find their way home.

As his meeting with Donna Spencer came to a close, an aide approached the table, announcing that Danny's mother had been returned to her room, the hair appointment complete. The two old friends said their farewell, hoping that they might see each other again during the days ahead. Danny returned to his mother.

Jean Stone was in good spirits, not yet ready for her afternoon rest. Danny suggested a ride in the car, to which his mother readily agreed. For a couple of hours that afternoon, they took a drive by familiar places, including the old family home, as well as the recently sold townhouse, each wondering who might now live inside. They visited the cemetery where a husband and father had been laid to rest, a vacant plot of ground remaining beside. Many memories filled both the mind and heart of a mother and son. Returning to Windsor Hill, Jean Stone was obviously fatigued. Danny placed his mom comfortably in her chair, her eyes beginning to close before he even left the room.

JEAN

Jean Stone awoke the following morning. Like other days, her body felt sluggish, her thoughts disoriented, her feelings depressed. After yesterday's car ride with her son, she had slept through the dinner hour in her chair, awakened by the phone ringing on the table beside her. The evening call had come from her daughter. Jean couldn't remember much about the call, or whether her son might have come back for a visit. She did seem to recall that some dinner had been brought to her. And maybe she had watched Larry King on television before going to bed. Everything was a little unclear. Shafts of morning light slipped through the window curtains. It wouldn't be long before someone would be coming to make her get up, to dress and bring her coffee. It would be the same as every other day. She would have to summon the strength to get herself upright, whenever the aide arrived.

Recollections of the previous day began to find their way. Jean had loved going for the drive in the car with her son, to get outside and be part of the world. It had felt so good for her and Danny to reminisce together, to remember some of the good times in her life. But now, lying in her bed, an empty sadness overtook her. Both the family home and townhouse residence were gone from her, each occupied by strangers with lives and families of their own. All the pleasant memories she had shared with Danny could never be returned. Instead, on this useless morning, she lay here alone and so inadequate. It hurt to recognize this truth, the hopelessness of knowing she could not go back again.

There had been the visit to the cemetery, where her husband of over fifty years lay buried beneath the ground. She missed Tom in so many ways, the good Tom, the only man she had spent her life with, the father of her children. Seeing the grave site, his presence in her life marked only by a sculpted headstone pressed to the grass. She felt breathless in her emptiness, knowing the vacant plot beside would one day be for her.

There was nothing she could do or say that might bring back the happier times. Nor could her weakened memory ever forget the shameful moments that each of them had perpetrated upon their marriage and their children, including the loss of their second son. She silently petitioned a prayer for forgiveness, seeking absolution for their sins together, and hoping that her creator might gracefully grant the same. These thoughts would have to be her penance this morning, to simply wake up and face another day.

DANNY

Two more days went by. Danny awoke on Thursday morning, a little hung over from the night before. After visiting with his mother earlier that evening, he had driven north to meet some old neighborhood buddies at a local tavern, one they had all frequented over the years. The reunion had been good. Thankfully, no one in their group was dead yet, although it was probably the first time that medical infirmities had ever been discussed between them. For the most part, all his buddies were generally well. Kids had grown up and were on their own. Retirements had either come or were on the horizon. Sports and travel were reviewed, boyhood memories shared. It had been a full evening, a warm and valued link to his past.

Danny stretched his body in the bed. Duty would be calling soon. He had only two more days on this journey before heading back to Denver. He felt a little guilty making such a desired acknowledgement, but he was ready to travel back home. He felt almost in a rush for the next two days to pass, to be able to get back to living his own life again, feeling strangely as if he was running out of time. He knew where this feeling was coming from. The clock was ticking every single moment. For the past five days he had been daily observing a probable but unwanted future before him. It felt all too certain that time was of the essence. That was enough. He threw off the bed covers and began his day.

He gave Freddie his morning walk, feeding both dog and cat as the coffee brewed. Sitting at the kitchen table, he pulled out the sports section of the morning paper. Then, scanning the rest of the news, he turned eventually to the obituary pages, a section he rarely chose to read. But today, he peered at the faces in the pictures, seeing the dates of birth and death, each with a different story to tell.

Each of the obituaries seemed a positive story, a highlight reel of the best that could be written, as if confirming the value a life well-lived. But once again, his occasional dark humor returned. He had to figure that even criminals and assholes must be getting a good review. It was important that all the failures, mistakes, and regrets of a person's life needed to be faithfully ignored.

But why the hell not deliver a good review? Whenever a person had reached this particular section of the paper, it was far too late for any sorrowful admissions. Short of making a written public apology, what would be the point?

Instead, a service of respect would be scheduled. In lieu of flowers, a charitable contribution requested, perhaps a literary quotation expressed. Soon enough, a casket would be lowered, or cremated ashes spread. Sometime after, a lawyer would settle all the details, any leftover cash or property split amongst the living. And then, as time passed and grief abated, an unintended forgetfulness would ensue. For a quiet truth remained. Time itself was only for the living, while memories were always meant to fade. Nevertheless, in the end, the mystery of life and death would forever remain.

With such unanswerable questions wrestling in his thoughts, Danny made ready for another day at Windsor Hill. He and Kelli had spoken the night before. Diligent as ever, his sister reminded him that every Thursday afternoon would be time for the 'Wedding of the Week'. Apparently, each Thursday afternoon, in the hours before dinner at Windsor Hill, his mother and Lucy would join Bernice at her apartment. Bernice's daughter would be coming to the facility, carrying with her the style-section of the previous Sunday paper. She would read to the ladies the latest edition of the 'Wedding of the Week'. This regular event had become one of their mom's favorite social activities. It was important for Danny not to forget.

KELLI

With the morning sun climbing above the Atlantic horizon, Kelli walked the beach alone with her thoughts. She had driven several miles to a more secluded section of oceanfront, farther away from the tall hotels and boardwalk that now lined the center of this resort community. The ocean waves rolled languidly toward the shore, the steady sound of their break repetitive in her ears. She let the chilled rushing whitewater spill against her naked ankles and over her feet, the sand bubbles whispering softly as they reached the ever-changing tide line. She breathed in the salted morning air, felt the warmth of the sun against her skin, as the pull of each wave retreated to the sea.

It had been such a blessing to be back on the Atlantic shore the last several days. Ever since her childhood, Kelli had always loved the ocean, the solitary calming effect it could have on her, the grand blue sky above. Ahead of her stretched nothing more than sand and beach, except the remote forms of other walkers scattered far into the distance. These were the peaceful moments she had wished for, and now they had come to pass. The beach never failed in helping Kelli return to herself, to remind her that she was lucky to have this life, despite the challenges that must be faced in living the same.

She had slept well the last two nights, the rush of her anxieties beginning to temper with her time away. But upon her leaving, they would more than likely surface again, returning home to the pace and obligations that must be met. Still, she was grateful for this tiny dose of freedom, of being able to catch her breath from the duties of work and her mother's care.

It was impossible to wish for a sooner release. For such a request would only come with a deeply felt loss she would have to accept. Her mother was her most intimate friend, their lives shared together as two women in the family, a bond that both her father and her brothers could not share. Of course the men carried their own histories together, although each in their separate ways. But to eventually lose that bonded intimacy with her mother, it would leave an incredible emptiness she could not imagine, and one she could never hope to fill. And yet, in not too long a time, her mother's final passing would sorrowfully come. And despite a burden being lifted, an equally devastating emptiness would descend.

Reaching a familiar landmark, Kelli turned and headed back the way she had come. With this change in direction a resolution prompted within her. There would not be much time left. Perhaps within the year ahead her mother might pass away. So upon her return home, she would contact her younger brother, Ronnie, asking him to visit whenever he was able. But more important, she vowed to write to her missing brother, Billy. Although no one else was sure of his whereabouts, she had recently found a current address with the use of the internet. She would try and reach out to him, asking him to come. However, she would refuse to plead with him, or try to shame him in any way. But she also knew she couldn't live with herself if she didn't make the effort, to make this one last attempt. At least then she could put it all to rest, whatever the outcome might be. She would do this one last thing, on behalf of the mother she loved.

DANNY

Back at Windsor Hill, Danny caught sight of Donna Spencer working by her cart of daily medications. Donna would not be working the following day, so Danny thanked her for her help, the two old friends saying their good-byes. At the noon hour, he rolled his mother down to the dining room. Once again, he and the women sat at the dining table, along with the one empty chair. No new resident had yet been brought to join them, but each woman's concern remained a topic of conversation. Across the room, Danny could see Janice being fed by an aide. And today, sitting beside Janice was the man with the meaty hands. Danny watched as a second aide did her best to plant some food in the man's mouth. With a cloth napkin at the ready, she quickly wiped away the drool at the edge of his lips.

It was still hard to imagine, to see oneself at the mercy of such a disability. Before this present journey back home, whenever most people had thoughts of death, it would have likely been the misfortune of an auto accident, a plane crash, an earthquake, a terrorist attack, or some other horrendous circumstance where there could be no escape. Certainly, there were the worried fears of losing a loved one, his wife or sons, his brothers and sister, or perhaps a cherished friend. But it had never crossed his mind that someone might die while never knowing they were still alive, like the man with meaty hands. A final condition where one's mental capacity was a total blank, and yet the heart still beat and the blood still flowed. That each day, someone would have to be there to wipe your ass, or grab you before stumbling down the stairs.

Shoot, wasn't it bad enough to no longer be a contributing member of society; to no longer be capable of some ambition in life; to be passed by and ignored as you struggled down the street because somebody took your driver's license away. Or perhaps be freezing cold all the time, in a home where you can't even open a can of soup, and all your friends are dead and the phone never rings. Wouldn't that potential reality be simply bad enough? Once again, Danny had to humorously shake himself from this moment of miserable contemplation. And yet, here in this dining room at this place called Windsor Hill, on a beautiful autumn afternoon, sitting here with his mother, and with Lucy and Bernice and all the others in this weirdly captured reality, the potential expectations for his own life were no longer becoming a hypothetical. Rather, the betting line today was heavily favored toward a personal future that might be little more than a foregone conclusion.

When lunch was finished, it was back to the apartment. After helping his mother use the bathroom, Danny settled her back in her chair for an afternoon rest. He then took his leave, planning to return later in the afternoon.

JEAN

Back in her apartment at Windsor Hill, Jean lay back in her recliner chair, falling asleep for a couple of hours. Upon awakening, she checked the time on the light-table beside her. It was shortly before four o'clock. Although her memory continued at times to desert her in these recent months, she did recall that within the hour her son would return, joining her and the girls for their weekly reading of the 'Wedding of the Week'. The reading was something she looked forward to, and she didn't want to forget. Bernice's daughter would be coming to visit. She would bring along the story from the Sunday newspaper, including a baked dessert and some sparkling cider to share.

There were very few things that she looked forward to in her life at Windsor Hill. She had slowly grown tired of the regular events downstairs, the crowded room of entertainment functions that would be held for the residents. She had never been one for games or group sing-alongs, the events that were so often part of the daily programs. In her past life before coming here, her activities had been more focused on raising her children. That had been followed by her work as a teacher's aide in the schools, then later her grandchildren, and finally the care of her husband in the time before his death. Along the way, she did enjoy an occasional game of cards with other women in the neighborhood. But unlike many of them, she had always been a sports fan. She had never missed watching both her children and grandchildren play on their athletic teams, as well as the college games on television, especially the teams where each had gone to school.

The Stone family had always been about team sports, whether it was playing or watching the same. Of the four, only Billy had shown little interest. He had been her second child, the one she believed she had failed to love enough, the one child that had always been the hardest to reach or understand. It would forever hurt her deeply that she had never found a way to love or comfort him in the ways he needed. It was another failure she would always regret, yet one she had never been able to fix. Without question, it was clear that Billy had been the child most affected by the infrequent disasters that both she and her husband had inflicted upon the family. And for these sins, her shame and guilt would never go away. She had tried to love Billy as equally as the rest. But sometimes there is that one child that a mother is somehow unable to reach and embrace, or be able to do the right thing.

Billy had always been a quiet boy. In fact, he was the easiest of the others to care for during his infant years. He had

never been a difficult child in any way, just so terribly distant
and internal in his presence. It was almost as if he was not
supposed to be part of the family, that he had somehow been
misplaced in some way. That he had sensed on his own that
some mistake had occurred. It was always so hard to know
what was inside of him, to comprehend his feelings, to be able
to show a mother's love. Maybe it was because he was so quiet
and effortless that she had taken him for granted, and thus
easy to ignore. Whatever the cause might have been, both she
and Tom had failed him, failed him in ways they could not answer, their own destructive tirades only making matters worse.
And so her son had taken up his own solitary activities. And
then suddenly he was gone, drifting away, away to another life,
with little more than an honest and respectful good-bye.

Billy's loss would always be a deeply held regret, but it was
one thing that her drinking had helped to overcome. But now,
the thought of her dying without some resolution, without some
way of saying she was sorry, was a cross too hard to bear. She
quietly wiped a tear from her eye, knowing she might never
have the chance to say good-bye.

At quarter to five, there was a gentle knock on the door. By
then she had wiped the tears away, a disguised smile greeting
the entrance of her oldest son. She pulled herself together,
forcing herself upright, her courage returning. She always had
the children to live for, including those desperate mornings so
many years ago when she had to respond. They were terrible
mornings, having to rise up after having been verbally beaten
to a pulp the night before. But the kids needed their breakfast,
they needed to be dressed and off to school. Her fortitude and
loyalty still stirred within her. Today, she demanded that Danny
spare the wheelchair. Taking the walker in her feeble hands,
she pushed herself forward down the hall.

DANNY

Danny sat with the other women in Bernice's apartment at Windsor Hill. An aide had helped him bring some extra chairs from a nearby activity room. Bernice's daughter sat before them, holding a section of newspaper in her hands. She had already distributed to each of the women a copy of a young couples' marriage photo from the story she was about to read. And so began the 'Wedding of the Week'.

As for their introduction, Karl and Lindsay had first met at the birthday party of one of Lindsay's friends. Karl was working for a landscaping company. Lindsay was finishing her final year of school at a nearby college. Lindsay was attracted to Karl from her very first sight. By the end of that evening she had given Karl her phone number. But over the next several weeks she didn't get a call. Sometime after, she joined her college friends for a night out to see a local band. Karl was present that evening. They spent more time together, with Karl once again saying he would call her, which he finally did.

Their first date together was a walk they shared at a local park. Their first kiss came later that day at the door of her apartment. As time went by, they began to go out regularly, to concerts, festivals, camping trips and the beach. Karl loved to fish, Lindsay was a bird watcher. Eventually they talked about buying a house together. Karl's proposal came on the two-year anniversary of their very first date. Having gone to dinner that evening, Karl had seemed a little nervous and distracted. He even forgot his wallet at the restaurant. But later that evening, Lindsay was surprised and overjoyed as he struggled to make the proposal. She immediately gave her assent.

The couple decided to wait on a marriage date until Lindsay finished her master's degree at the college. Lindsay's parents still owned an old family farm. The house and grounds needed a lot of work, but the couple decided to have both the ceremony and reception at that location. All the following summer, with the help of family and friends, the farm was made ready for the occasion. By August the corn was tall, the temperature warm and dry. Fluffy white clouds floated across the sky. Close friends performed several readings, with Lindsay's brother performing the ministerial duties.

Lindsay wore an ivory fit and flare gown, trimmed with ruche and silver crystal accents. Her grandmother's engagement ring was tied to her bouquet, as well as a 'mother's ring' which was featured with special birthstones. Lindsay chose to wear 'something blue', although it never could be seen. It happened to be her underwear.

The reception was held on site. Using old mason jars from the farmhouse, the tables and yard was adorned with flowers. Party favors for the guests were dispensed from the jars as well. The toppers on the wedding cake were the silhouette of a groom holding a fishing pole, and behind the bride's topper was a bird sitting in a tree. The honeymoon would be a short trip to the Pocono Mountains, where the happy couple would canoe and enjoy the outdoors. A longer tropical honeymoon was planned for later that winter.

The funniest part of the ceremony occurred when Karl dropped a piece of the wedding cake down Lindsay's dress while feeding her. He then used his mouth to scoop it out over her breasts. After the ceremony, the couple returned to their daily lives and work, living together with their pet birds and cats. And with that, the latest version of the 'Wedding of the Week' came to its end.

When the reading was finished, the women in the room began to chatter together as Bernice's daughter fed each of them some coffee cake and sparkling cider. Danny was little more than a fly on the wall as the wedding story was discussed. To his surprise, his mother began to happily tell of Danny's own wedding so many years ago. It had been a late September wedding on a similar blue day in Colorado. The location was an aspen grove, the leaves having just begun their brilliant yellow run. At the time, it had been a wonderful event, one that Danny would never forget, although the vagaries of time and circumstance had slowly weathered its effect. Still, as a courtesy to both his mother as well as his ex-wife, he joined in helping to retrace the events as best he could.

It was easy to believe that certain moments in life would always retain their luster for recollection. Whether it be a beautiful wedding, the birth of a child, or other singular moments where an indelible sense of joy and contentment had made their mark. Upon such memories, it made no sense to recall the more difficult outcomes that might have come after. For such tribulations were only destined for the future, and thus unknown at the initial moment in time. And there was no good reason to rob such moments of their place in one's journey, to ever allow misfortune or regret to shade their light. For those instants of true happiness can often be a sparing sensibility within the longer scheme of a lifetime. It was best to hold them clear and dear to the heart for as long as one was able. Eventually, the time would come when their memory would fade like a candle melting away, the flame flickering towards the dark, gasping for air.

KELLI

On Friday morning, Kelli and her husband woke up early. They packed quickly and were on the road for the long drive north. Like most men, Jack preferred to do the driving, so Kelli settled in as a passenger for the trip toward home. Once again, between the scenery and small-talk in the hours ahead, Kelli would be left alone with her thoughts.

The 'sandwich generation', that's what they called it, that time in life when an adult must be both engaged in the care of one's own children, as well as the care of aging parents who needed their help. Although Kelli was approaching her mid-fifties and the children mostly out of the home, the feeling of being 'sandwiched' in her life had not given way. She had her youngest son at home whose future still worried her, and a mother whose care had essentially begun with the death of her father. And there was of course her work, which continued daily with its own set of demands. She knew these circumstances would continue to persist in the months ahead, a life controlled by the burden of their necessity. Still, she longed for some sense of freedom from it all, for a time when she and Jack might wake up in the morning, with nothing more than a plan they might choose to share together. It would become a new chapter in their marriage, with a bucket list waiting to be filled.

But today, there was still a ways to go. Kelli felt somewhat rested, this modest break from her current routine providing some relief. Her anxiety had tempered with just the change of place. It was great to know that a feeling of calm might still exist within her. Nevertheless, she knew herself well enough, that her stress was only temporarily dormant under her skin. And although she felt confident she could manage those effects, it was always such a toll to maintain.

She loved her mother dearly, despite all the troubles and challenges that had come before. They were like two peas in a pod, each of them an appendage of the other, always there for each other whenever difficult moments arose. But the thought of one day being without her mom, to be without the intimacies that existed between them, seemed almost impossible to comprehend. Surely her mother's death was coming, as indeed it must. There was no escaping the outcome, the eventual loss of this bond between them. Meanwhile, they would have to carry on, knowing the ultimate hardships each would have to endure.

JEAN

Once again, the morning awoke with the afflictions of age and restless fatigue needing to be overcome. Jean silently said her prayers. It would be another day of accepting her condition, another day of accepting her fate. Some mornings she felt too weak to go on, wishing that God might gently touch her with his blessed hand, and release her from this place. Although not today she hoped, for today her son would be coming one last time, and she wanted to say good-bye.

And so the present routine would play out again. Today was a shower day, followed by the dressing, the feeding and the pills, the television, before Danny arrived at noon. They had lunch together downstairs, where her son said his farewell to Lucy and Bernice. Then they made a phone call to Jean's sister in New York. For a time, Jean forgot about her future, watching her son chat happily with her sister, asking about the cousins, and wishing all the best. Outside the building, they made another roll around the grounds of Windsor Hill, the chilled air brushing across her face.

After Danny headed for home, she fell into her afternoon nap. Later she watched the evening news before taking dinner inside the apartment. Around seven in the evening, Danny returned with Kelli and Jack, her daughter finally home from her trip. She listened to the summary of her daughter's vacation. Then she and Danny told them more about Janice being taken away, of Donna the nurse being one of Danny's old friends, as well as Danny attending the latest edition of the 'Wedding of the Week'. But far too soon Sharice arrived to dress her for the night. Danny and Jack went into the hall. The evening visit had been special until the final moments came to pass.

Her son was going away, leaving tomorrow to go back home. Jean held him close with all the strength she had, feeling the warmth of his lips on her cheek, her tears beginning to swell. When all were gone, she struggled into her bed. Lying in the dark alone, she simpered under the covers, her heart sunken in her chest, the emptiness so deep she could hardly take a breath. Her silent prayers seemed useless in the night, amidst the shameful wish that tomorrow might never have to come.

DANNY

The jet airplane gently circled over the front range of the Rockies as if suspended in air. Seated within the flatlands of Colorado, the city of Denver spread below. In the distance to the west, the mountain peaks had begun to take on the whitened cover of a coming winter ahead. Further down, the blonde foothills were bathed in an aspen glow, amidst the timbered green of Ponderosa pine reaching toward the sky. It felt good to be so near to home.

Danny's emptiness at leaving his mother behind was slowly beginning to fade, although he knew an ever-present sense of guilt would remain for a time. Sorrowfully, there wasn't much more he could do? It was true. Sometimes there are circumstances in life that must go wanting, despite the desire to fix. Part of him felt the need to bring his mother here, to have her nearby, to continue this necessary cause on her behalf, to repay some undefined debt that needed to be paid. But that was not about to happen, and surely it was not the answer in the end. His mother needed to be close to her daughter's world, close to the tethered bond they had shared together for such a long time. Even more so, the memories of Jean Stone's life needed to be near to her, to remain set upon the terra firma of her family's becoming. Somewhere near home, always close to home.

As the jet began its slow descent, Danny Stone wondered whether he might see his mother ever again. He felt some hope about the chance. But if not, he knew it would be okay. For near the end, certain understandings must come. Often in life, there are events that must remain devoid of resolution. For those happier moments, much like the week just passed, they can never be freed from the others. The good times would always be wedded to the mistakes of the past, those moments of grace inextricably attached to specific errors incapable of reverse. In a way, each must stand the test of time together, for better or worse. Danny could only hope that his mother's last thoughts might be joyful and beneficent, perhaps embraced by a warm white light surrounding her, offering a beautiful and youthful future ahead. Maybe, he began to wish to himself, perhaps that his lovely mother might once again return to her very own 'Wedding of the Week'. And in so doing, live happily ever after.

THE LAWS OF NATURE
ACCORDING TO
BALLPARK FRANK

(Pollard Creek, Oregon / Summer 1979)

THE LAWS OF NATURE
ACCORDING TO BALLPARK FRANK

(Pollard Creek, Oregon / Summer 1979)

The month of May had reached a full spring bloom in Pollard Creek. Each day stretched longer toward the apex of summer light, the Solstice soon to come. The early evenings grew comfortably warm. It was a time to be outdoors as much as possible, for whatever reasons one might choose.

Sean McAllister and Marty Johnson sat lounging on the porch of the Pollard Creek Country Store, taking in the extended light of day. McAllister chewed on a swizzle-stick of red licorice. Marty Johnson licked his fingers after wolfing down a chocolate Ding Dong. Ralph Swanson, the owner of the Country Store, stepped outside and joined the pair, lighting a cigarette. The men casually made small talk, lazily gazing across the triangle of roads that intersected through the center of Pollard Creek. During their idle conversation an occasional vehicle would pass before them. Off to their right, the tractor trailers geared up or down the access road, heading either for the Hungry Dog truck stop or returning back towards the north/south freeway entrances at each edge of town.

The men paid no mind as an automobile approached from the northern exit of the freeway toward Pollard Creek. Rumbling along, the car began angling slowly to its right, appearing to head across the triangle toward Lower Pollard Creek Road. But suddenly the vehicle swerved abruptly back toward the access road.

This quick change of direction caught the men's attention. They watched as the vehicle motored before them, approaching the stop sign at the crossing to the access road. With another sharp swerve to the right, the car plowed smack into the stop sign. A loud metal whack broke through the air, the impact of the collision bending the signpost halfway back toward the road. Startled by the event, the men remained frozen, watching as the automobile idled in front of the sign, the driver's silhouette behind the wheel. The driver slowly reached for the shift lever on the steering column, placing the car into reverse. As the vehicle started backward, the stop sign sprang wildly toward its hood, the metal signpost shuttering as it tried to return upright.

Finding his voice, Ralph Swanson cried out, "What the hell? Jeepers, look at that!" Sean McAllister remained silent, his jaw ajar. He turned his head toward Marty Johnson as if seeking some response. Marty continued to stare at the vehicle. All three men watched as the driver moved the car back from the stop sign before sliding the shifter back into forward gear. The car motored slowly forward. Turning right onto the access road, the driver resumed speed toward the freeway ramp at the south end of town.

Sean McAllister leaned back on his bench seat and burst out laughing. Marty Johnson sat silent, shaking his head as if nothing particular surprised him. But Ralph Swanson didn't think anything was funny. "Hellfire, we got to do something," he spoke excitedly. "I'm calling Sheriff Haines. We got to get that guy off the road."

Marty Johnson leaned back against the porch bench, before looking up at Ralph, speaking calmly. "Now wait a second, Ralph. Slow down a little. There's no sense bringing the law into this. If the guy happens to kill himself, he kills himself. The law can't do anything about that."

Ralph turned quickly toward Marty. "What? For crying out loud, boy, what if he ends up killing somebody else? Jesus H.

Christ, Marty, we can't let that happen. What kind of car was that anyway? I got to try and give Haines a description."

"Come on, Ralph," Marty soothed, "settle down a little. It's a brown Ford Galaxie if you need to make the call. But hell, I happen to know that guy. He lives over in Glendale. If you want to call Haines and have the guy end up the slammer, go right ahead. I also happen to know he just recently split with his old lady. From what I've heard, he's been having a pretty hard go. Now I wouldn't advise it, but if you want to add to those particular troubles, then go right ahead and do what you got to do."

"Goddamn you, Marty. You can't have a guy like that driving around shit-faced all the time. Jiminy Christmas! So what do 'you' propose we do about it, before he runs over somebody else, or maybe even Sean here? Who the hell wants that?"

Marty Johnson quietly raised his hands up with acceptance. "All right, Ralph, all right, relax, would you? I'll tell you what. How about if I try to take care of it? I'm pretty sure the guy is headed over to the tavern in Solace Valley. I've been seeing him there off and on the last week or two. Listen, if I follow on over, if I talk with him and get him home all right, will you leave Sheriff Haines out of it for now? Then, if you happen to see him driving through town all fucked-up again, you can hand it over to the law. What do you say, Ralph, can you be cool with that?"

Ralph Swanson turned and flicked his dead cigarette out into the street. Letting out a deep breath he gathered himself. He turned back toward Marty. "I know what the hell it is, Marty. That guy is a goddamn vet, isn't he? You goddamn Vietnam boys are always covering for each other, whatever your behavior, whatever the mess you're dealing with. Am I right?"

Marty Johnson seemed to tighten a little, staring back at Ralph, but keeping his cool. "Sure, Ralph, whatever you say. Yeah, we stick together all right, at least up to point. But for now, I'll take that remark as a 'yes'. So we got a deal?"

Ralph Swanson turned his head and looked hard at McAllister. "And what the hell do you say about all this crap, mister everything's-so-funny? Are you in on this, too?"

McAllister looked up at Ralph before shrugging his shoulders. "Well, I'm not a veteran, Ralph, so what would I know? But come on now, you know that Marty will try to help the guy. And if it doesn't work out, he'll let you know."

Ralph Swanson's face gripped with frustration as he reached for the door handle to the store. "You goddamn boys! I just don't understand you long-haired idiots sometimes. But do me a simple favor, will you? Before you leave, see if you two knuckleheads can bend that goddamn sign back up straight. That's the least you can do, for crying out loud." With those words, Ralph Swanson stepped through the door of his store, slamming it from behind.

With Ralph out of the picture, McAllister turned back toward Marty. "So is that all true? You know the guy, and he's a vet?"

"Yep, Air Force from what I hear, flew jets over the North." Marty paused. "But you know him too, don't you? He's kind of a big talker and a jokester most of the time. He's sort of crazy-wild like most of those flyboys, but not in a bad way. But you know him, he plays guitar and sings in that house band over at the Village Inn in Glendale. And his old lady is the dark-haired lead singer in the group. But from what I hear, she's his ex-old lady these days."

Marty Johnson continued. "I briefly met him at a party one night last year. They had this big campfire, and he was playing guitar and singing. He's got like the whole Neil Diamond songbook down pat, and can really sing them well. But on the other side of things, I also heard that when he and the chick broke up last month, he took out a chainsaw and tried to cut their house in half."

"What? Are you kidding," McAllister questioned, cocking his head sideways?

"Yeah, that's what they tell me. I guess the chick's brother and another guy in the band happened to be over at the house that day, and they were able to stop him. But apparently, he had that chainsaw all fired-up and was ready to rock and roll."

Marty Johnson broke into a laugh, as if imagining the scene. But he quickly settled, returning serious. "Yeah, as I was trying to tell Ralph here, the guy is just going through a tough time right now. He's kind of on a loose screw. Like I said, he can really talk some shit. But he's not a troublemaker, not like some other assholes in these parts."

"Unless he's behind the wheel of a car," McAllister noted dryly. "But yeah, I do know that guy. I only know him to see him, that's all. Are you really going to follow him over to the tavern like you said?"

"Yeah, why the hell not," Marty seemed to question himself. "I suppose duty calls. And now I've told Ralph I would do it. Of course, maybe the guy has already found a guard rail to punch out, and then gone rolling down the mountain." Marty stood up and spit toward the street. "What can I tell you, Sean? He's just another brother going through some shit. What would you expect me to do?"

"I wouldn't expect anything to the contrary, Marty," McAllister confirmed. "And as far as Ralph goes, he's just one of those law-and-order guys, you know that."

"Yeah, I know", Marty answered. "Hey, let's go over and see if we can bend that goddamn sign back up. We don't need Ralph coming further unglued. I think that maybe with the two of us, it just might work."

McAllister followed behind, walking across the street towards the stop sign. "So what's that guy's name anyway," McAllister asked?

"Frank, I believe, Frank Mayer. People in Glendale call him Ballpark Frank."

"Like the hot dog," McAllister joked?

"Yeah, like the hot dog," Marty deadpanned. "But his mother calls him 'Oscar'! Now don't be a wise-ass. Just put your weight right here, and we'll try to bend this damn thing back up straight."

Two weeks passed. The days of spring grew longer. The calendar turned from May to June. On a warm twilight evening, Sean McAllister drove back home, winding his truck up London Ridge Road, returning from a softball practice with the local Pollard Creek team. Reaching the property, McAllister parked near the main house. He grabbed his glove and cleats before climbing out of the truck. A visiting car sat nearby in the drive. It was Dianne's vehicle. Dianne was a friend of Brenda, who now lived in the main house with his buddy, Robert Sage. Robert owned the eighty-acres of land situated on this south side of London Ridge. The property also had a small one-room cabin that sat further up the hill. It was this little cabin that Sean McAllister presently called home.

Robert Sage was out of town. Once again, he was on a business trip that nobody needed to know, and everyone knew better not to ask. McAllister decided to knock on the door of the main house, if nothing more than to say hello and see what was up. Hearing a return salutation he let himself inside.

At the far end of the large open room, Brenda and Dianne sat at the kitchen table with a bottle of wine, facing McAllister. Sitting across from the two women was a bushy-haired man, a can of beer in his grip. At first, McAllister didn't recognize the man as someone he knew. But as Dianne said hello and introduced the man as Frank, it quickly dawned on him. This was the musician guy from Glendale, the driver of the car from a couple weeks back, the man they called Ballpark Frank.

The two men shook hands. As McAllister took a seat at the table, he accepted a smoking joint from Ballpark Frank that was being passed around. While McAllister took a hit, Ballpark Frank quickly jumped up from his seat. Heading for the refrigerator, he asked McAllister if he wanted a beer. Before McAllister could reply, a can of Budweiser was being placed in his hand. Then, returning to sit at the table, Ballpark Frank caught sight of the baseball gear that McAllister had placed on the floor.

"You play ball," Ballpark Frank inquired? "You guys got a team over here?" McAllister answered in the affirmative. It was not much of a team he admitted, but a team. In fact, they had just begun playing in a league up in the Tri-Cities, thirty miles north of Pollard Creek. As McAllister answered the question, he could immediately sense that Ballpark Frank was all ears. It didn't take long before Ballpark Frank was telling McAllister that he had a long baseball history down in Los Angeles. And from the substance of his fast-paced rap, Ballpark Frank sounded like a guy who knew how to play. So it didn't take long for the inevitable question to arrive. "You guys need any more players," Ballpark Frank asked?

McAllister answered in the affirmative. But he also was thinking to himself that the operative word to this particular question was 'play', especially when it came to the scarcity of athletic talent in this part of the world.

There were certainly more trees in Southern Oregon than one could shake a stick at, but that surely didn't mean there were many adequately talented ballplayers growing on them. If one happened to need a team of stoned-out pot growers, drunken loggers, or other inebriated no-counts, there were plenty. But ballplayers, that would be something else altogether. So in measured response, and with a wee-bit of reticence, McAllister asked if Ballpark Frank had ever played any second base, a position where this current band of Pollard Creek misfits definitely needed some help.

It took only a moment for Ballpark Frank to begin selling himself as the second-coming of Joe Morgan of the Cincinnati Reds. Morgan, of course, was already destined to be a sure-fire Hall of Famer. But by the time Ballpark Frank had managed to take a second breath, he had attempted to convince McAllister that he alone was nothing short of what scouts in professional baseball call a 'five-tool' player.

A 'five-tool' player was a rare species, a young man who could do it all. He could run, he could throw, he could field, and he could hit. But often the final tool was the difference maker. He could hit with power. Every major league team in baseball was constantly in search of the next five-tool player. Throughout the history of the game many had come bearing that label of potential, but only a few had ever accomplished such status on the field of play.

So now, who could have ever imagined, that right out of the clear-blue sky, sitting in a cabin on the edge of a mountain hillside, deep in the forests of this Oregon timber country, there just happened to be a guy who could both run and throw? In addition, he could field, he could hit, and even hit with power, those veritable five-tools. Ballpark Frank Mayer was becoming so surely insistent of his own capability, it would be difficult for any person, the least of all Sean McAllister, to question the man's veracity. Whatever the truth might eventually become, one thing was certain. Ballpark Frank Mayer was not to be deterred. If he had made up his mind he wanted to play some summer softball with a bunch of mountain hippies, then in doing so, he would leave not a single stone unturned.

At first, Dianne and Brenda courteously listened to Frank's impassioned delivery. Dianne especially, as McAllister found out later she had just met the guy. But soon enough, Dianne and Brenda grew bored with the sports talk, instead returning to their preferred conversation about spring garden plantings and other feminine interests, leaving McAllister to engage with Ballpark Frank's enthusiastic presentation all on his own.

Continuing to listen, McAllister kept thinking to himself. Here was the same guy who Marty and he had watched run down a stop sign a couple weeks back, the same guy Marty had said was a jet pilot in Vietnam. The very same guy who had recently lost his old lady, then tried to chainsaw a house in half. The same guy who played guitar in a band, and who some folks in Glendale referred to as 'Ballpark Frank'. McAllister hadn't seen Marty Johnson since that particular evening, so he still didn't really know if Marty had perhaps found the guy that night and helped him out.

About the only thing McAllister did know, was that this dude obviously hadn't yet crashed over the side of a mountain. Nope, instead he was a living and breathing man of considerable athletic consequence, complete with Hall of Fame credentials at America's favorite pastime. As Marty had previously mentioned, Frank Mayer could definitely talk the talk. And even though McAllister knew that 'talking shit' was a commonplace commodity in the land of Pollard Creek, still, he had no choice but to give the man his stage.

So the dates were set. Practice on Friday, followed by a league-sponsored tournament on the upcoming week-end. Ballpark Frank Mayer would meet with the rest of the team at their practice in Glendale, then head north with them for the tourney the following day. At least Frank Mayer looked the part. He was stout, strong, and forcefully confident, an ex-fighter pilot in Nam, with the tattooed forearms to show for it. He appeared to be some years older than McAllister and the rest of the team, perhaps a bit past his prime. But what the hell, if the guy could play ball, then he would be a welcome addition to the club.

But after the practice on Friday, McAllister was the one who had to break the unfortunate news to Ballpark Frank. In so many words, Frank Mayer would never be confused with Joe Morgan, despite his five-tool highlight reel from several evenings before. The team would instead use him as a catcher on Saturday. Catcher would undoubtedly be a better fit.

In slow pitch softball, the catcher position did not necessarily require great skill. Most of the catcher's duty was to simply return the ball to the pitcher. However, he did need to be adequately capable of catching and making a play at the plate. And equally important for the catcher was to talk a good game, to make friends with the umpire, and whenever possible distract the batter while he stood ready to hit. By the end of their Friday practice, it was abundantly clear that Ballpark Frank was more than endowed with these particular skills. Indeed, there appeared to be no shortage of *talk* in Frank Mayer's athletic repertoire. During the evening practice, Frank Mayer had placed himself easily at the center of attention, meeting all his new teammates with ease and gusto, without a speck of personal deference needing to be displayed.

Still, McAllister couldn't be sure how Ballpark Frank would respond to the news of his positional demotion. And since it was solely McAllister who had brought Frank Mayer to this particular dance, he would be the one expected to deliver the verdict. They were standing in the high school parking lot after the workout. Being up in Glendale, McAllister figured that Frank probably wouldn't have to drive very far to get where he was going. Although as far as McAllister knew, the guy could be living in his car for all anyone might know.

So McAllister was relieved when Ballpark Frank simply responded by saying, "That's cool, so I'll be starting as catcher. I think catcher will be good for us. I like catcher." McAllister reminded Ballpark Frank that they would pick him up the next morning at the freeway rest stop a little before eight-thirty. The team would then head north to the Tri-Cities for their first game at ten. Saying farewell, McAllister headed for his panel truck. But as Ballpark Frank reached the door of his familiar Ford Galaxie, he shouted back at McAllister. "Hey, Sean, not to worry, it's all good, brother. And remember this. It happens to be one of my natural laws ...."

"If you can't dazzle them with your brilliance, then baffle them with your bullshit!"

"You got that?" Ballpark Frank questioned, chuckling to himself as he slipped behind the wheel.

"Yeah, I got it," McAllister answered. Starting his car, Frank Mayer gunned his vehicle out of the parking lot, headed for god-knows where.

Shortly after, as McAllister drove his own truck back over the mountain pass to Pollard Creek, he wasn't exactly sure what he might have 'gotten'. But he pretty much figured he'd 'gotten' it already. And whatever it might be, McAllister was certain about one thing. This guy known as Ballpark Frank Mayer was likely going to be a story all his own.

On Saturday morning the team caravan out of Pollard Creek was running late. But just as promised, Ballpark Frank was waiting at the freeway rest stop, wearing the uniform he'd been given the previous evening. With a small athletic bag in hand, Ballpark Frank pressed himself into the front seat of the station wagon, joining McAllister. At the wheel of the station wagon was the pitcher, Jimmy Lacovski. In the backseat were 'Little Al' Miller and Rickey 'The Rocket' Rucker, outfielders, as well as Harry "Wheels" McClanahan, the shortstop. A second car of teammates sat idling behind the first.

The usual reason things were often running late was always due to Lacovski, the world's preeminent cheapskate. Jimmy Lacovski's car never failed to be out of gas on game day. From his previous trips to the Tri-Cities, Jimmy Lacovski had already figured out the exact amount of petroleum necessary to get to the fields and return back home. He would pull up to the pumps at the Hungry Dog truck stop in Pollard Creek, immediately beginning to wrestle as many dollar bills as he could muster out of his ridership. Lacovski had one and only one purpose in mind, to make a profit out of the trip.

Despite having met Ballpark Frank Mayer only the day before, Lacovski wasted no time in setting down his rules of the road with the team's newest member, exacting three bucks to pay for the ride. Ballpark Frank gave McAllister a quick glance, before whistling toward the windshield. "Three bucks, huh. A little stiff, don't you think." The statement immediately drew a laugh from the rest of the car. Sensing this response, Ballpark Frank was quick to get to the point. "Hell, I didn't realize I was catching a cab today. But I guess I got no choice, huh boys."

Everyone but Lacovski cackled again, with Rickey the Rocket chiming in, "Yeah, Frank, welcome to Lacovski's Limo Service. Lacovski be his name, and extortion be his game." Searching into his athletic bag, Ballpark Frank counted out three singles, before reaching over to hand them to Lacovski. As Lacovski reached a free hand to receive them, Ballpark Frank quickly pulled back the money, before speaking to the group ....

"You know, boys, if the good Lord didn't want them sheared, he wouldn't have made them sheep."

Ballpark Frank pushed the money into Lacovski's hand. Lacovski stuffed the money into his pocket. "Thank you, Frank. Now where is it you wanted to go?"

"To the ballpark, my man, to the ballpark. To kick some logger ass." As he spoke, Ballpark Frank nudged McAllister in his side. McAllister took the cue. Turning toward Ballpark Frank, he whispered, "That wouldn't be another one of your so-called 'laws', would it?" Ballpark Frank simply smiled and nodded at the question. "You know, Sean, I got a feeling that nothing much gets by you. Am I right? Yep, I got that feeling. But be prepared, there may be other laws you might want to consider living by."

Heading north toward the day ahead, Sean McAllister had little doubt about Ballpark Frank fitting in with the team. He wondered if Marty Johnson might have perhaps felt the same, after checking in on this dude after the stop-sign fiasco a couple weeks back. It was now pretty clear that nobody needed to seriously worry about old Ballpark Frank Mayer. The man could easily take care of himself. As well, McAllister figured, there was a good chance this guy would be busting more than a few softballs before this season was done. He would likely be busting some other balls as well.

The tournament started on a positive note. The team managed to get a good draw for its opener, winning the game six to three. Everyone played well. Ballpark Frank wasted no time is settling into his new position. He engaged and encouraged Lacovski with the pitching. He added positive energy in the dugout. He was entirely focused and playing ball again for the first time in a long while, thoroughly enjoying being part of the competition. Although he was a little rusty at the plate, and proved to be rather slow on the bases, he managed to reach on an error, later scoring a run when 'Wheels' McClanahan ripped a two-out triple into the gap in right-center field. It was an auspicious start for the ballclub, as well as the team's new player.

For game number two, the team was again a recipient of good fortune. They only had to wait a short time before being back on the field, and they were ready to play. Under a sunny and warm late-morning sky, McClanahan and McAllister both had three hits, leading the club to a second victory over another familiar opponent, a team that had beaten them earlier in the regular season. Ballpark Frank immediately anointed the duo the "Big Mac Combo".

The whole team was feeling great. It was the first time the group had ever won two games in a row in the winner's bracket. Spirits were high. With a third win later in the afternoon, they would get to play in the winner's bracket final on Sunday morning, farther than they had ever gone before. But after the game, when the team studied the tournament bracket to see who they would play next, a thing called 'reality' began to sink in.

The Tri-City Bombers! Wouldn't you know it, the Tri-City Bombers! Nobody ever beat the Tri-City Bombers, at least not in this part of the state.

The Bombers were the Southern Oregon heavies, a team from right here at home in the Tri-Cities. The Bombers were known to be one of the best teams in the region, a collection of logger-sized assholes who could bash slow-pitched softballs deep into the sky, before jogging arrogantly around the bases till they reached home plate. Whenever the Bombers did finally make three outs, and were forced to take the field, they appeared like a brick wall. Every ball that an opponent would hit seemed to go directly to where they were standing. The Bombers could often knock you out in no time flat. Damn. It had to be the Tri-City Bombers!

McAllister knew the Bombers well from playing in tournaments in Grants Pass during seasons past, and so did McClanahan and a few of the others on the team. But adding to their misfortune, the game would not be played for at least a couple of hours. So when Lacovski started to take orders for a food run to get some lunch, everyone threw in some extra dough for a case of beer.

However, having sensed the foreboding pall that had taken over the team, Ballpark Frank Mayer pounded his fist hard into his glove, striding into the center of the group. "What's this all about, boys? You mean to tell me we're giving up on this thing? Well, that sure ain't going to happen. No damn way. Let me tell you this ....

"You show me a good loser, and I'll show you a constant loser."

Upon this remark, every head on the team sank a notch, followed by the shuffling of feet. After some moments of uncomfortable silence, McAllister took Ballpark Frank aside, pulling him away from the team. For a minute or so, McAllister whispered some confidential words of explanation into Frank's ear. Ballpark Frank appeared to listen intently, although showing no expression. Then, as McAllister stepped aside, Ballpark Frank turned back to the team. "Okay, okay. Never mind, boys. Never mind. Are we sure that one case of beer will be enough?"

With the question, everyone on the team breathed a sigh of relief, before reaching further into their wallets to help increase the beer order. Lacovski was all smiles as he happily collected the bills.

With the early June afternoon growing hot with the sun, and while empty beer cans piled up higher in a recycle container near the side of the dugout, the winner's bracket game between the mighty Tri-City Bombers and the Southern Oregon Grower's Association got under way.

The silent financial sponsors of the Pollard Creek team had actually never witnessed their community softball club compete on the field. Rather, they remained hard at work back at home. Hidden in the hills of Southern Oregon, they would be busy checking their water lines, mixing compost tea, weeding the male plants out of their patches, while stocking their ammo and otherwise feeling completely comfortable remaining out of site.

Nevertheless, these illegal farmers certainly understood the inherent humor of a play on words. And thus, their local softball team had generously received its team name, as well as its league fees. Most of the Grower's opponents in the straight world of competitive softball had never figured out this inside joke. For all they knew, these dumb-ass hippies were probably trying to grow fields of wheat germ or brewer's yeast in the narrow and barren hard-rock valleys of Pollard Creek.

Per the usual, the Bombers strode over to the field with an easy confidence, their expressions stern and sanctimonious. Their shoulders and chests were wide and burly, their forearms solid as sledgehammers, their short legs stout as corner fence posts. The Tri-City Bombers appeared like a corn-fed Midwest football team, ready for battle. Although they didn't look anything like natural baseball players, it didn't matter. For this was slow pitch softball. And in slow pitch softball, all that might be needed was some basic hand-to-eye coordination plus two-hundred and fifty pounds of wallop. The kind of wallop the Tri-City Bombers definitely had in spades.

For a fleeting moment, even Ballpark Frank Mayer seemed duly impressed with the Bombers. But by game-time he had rammed down several cans of beer and didn't give hoot. During the pre-game warm-ups, McAllister noticed that Ballpark Frank was talking it up with an attractive big-breasted woman, scantily clad in an orange halter-top and shorts. The woman had placed her lawn chair near the edge of the back-stop behind home plate, on the Bombers side of the diamond. She held a pencil within her fingers, and what looked to be a scorebook rested upon her lap. As both teams returned to their dugouts prior to the game, Ricky the Rocket began to inquire, "Hey, Frank, so who's the hot chick over by the fence?"

"None of your business, Rocket," Ballpark Frank answered, "can't you see I'm working?"

"Come on, Frank," the Rocket countered, "you got to at least give us her name, so we can all introduce ourselves? This is a team sport, remember? One for all, and all for one, isn't that right, guys?" Everyone in the dugout echoed their assent.

"You want to know her name, huh. Well, I got a name for you," Frank returned. "Let's just call her Big Tits Jackson. Hell, boys, I don't know her name yet, I'm still getting to that."

Then, Little Al Miller meekly piped up. "You know, Frank, I saw that's she's got a nice big rock on her left finger. I bet she's most likely married to one of those Bombers. You better watch out."

Ballpark Frank turned and stared at Little Al, the team's youngest player. "Now, listen to me Little Al, have you graduated from high school yet? That's not a wedding ring she's got, it's an engagement ring. And those kind of rocks don't mean nothin' at all. Come on, Al, didn't they teach you any of the true natural laws of this world? Like, for example ....

"The ring don't plug the hole!"

For a long moment there was a uncertain silence in the Grower's dugout, as the understanding of this remark began to sink within the players' minds. Then McAllister burst out laughing, while raising and cocking his fist at Ballpark Frank Mayer. The rest of the team followed suit, as the disguised impact of the statement began to take its effect. But when the hilarity subsided, McAllister tried to regain the attention of the club.

"Now, come on guys, let's get it together, we got a game to play, or at least try to play. It's only the Bombers for crying out loud!"

Yes, it was only the Tri-City Bombers. And 'bombs away' it became. Right from the jump, those big boys sauntered up to the plate. Digging into the batter's box, they each leaned their huge torsos back on their rear foot, waiting patiently for something they liked. When Jimmy Lacovski delivered the pitch desired, they leaned back further before exploding forward with an audible grunt and letting things rip. The result was either a screaming line drive over the infield, or a towering moon-shot far into the sky, sailing easily over the outfield fence.

Whenever each of their homers was smacked, the Bombers would casually stroll around the bases, their stubby legs making them appear like top-heavy stick figures as they circled for home. By the fourth inning, Ricky the Rocket had taken a white handkerchief out of his pocket, waving it over his head in deep center field. On the pitcher's mound, Jimmy Lacovski was in the midst of a nervous breakdown, his long blonde hair damped with sweat, his bulging dark eyes as round as golf balls, his voice muttering in tongue.

By the time the fifth inning came to an end, the game was halted at eleven to one, compliments of a ten-run mercy rule taking effect. Most of the Grower's team walked slowly off the field, their shoulders shrunk, their spirits depressed, their heads hurting from the heat of the sun and the earlier beers. Although they had avoided a shutout, due to McAllister and McClanahan bunching a couple of doubles back-to-back, it was of little relief.

What followed was another long wait until their next encounter, a game from which they could not recover. Failing in the loser-out game, they were knocked out of the tournament. From their earlier morning joy of being in the winner's bracket, and perhaps challenging for a trophy on Sunday, they were now glumly picking up their gear and heading for a long ride home. Even though the fading evening sun was warm and sublime, it provided little solace for their painful defeat.

Only one member of the team appeared free of discontent, and his name was Ballpark Frank Mayer. During the earlier Tri-City Bomber barrage, Ballpark Frank had been playing a game all his own. Sitting behind the plate, Frank had chattered and joked with Bombers, even shaking their hands when they crossed the plate after belting a homer. In addition, he continued his constant repartee with the woman named Big Tits Jackson, helping her with the scoring of the game, trying to make small-talk whenever possible. He appeared to be having the time of his life.

So after the game, Sean McAllister honestly confronted Frank Mayer about his behavior during the fiasco. He demanded that Frank take the game more seriously, to have at least tried to help Lacovski manage his pitching issues. In response, the man simply grinned at McAllister in a strange way, before giving him a wink.

"Don't worry about it, Sean," Ballpark Frank responded. "I know what I'm doing. Trust me, there will be another day." McAllister didn't have the energy to argue further. Instead, he walked back to the dugout, before tossing his glove in disgust.

Spring turned to summer in Pollard Creek. Framed against a sky of clear brilliant blue, giant cumulus formations drifted silently over the mountains and valleys below. Mostly freed of these occasional interventions, the sun bore down hard and hot, the orange-red clay of winter transforming itself to a tarnished white. Whenever vehicles passed on the dirt-hardened mountain roads, clouds rose-up from behind, leaving misty residues of hazy-floured dust in their wake. The sound of chainsaws and equipment whistles sung throughout the timbered hills, the dangerous roar of logging trucks barreling around roadside curves, speeding toward mill towns whose screaming industrial teeth ran night and day. This was the annual song and currency of Southern Oregon in the season of its height.

Meanwhile, homestead vegetable gardens began to reach full-bloom, while mysterious drip lines reached deep into forest clearings, hoping for disguise. The quiet work of weeding and tending the crop, both legal or not, could fill a summer day. Evenings were soft and gentle, the happy voices of children playing late under twilight-gray skies. Men rose to guzzle from perspiring aluminum cans, the women sipping from tinkled cubes of liquor in a lime-garnished glass. In the air, the fragrant odor of a marijuana cigarette burned between finger and thumb, before being passed easily along. In such pensive moments, all thoughts of life were good, and any notions of trouble seemed a thousand miles away.

Sean McAllister, like many others in the world of Pollard Creek, lived only the day-to-day. Work when possible, play when not. Coffee in the morning, steady work until the heat grew harsh, swimming holes in the afternoon hours, and perhaps a woman at night.

Except for their practices and game days, McAllister and his teammates lived their separate lives, before coming together on scheduled evenings to share this game they loved. Win or lose they played together as boys, their bodies running and swinging in flight, their manly competiveness allowed to soar free, their humor and naughtiness given the space to reveal itself without restraint.

As the weeks passed and games were played, the season and its high jinks continued along, with Ballpark Frank Mayer the hit of the show. And oddly enough, Sean McAllister and Ballpark Frank grew closer as friends. Within this strange accommodation, McAllister began to experience more about this man who had entered his life. Still, McAllister understood that the questions of what might be fable or fact about Ballpark Frank Mayer remained an unknown.

Although Frank Mayer's daily assertions never lacked for certainty, mystery seemed to follow him. So it was best to simply give Ballpark Frank the stage, to take things for what they were. Most notable was the content and outrageous opinion of Ballpark Frank's performance in this world, the complexion and personality of this man as he rode upon the moment. Perhaps the luxury of any truthful verification would be missing. But in the end, what did it matter? The truth was of little consequence.

Nevertheless, a life story had begun to take shape. Frank Mayer had been born and raised in Dubuque, Iowa, the child of German-Catholic parents. He might have had a brother and sister. But whatever had happened in his Iowa childhood, only complaint and distrust remained. The single resulting perception that McAllister could possibly apprehend was that Frank Mayer's birth family was no longer part of his life. This earlier period of childhood seemed to have been dutifully erased. Whatever regrets there might have been, they were buried deep inside, and never allowed to escape. For reasons unknown, Dubuque, Iowa had been purposely left behind.

Frank's service in the military appeared more reliable, where he played cornerback in football for his base team before taking to the skies. However, like most of the veterans who had endured Vietnam, any personal histories in that regard were mostly kept in-house, and no outsider need apply. But Frank did claim that the earlier football thing had later led to a failed tryout with the Denver Broncos, before their merger with the NFL. Sometime after his release, he drifted to California where he met a Mexican girl in Los Angeles. It was there that he got married and spawned two children, a daughter and son. In order to raise his family and make ends meet, Frank found work at a Budweiser plant.

But the marriage didn't last. After the separation, he disappeared from his home in the barrio section of LA. Purchasing a van, he began living as a hippie along the beaches of Ventura County. There, he began to fish the surf, took odd jobs whenever they were offered, and began to play the guitar. Eventually, he met another woman on the beach while playing music with friends. The woman was a sister of one of the musicians. She had a beautiful voice and a young daughter to care for.

At some point, talk of Oregon ensued. It was decided that everyone would move north and start a band. So the extended family headed to Glendale, a mill town in Southern Oregon. They found places to live and began to practice. Frank got a job at the lumber mill, working days. Sometime after, the band got the Village Inn gig on the week-ends. Things were good for awhile. But again, far-too-often many good things never seem to last.

Sean McAllister couldn't be sure if this sequence of events had any basis in reality. It wasn't as if Ballpark Frank had sat down with him and told this tale. It was more that McAllister had quietly compiled the scenario, in bits and pieces whenever Ballpark Frank had an anecdote to relate. Whether it was on the road trips to the Tri-Cities, conversations in the dugout, or at a bar after the games, Ballpark Frank Mayer was a man who could talk. More often than not, it wasn't about any life story he needed to tell. Rather, it was usually about particular grievances he needed to share, including barbs aimed at his teammates to keep them off balance. And of course the peculiar philosophies of the world in which he roamed, including his laws, always his laws!

You might as well go for murder as manslaughter!"

"Why wish for a loaf of bread, when you can wish for the whole grocery store!"

"Never get even, get ahead!"

"Always be reasonable, demand the impossible!"

"Anything worth doing, is worth overdoing!"

"There is no such thing as bad sex, just good, better, and best!"

"Reality is only for those who can't handle drugs!"

And one day, just to mess with Little Al ....

"Roses are red, violets are blue, your streamers are pretty, But you still come from Stockton, California!"

And finally, a bumper sticker he felt everyone should have ....

"HONK, IF YOU LOVE BALLPARK FRANK!"

When it came to Ballpark Frank Mayer, almost nothing and no one in this world was sacred. Even God had been put on notice that whenever Frank Mayer had picked the locks to the gates of heaven, you could be sure somebody new would be taking over the throne. He seemed to be a man without fear or filter, full of independence and boastful self-reliance.

For McAllister, the most appropriate descriptive was 'appetite', a man of voracious appetite. Whether it be fishing or guns, softball games or music, political opinion or human philosophy, or just simply sex, drugs and rock and roll, Ballpark Frank Mayer might just have been the most 'free' human being that Sean McAllister had ever met. He was a man who couldn't be restricted. The common conventions and expectations of this world were more than he could accept, and no match for him whenever the day was done.

Frank Mayer could easily have become a sociopath in another world gone mad. But no, he understood the ultimate limits of the world in which he inhabited. His deeper distrusts and anger at the world, his pain and regrets over wounds and rejections suffered in his life, these failings seemed to live only on the surface, and never deterred him. But there was a deeper thing here, an elemental pathos and love of life that could not be hidden or disguised.

And to fully understand this reality, there was only one singular thing another human had to do. And that was to hear Frank Mayer sing and play. To see him with guitar in hand, to feel the depth and love that rose from his soul in music and song. That was the ticket that suddenly let others inside, whenever the time was right. The rest of his daily performances were nothing more than the fuel that made him run, the attributions one must collect to safely make their way through the forest of a hypocritical world. In the end, Ballpark Frank Mayer was just another weird traveler on a journey towards an unknown destination we all would one day reach. And yet, he had become one hell of an interesting dude to meet along the way.

Shortly after their tournament defeat to the Tri-City Bombers, the Southern Oregon Growers had lost a second game to the Bombers in regular league play. This time they had managed to score enough runs to take the Bombers the full-seven innings, before leaving the field with a thirteen to six loss. By the end of this second game, Ballpark Frank Mayer and the woman known as Big Tits Jackson were comfortably on a first-name basis. During the third week of June, Ballpark Frank had traveled to Eugene, trading in his Ford Galaxie for a powerful Japanese motorcycle. He had also gotten a job in Grants Pass as a service attendant, working days at a gas station near the freeway.

On a summer Friday night, McAllister and a few of his teammates were drinking during Happy Hour at the local Solace Valley Tavern. The tavern was busily crowded with people seeking respite from a week of work and heat, a usual occurrence during this time of year. Wheels McClanahan wedged himself up against McAllister at the bar. "Hey man, did you see whose here, at the other end of the bar?"

McAllister hadn't noticed, but as he strained to get a look, he could see Jimmy Lacovski and Ballpark Frank at the other end of the room. Between them was a woman that McAllister didn't immediately recognize. But McClanahan leaned in closer, whispering in McAllister's ear.

"And do you know who the chick is," McClanahan inquired? McAllister took a harder look, staring at the woman. Then, he turned his head back toward McClanahan and spoke. "No way!"

"Yes. Way," McClanahan answered. "Big Tits Jackson...... or whatever her real name is."

At the very same moment, Ballpark Frank and McAllister made eye contact from across the bar. With a knowing grin on his face, Ballpark Frank quietly raised his glass of beer, before forming his other hand into a fist and raising the thumb. McAllister could do little more than shake his head in return.

"I told you not to worry," Ballpark Frank reminded McAllister later that evening. "I've got the secret weapon. See you at practice on Sunday."

When McAllister arrived at practice on Sunday afternoon, Jimmy Lacovski and Ballpark Frank were already at the field. Between the pitcher's mound and the plate they had raised a twelve-foot two-by-four. It was nailed to a wooden stanchion on the ground, keeping the stick of lumber standing up straight. Lacovski was raining pitches at the height of the two-by-four toward his catcher at the plate. "She says they have trouble with the high stuff," Lacovski related. "And if I put just enough spin on it, they can't square it up. We call it the 'Skylab' pitch."

McAllister had to laugh. The recent news in the United States and across the world had been focused on the damaged American space station called Skylab. Despite a number of attempts to save the space module from falling and breaking up in the atmosphere before a fiery crashing to earth, nothing could be done. According to the authorities, the odds of any-one being killed by tons of falling space debris were minimal at best. But others had reported that there was a one-in-seven chance that such dangerous tonnage might rain upon a city of a hundred-thousand people, at a location anywhere on the planet earth. Although the projected break-up of the Skylab would likely not be over the mountains of Southern Oregon, there was hardly a human on earth, if they had heard about the event, that wasn't occasionally looking up at the sky with a measure of unease. Nor was there any surprise that characters like Ballpark Frank Mayer and Jimmy Lacovski would come up with such a moniker.

So this was the secret weapon, for what it was worth, the ticket to the upset of the undefeated Tri-City Bombers in the final league game. Yet, by this time late in the season, Sean McAllister had come to figure that any particular event was possible when it came to the matter of one Ballpark Frank Mayer.

Somehow, Ballpark Frank had obtained the phone number of Big Tits Jackson, before convincing her that she needed to spread her wings a little before walking down the aisle. In fact, Big Tits had driven with him to Eugene to purchase the mo-torcycle, and had surreptitiously been riding with him the last couple of weeks. McAllister preferred not to have an opinion on the circumstances at hand. He only hoped he wouldn't be acci-dentally killed while an innocent bystander during a domestic dispute. Still, he figured that someplace, or somewhere, one of Ballpark Frank's natural laws likely had to apply.

On the evening of the final game of the season, Big Tits Jackson curiously did not sit at her usual place with her scorebook near the side of the backstop. Instead, she placed herself somewhere high in the aluminum stands. And Ballpark Frank Mayer never gave her a look. No one on the Grower's team knew exactly which one of the Bombers was her engaged husband to be, and whether or not Ballpark Frank's jig might finally be up. Nevertheless, it was decided by the team that all of their cars would be left idling in the parking lot, just in case.

When the game began, the practice scheme that Lacovski and Ballpark Frank had dutifully worked on all that week was having incredible success. Lacovski was arching the ball high into the air with just the right amount of spin. And although the Bomber hitters were rearing back and customarily swinging for the hills, they were merely undercutting the ball and floating lazy pop-ups far into the sky. As a result, the Grower's confidence began to rise and everyone began to put the ball in play. Through the early innings the pressure grew, the Bombers only blasting a solo homer, while the Growers themselves banged out a succession of hits to take a three to one lead.

In the top of the fifth inning, while taking his position at first base, McAllister noticed Big Tits Jackson coming out of the stands. She strode over to the dugout, leaned in and spoke to one of the Bombers. The discussion went on for what seemed like a long time, the Bomber player appearing angry before throwing his hat in disgust onto the dugout floor. McAllister turned his attention to Ballpark Frank who was standing behind the plate. Frank caught McAllister's expression, simply shrugging his shoulders in return.

"Uh oh", McAllister muttered only to himself. It was more than likely that some strange form of confession had taken place. Immediately, the Bomber manager came stalking out of the dugout. He approached the plate umpire and took him aside, getting into his face in no uncertain terms. Ballpark Frank attempted to edge in on the conversation, but the Bomber manager pulled the umpire further away, continuing his argument. Something was up, and it wasn't long before the impact was felt.

As play resumed, Lacovski delivered the first pitch of the inning. But before the ball had even reached the plate, the umpire raised out his arm, calling the pitch a ball. "Illegal pitch," the umpire stated, "over twelve-feet in height." Ballpark Frank and Lacovski argued the call. But on the next three pitches came the same result, with the Bomber hitter jogging to first on a four-pitch walk. The rest was history. Lacovski became unglued, his anger and mental state beginning to fray. By the time McAllister got to the mound to calm Lacovski down, Ballpark Frank had been tossed from the game, the umpire's shoes covered with red Oregon dirt.

The fix was in. Forced to lower his pitches, Lacovski was snake-bit. The Bombers went on a terror, once again driving balls into the gaps and over the wall. The final score was of little consequence. The Tri-City Bombers, on very their own home field, and in their very own home town, were undefeated league champions once again. It might be safe to say the following: there would be no way that a bunch of pot-smoking hippies from Pollard Creek were ever about to spoil such a desired and predictable outcome. In other words, all remained right with the world.

As the game dragged along toward its pre-determined end, McAllister had surveyed the stands on the Bombers' side of the field. And the woman known as Big Tits Jackson was nowhere to be found. Later, a police escort arrived, the umpire catching a ride. Out in the parking lot, Ballpark Frank sat on hood of one of the team's vehicles, drinking a beer. When McAllister inquired, the team's catcher remained his eternal self.

"I guess she had a change of heart," he flatly stated. "Let me tell you, Sean, the word 'trust', and the emotional context of which it implies, in the end can never be trusted. Trust will always be as vagrant as the blowing of the wind."

"Well, that sure is a life-affirming aspiration," McAllister replied. "Another one of your laws, I suppose?"

Ballpark Frank pushed himself off the hood of the car. "Not really," he yawned, "but I will tell you this ...."

"The sun don't shine on the same dog's ass every day."

"Yeah, sure," McAllister objected, "unless you're a Tri-City Bomber."

Ballpark Frank laughed in response. "Well, you got me there, bud. Like I once told you before, you don't miss much, do you? Still, as Kojack says, 'Life is life, baby'. And I figure that's all we can ever expect. But I'll tell you this, my friend. We sure as hell had them boys shaking in their boots for a good long while. Now, it's time to let it go. Let's pack it up and get to the bar."

With the ball season over, the members of the Grower's team returned to their personal lives. The long hot summer continued in Southern Oregon, a time for work and other outdoor activities. McAllister did not see much of Ballpark Frank Mayer.

But one week-end night, they ran into each other at the Solace Valley Tavern, before deciding to carry the evening further by traveling south to a music club near Grants Pass. McAllister climbed onto the back of Ballpark Frank's motorcycle. Roaring over the mountain pass and into the Rogue Valley, Ballpark Frank leaned the bike forward at high rushing speed. McAllister held on tight, questioning his decision, thinking of his life, before accepting the fact that it might end suddenly at any particular moment, and this might be the one.

On several other occasions, while making a town trip, he caught-up with Frank at the gas station in Grants Pass. Mostly, they talked about sports, or general updates on the guys from the team, although as usual, little about themselves.

Not surprisingly, Ballpark Frank hated his job, hated the corporation who owned it, and hated most of the clientele that were filling up their cars. Unless of course the customer might be of the attractive feminine gender, whereupon he would faithfully provide superior personal service.

In between, he was crashing up in Glendale, or with his friend, Dianne, who lived in Solace Valley. Apparently, the former relationship with the singer in the band was definitely over, and the band itself another part of his past. If a next move might be in Ballpark Frank's consideration, he never let on. Life seemed like nothing more than the simple day-to-day.

On the first Monday of September, Labor Day, Sean McAllister was up at his cabin on London Ridge. In the early afternoon, he could hear the sound of a motorcycle winding its way toward the property. Stepping out onto the porch of his cabin, he waited for the vehicle to appear in sight. As it escaped from the tree-line and out into the meadow, it was none other than Ballpark Frank. McAllister watched from a distance as the motorcycle slowly bounced through the potholes on the road. He could see that something of an odd shape was strapped to the back of the bike, but it was hard to tell.

Ballpark Frank parked the motorcycle by the main house down below, before removing his cargo. McAllister could now see that it was a guitar case, which Frank carried by its handle as he trudged further up the hill. As Ballpark Frank approached the cabin McAllister spoke down to him.

"So, have you come to serenade me? My, how sweet of you."

"Sorry to disappoint you pal," Frank answered sharply "but I'll never be that hard-up."

"So how you doing, Frank? What's up?" McAllister sat down on top of the porch steps. Ballpark Frank stood below him, his foot unconsciously pawing the dirt.

"Well, I got a special favor to ask," he began. His voice had changed, appearing serious. "I got to head down to LA pretty quick. Just some family stuff, but I might not get back for awhile. I was wondering if you could take my guitar down to the bus station next time you drive into town? Send it down to Los Angeles." Putting down the guitar, Ballpark Frank reached into the pocket of his jeans, pulling out a piece of paper and some money. "Here's fifty bucks and the address to send it to. This should cover the postage and the trouble." He stepped forward toward McAllister, reaching out with the paper and cash.

"Sure," McAllister answered. "Anything serious?"

"Nah, nothing serious." Ballpark Frank turned his head back toward the house below. "You folks got a telephone way up here in this place?"

"Yeah, there is one down at the house. So when are you leaving?"

"I got to leave right away. Give me the phone number and your address and I can let you know whenever it arrives."

"Not a problem," McAllister responded. He decided not to inquire further about the circumstances. It seemed like Ballpark Frank did not want to speak to it. McAllister went inside the cabin, writing down the number and address. Stepping back outside, he handed the information to his friend. Ballpark Frank reached out and exchanged the guitar.

"Thanks for doing this," Frank said quietly. Then he paused. "So have you heard from the girl up in Seattle?"

The question caught McAllister by surprise. He had forgotten that he had ever mentioned her. It must have been sometime back, in one of those infrequent encounters where they had spoken about their personal lives. For most of their time together during the summer, any discussions between them had been little more than useless banter, and more often than not about Ballpark Frank living large.

"Not lately," McAllister admitted, "but you know how those things go."

"Yeah, I know," Frank admitted. "Anyway, I hope it works out." Once again, a pause ensued.

"Listen, Sean, I want to thank you for letting me play with the team this summer. It meant a lot. It helped me get over a rough patch. Get back to being myself. It was a blast, brother."

McAllister smiled in return. "Yeah, no doubt about that, my friend. It sure was good having you along for the ride."

Feeling a little uncertain, McAllister wanted to inquire about the whereabouts of Big Tits Jackson, if only to hear Ballpark Frank rail about something like he always did. Perhaps just to get things back to normal and have a laugh. But at the moment, it didn't seem like the time. McAllister stepped down off the porch. The two men embraced and said their farewells.

Holding the guitar by his side, McAllister watched as Ballpark Frank returned to his bike, kicking it to start. The motorcycle renewed its bounce over the potholes before disappearing from sight. Sean McAllister wondered if he would ever see the man again.

Certain stories in life need a postscript ending, an anecdotal moment after the fact. The preferred literary ending would be to leave the reader to wonder whatever outcomes might have occurred after the story was told. It might be an ending that would perhaps leave some ambivalent questions, ones the reader might reflect upon whenever the story might come to mind. But this could never be the case for the story of Ballpark Frank Mayer.

On that Friday of Labor Day week-end, Ballpark Frank Mayer went to work as usual at the service station along Interstate 5 in Grants Pass. On this particular week-end he worked the closing shift for three straight nights. Each night, his last duty was to account for the day's receipts. He would then make a drop-deposit at the bank just down the street from the station. On this particular week-end, the gas station was extremely busy, with holiday travelers heading north and south, enjoying the last of summer before the school year would open in a matter of days. The banks would be closed until Tuesday morning.

For each of the first two nights, Frank Mayer made the normal deposit at the bank. However, he had consciously made a mistake. He deposited only the checks, while leaving the cash in the safe at the station. On that final Sunday night, he did the very same, before placing all the cash into his rucksack instead of the bank drop. At this point, there would be no turning back. He would be on his way to LA. The following Monday morning he packed up some clothes in a duffel bag, preparing for the trip. Just before his leaving he grabbed his guitar, deciding to pay a visit to his friend Sean McAllister to say good-bye. Then he returned for the duffel bag, loaded things up and hit the road.

For twenty straight hours he drove the motorcycle, fighting to stay awake and not die on the highway. By the following Tuesday afternoon, he arrived into the bowels of Los Angeles, California, his life in Oregon now left far behind. It was still likely the banking error had yet to be discovered. But if this error might ever have been correctly tabulated, it would have totaled in the neighborhood of thirteen thousand dollars.

Human survival in this world can take many forms. And when it becomes desperate, morality and ethics often get left in its wake. At least for some. Necessity is the mother of invention they say, one of those ancient laws to live by. Perhaps it was a law that a man named Ballpark Frank Mayer might have failed to mention, but one in which he obviously believed.

When McAllister learned of the escapade, he understood that a certain line had been crossed, and that perhaps some consequence or karma would eventually find its way. And now, he felt truly certain that he would never see Ballpark Frank ever again. And yet, something of a strange notion seemed to follow him in the September days ahead. It was a simple little law, one that everyone knew, and perhaps often came true. *"Never say never"*.

Sean McAllister figured it might be best to write this one down as well, if only to keep it with the other laws that he had chosen to transcribe.

THE
SECRET

THE SECRET

The bright noontime sun pierced its vertical light between urban buildings of brick and mortar, reaching the speedy hustle of the New York City streets. But on this late September day, the solar rays brought little warmth to the busy hum of humanity below. For a cold autumn breeze swept steady through the paved canyons of the populace, its chilling effect prompting those on their daily lunch-hour excursions to pull themselves ever closer within. As the month of October approached, an autumnal season of change was now underway. The heat of a waning summer had begun to disappear with the pages of a calendar, prompting subtle reminders of a darkening winter ahead.

Eighteen year-old Katherine Flynn hurried herself down a Fifth Avenue sidewalk, her hand unconsciously pressing the collar of her coat tight against her skin. Katherine remained thoughtless to these early signs of an annual reckoning ahead, for much more worried concerns pressed upon her mind.

Katherine had only an hour to accomplish this unwanted task before her. She hoped that she wouldn't find additional trouble by possibly returning late for work. She deftly weaved through the crowded tangle of pedestrians in pursuit of her destination. She could hear the short heels of her shoes knocking on the sidewalk.

At the intersection of 5th and 51st, Katherine was halted by a traffic light. Along with several others pressing on the corner, she silently raised her head. Above her, the grand spires of

St Patrick's Cathedral stretched like pointed spears far into the cloudless blue. At the sight, a panicked rush of anxiety ran through her body. This fear was coupled by a desperate wish that she might only turn back from this unwanted responsibility before her, a wish that maybe someone, or something, could make her troubles go away. But she knew such vain hopes were not meant to be. Taking a deep breath to steady herself, she crossed the street at the light, knowing that she must go on.

Katherine forced herself up the steps towards the Cathedral entrance, before leaning against the heavy bronze doors and into the Church. Only a week before, she and her sister, Maggie, had visited the Cathedral for the very first time. During that visit, Katherine had secretly noted that the confessional boxes were located just to the left side of the church's majestic interior. And unbeknownst to her sister, she had quietly learned that week-day confessions could be heard at noon.

Slipping past the statues of St. Peter and Paul, Katherine dipped her fingers with holy water, making the sign of the cross. Then sitting down into a nearby pew, she sought to gather herself, wordlessly mouthing a prayer of forgiveness. Moments later, she forced herself up, seeking a vacant confessional box. Entering its dark interior, she began to kneel. Behind a screen shadowed in soft yellow light, the voice of a priest acknowledged her presence. He blessed himself as he greeted her in the name of the Lord. Feeling her heart thumping within her chest, eighteen-year old Katherine Flynn began to confess. "Bless me Father, for I have sinned, it has been over three months since my last confession ...."

Long before this day, Katherine Flynn's ancestors had fled from the shores of Ireland in the years following the Great Famine. They were amongst the thousands of immigrants hoping to escape the crushing poverty and religious persecution of the

English crown's power and control. Arriving through both New York and Boston, these early members of her family found their way to Riverton, Massachusetts, a city on the western banks of the Connecticut River. There in Riverton, work could be found in the growing paper-making industry that was flourishing in the late 19th and early 20th century America.

James Flynn, Katherine's father, was born a United States citizen, later finding work in the mills that lined the river's banks. In 1911, he met the niece of a funeral director within the Irish wards of the city. Molly O'Conner, who also hailed from County Kerry, had emigrated only several years before, having been sponsored by her uncle in order to reach the United States.

Both the Flynn and O'Conner families were Catholic members of the Irish Temperance Societies that had been founded in their former homeland, and were now established in Irish strongholds throughout America. Sponsored by the local parishes, these societies were often more like Catholic social clubs, places where like-minded teetotalers could gather together and meet. As Molly Flynn would later express to her children, the society gatherings were a place where a young woman might be able to find a 'good living and sober' man. In those days, Katherine's mother had explained, it was difficult to meet an Irish man who didn't drink. In fact, Riverton, Massachusetts, a community of hard labor and tough Irish ways, was especially known for having more drinking pubs per person than any other city in the state of Massachusetts.

Two years after their first meeting, James Flynn and Molly O'Conner were married. Over time, the couple birthed and raised four children, one boy, the oldest, and three girls, of which Katherine was the youngest. James Flynn worked hard, eventually rising to a well-respected supervisor of men. As the years went by, the family was able to move out of the rough Irish wards to the edge of the Highlands district in Riverton. The Highlands was a locale where most of the more prosperous citizens of Riverton called home.

The Flynn's remained devout Catholics and active members of their parish, with their children attending the local Catholic schools. The use of alcohol continued to be disdained, amidst a myriad of church activities. Still, they were an otherwise typical Irish family, suffused with the constant exchanges of Irish humor and idiom amongst their extended family and friends.

And then, quite unexpectedly, two difficult events would inflict the Flynn family's life. Neither of which was anticipated, nor could they be overcome. The first was the Great Depression, a period of life the Flynn's shared with all America. The second, in the year of 1936, came an event that could only be endured by the Flynn family alone. James Flynn, 'Daddy Jim' as he was known by his family and loved ones, had suddenly collapsed while working at the paper mill. He was immediately rushed to the hospital. With the onset of this event, a long and trying journey was about to begin.

The doctors at the local hospital in Riverton were unable to diagnose the condition of their patient. But they believed some form of stroke had undoubtedly occurred. After serious consultation, it was determined that more expert analysis would be necessary. James Flynn had served in the military during World War I. And thus, it was decided that the Veteran's Hospital in New York City would be better equipped to discern the medical issues at hand.

James Flynn was transferred to the Veterans Hospital in the Bronx, New York. There, the diagnosis was made that Katherine's father was suffering from a tumor on the brain. This was shortly followed by a dangerous and life-threatening surgery to remove the cancerous growth. Fortunately, after an extended period of recovery, James Flynn had been able to return home. But serious damage had been done. The man and father known as 'Daddy Jim' would never be the same. At the time of this family tragedy, Katherine Flynn had been a ten-year old child.

With James Flynn's return to Riverton, the paper company that had employed him for so-many years managed to find a spot for him. He became the night watchman at the mill site. But this was the very most the company could do. For James Flynn's physical and mental abilities had suffered permanently from the illness and surgery. With the consequent reduction in his wages, the Flynn family struggled to get by. Molly Flynn began to work, and her three oldest children took part-time jobs after school to make ends meet. The youngest, Katherine, contributed with daily chores at home. Despite these unfortunate setbacks, the family persevered, remaining close and making the best of their circumstances.

Five years went by. The oldest brother, Denny, and the first daughter Ellen Marie, graduated from high school. Each left the family home, finding jobs, while beginning to further their educations part-time. Maggie, the second daughter, and Katherine remained at home.

Meanwhile, far outside the daily lives of their family, the United States and a greater world were about to change dramatically. And no living American would ever forget one day in particular, December 7th, 1941. From that day forward, the United States of America had once again become a nation at war.

Denny Flynn entered the Coast Guard, eventually being stationed in nearby Boston. Ellen Marie, having studied to become a nurse, entered the Navy and was sent to California. Maggie, having just finished high school, found her way to New York at a nursing school for girls. As children, now only Kathcrine Flynn remained at home, having just entered her first year of high school.

Several more years passed, while both the war in Europe and the Pacific raged onward. In April of 1944, James Flynn's health began to suffer once again. He was forced to return to the Veterans Hospital in New York, being hospitalized for testing and recovery. Thus began several months of periodic trips to the city for treatment and care. With Molly Flynn traveling to be near her husband, Katherine Flynn would be left alone at home, while completing the latter months of her senior year in high school. In addition to her schooling, Katherine also worked part-time in the office of the church. Otherwise, she was on her own for several weeks at a time.

Katherine Flynn had grown to become a beautiful young girl with silken blonde hair. As James Flynn's youngest child, her father favored her dearly, while other family and friends would often comment about her beauty. Katherine enjoyed the attention her appearance inspired, although at times she felt embarrassed by the same. But as she became of age, the pressure and attention began to grow ever further with boys at school. And during her senior year, this pressure and attention would especially come from a boy named Jimmy Kane.

Jimmy Kane was a handsome strapping boy, and one of the best athletes at St. Jerome's Catholic High School. But his reputation was also that of a wild and careless youth, including being poor in his studies. Jimmy Kane's family hailed from one of the toughest Irish wards in the city, a hardscrabble section of Riverton known for fighting, and marked with a pub or bar on every single corner. Nevertheless, Jimmy Kane was tall and good-looking, and particularly smitten with Katherine Flynn.

With the spring of 1944 unfolding, Katherine and Jimmy Kane spent more of their time together. In the early days of their relationship, Jimmy had been respectful and charming. For Katherine, it had been fun and popular to be by his side.

As the final months of high school began to pass, with her father and siblings far from away from their home, and with her mother often absent on the trips to New York, Katherine's loneliness was eased by spending time with Jimmy Kane. And ever so slowly Jimmy Kane became more and more assertive with Katherine, trying regularly to take their companionship to a more intimate and dangerous place. At the beginning, Katherine made efforts to resist. But as the pressure continued, certain rationalizations began to take hold, having been given more credence when two young people might be falling in love.

In early June, Katherine's father and mother returned home.

Maggie came along to celebrate Katherine's graduation from high school. The Flynn family's life returned to some normality. And Jimmy Kane seemed to be accepted as Katherine's sometimes questionable boyfriend. The summer passed. The war in both Europe and the Pacific battled on. But as the month of September arrived, the hardships facing the Flynn family once again took a more troubled turn.

Behind the screen of the confessional box, Father John Doherty listened with cautious concern to a young woman's admission of sin. Sadly, the circumstances of her mistake and the troubles that now confronted her were not unfamiliar.

Father John had grown up in the city of New York, finding his calling to the priesthood shortly after high school. Eight years later he had reached his ordainment in the Church. During the twenty years hence, he had ministered within the parishes of the city, before his unexpected rise to the clergy at St Patrick's. In his pastoral work within this urban enclave, Father John had heard the admissions of almost every sin in this greater world of God's creation. And all-the-while he slowly had become skilled at offering advice and counsel to the fallen, before bestowing penance for the same.

Nevertheless, the fear and uncertainty of a young woman in this kind of trouble always tugged at the tendrils of his heart. For Father John had long ago come to understand that this singular mortal sin was rarely one of overt commission or intent. Rather, it was more often about wanting to please someone that the woman cared for, an unconscious and momentary loss of control. It was very difficult for any priest not to feel the utmost sympathy regarding the unfortunate results that would undoubtedly transpire. As well, Father John could foresee the lasting scars that would invariably be inflicted upon both the woman and her child.

Father John was also well-aware of other questionable realities. For he knew there were currently certain unspoken directives that the Church maintained within its silent and veiled interiors. These directives reflected both the culture of the times, as well as the cottage industry of which the Church had become dubiously engaged. Accordingly, it was best for an unmarried Catholic woman with child, and equally best for the child's future as well, to be separated at birth. This belief and directive would allow for the young woman to quietly go on with her life. It would also be better for the child to be raised within another loving family's embrace, where the child would have a married mother and father, without ever knowing the sin of their creation. Yes, Father John understood these directives. But whenever he was faced with such a circumstance, there had always been a dubious nagging within his own heart that left him in doubt. If only somehow there could have been a better way. And yet no satisfactory answer ever came. Therefore, when the young woman had finished her confession, Father John slowly began his counsel.

"Does the boy know of your situation?"

"No," was the answer he received.

"And are you planning to tell him," Father John inquired?

"That's why I am here today, Father, I don't know what is best. I don't want to tell him, Father, because I don't know what to do." A silence descended between them, as Father John paused in contemplation.

"My child, do you love this boy? Would you take the vows of Holy Matrimony with him, to love and cherish him for the rest of your life, so help you God?" Again there was a silence in the confessional. Finally, the girl responded.

"Father, I do not love him. Maybe I thought I did. But now I want to get away from him. He scares me, Father. He is angry I came to New York. He came down here from Massachusetts looking for me. I went with him to visit his relatives in Brooklyn last week-end. It was terrible for me, Father. They drank and shouted at each other all the time. My family is temperance. My mother says their family is 'shanty'. She is very angry at me, and says never to tell my own father, never to tell him about this trouble with me. I feel like I just want to disappear. Everything is just a bad dream for me, a dream I can't make go away. But no, I can't marry him, Father, I just can't. I don't know what to do. Please, Father. Please tell me what is right? Please ask God to forgive me for my sin."

Father John leaned back against the confessional box. This was the very reason the Church felt their directive was best. In the Church, marriage was likely the holiest of all the sacraments. A holy marriage was the foundation of the Church's survival, a life-long commitment of each to the other, as well as to the sanctity of God's human creation. But these real-life circumstances were not easy to administer. Each problem and its outcome could be fraught with complication and perilous effect. Nevertheless, in this particular situation, the only sensible outcome for this girl and her child appeared to be one of separation.

Father John leaned forward and spoke. "My child, if in your heart you do not love this man, if you believe you fear this man, then our Holy Father would not be in favor of consecrating such a marriage. His decision would be not to marry this man, not to marry any man until you are able to take the vows that I mentioned before."

"Yes, Father", the young woman answered, her voice seeming to express a sense of relief. "Thank you, Father, thank you so very much."

Father John Doherty once again let a brief moment of silence pass between them, before speaking again with a determinative voice.

"Now, as for the child.............."

Days after Katherine Flynn's lunch-hour confession at St Patrick's Cathedral, her sister, Margaret "Maggie" Flynn, quickly left her job after work. Her employer, Doctor Wagner, was an internist whose office was also located on Fifth Avenue. The late afternoon was cold, the sky tending toward earlier darkness every day.

With her working day complete, Maggie would now head south on the Avenue. She would then turn west toward Riverside. Having returned to New York, her mother had recently found a temporary apartment near the river, each day visiting her husband at the Veteran's Hospital in the Bronx. Only two days before, Maggie, along with her sister Katherine, had retreated from an apartment on 61st Street that Maggie had been sharing with her friends from nursing school. But the apartment had now become too dangerous to return.

After her confession with the priest at St. Patrick's, Katherine had told Jimmy Kane that she didn't want to marry him. Jimmy Kane had grown angry and distraught, while begging her to reconsider. Knowing that Katherine was staying with Maggie, Jimmy had found the apartment, pounding on the door, screaming that Katherine must see him. Frightened, the two young women had huddled inside, silently waiting until he went away. That very same night, Maggie and Katherine had escaped to their mother's temporary quarters on Riverside, while pleading with Maggie's roommates not to divulge their whereabouts. Should he ever find out Katherine's whereabouts, they fully expected that Jimmy Kane would seek to return.

Their situation was becoming desperate. Something had to be done. But any kind of answer remained an unknown. James Flynn was soon to be released from the hospital. Their mother and father would quickly be returning to their Riverton home. And only last night, Molly Flynn had turned to her second daughter, telling Maggie that for now only she could protect her younger sister. Molly Flynn's first priority must be the health and welfare of their father. And so Maggie alone would have to find a way to help Katherine, to try and keep her safe. All through the work day, Maggie had worried about what she might do.

Although three years older than her little sister, Maggie and Katherine had been extremely close all of their childhood lives. There was no question that Maggie would take care of Katherine in any way she could. But just how and where to protect her remained a fear without a solution, an answer Maggie struggled to somehow even imagine.

Katherine soon would be joining her at their mother's apartment, she herself returning from her work. Tonight, they would have to begin a plan, whatever it might be. Perhaps they could stay at the apartment their mother was renting, at least for awhile. Without question, the family had no money to send Katherine away. No place like Westfield, a home near Riverton where girls could disappear until a child was born. But Westfield was only for families who were blessed with means, families who could pay for such girls in trouble. And worse, everyone in Riverton would eventually know of Katherine's sin. She would end up being marked forever if she had to return home. And Jimmy Kane would undoubtedly find her, and perhaps hurt Katherine should she continue to resist him. Katherine had told Maggie of the things the priest had advised. But she and Maggie had not yet been able to discuss them. Getting away from Jimmy had been all they could do for now.

Maggie continued her walk down the Avenue. While passing the storefront of a travel agency, she halted for a moment, peering at the photos of faraway vacation destinations that were pasted upon the windows. At that moment she noticed a typewritten sheet posted near the door of the agency. Stepping closer, she began to read. By the time she was finished, her heart had begun to race with anticipation.

The job posting advertised positions for two young women. One position was for a waitress, the other position a switchboard operator. The location of both positions would not be New York City, but rather a hotel-resort in the state of Georgia. Each of the jobs required a year-long employment contract. And if the terms of the contract were successfully completed, all travel expenses to and from the location of the work would be paid by the employer.

Without hesitation, Maggie stepped toward the entrance door of the agency to see if it was open. The knob turned and she stepped inside. An older woman, sitting behind a desk greeted her appearance. Maggie immediately inquired of the job posting, could it still be available? The answer was 'yes', as far as the agent knew. If Maggie and her sister showed up early in the morning, they could make application. If everything was satisfactory, the agency would confirm with the employer. Then, if accepted, the necessary travel arrangements would be made.

Maggie quickly made the rest of the walk toward the Riverside apartment filled with nervous expectation. She had never done anything like this before in her life. She knew nothing of Georgia, only that it was a long distance to the south. But this opportunity just had to be their escape.

According to the travel agent, the destination would be a beautiful and well-known ocean-side resort. It was a place that catered mostly to the rich, especially to wealthy northerners traveling south for winter vacations. And the agent had also made a side comment as Maggie had begun to leave, saying that if her sister was as attractive as Maggie herself, they would be perfect for the positions offered. "You are just what they desire," the woman had explained. As Maggie hurried along, she could only knowingly smile at the thought of the woman's remark. Once anyone saw Katherine, the jobs would be theirs for sure. She prayed that this might be their chance.

At the apartment on Riverside, Katherine Flynn sat silently upon a chair in the kitchen, her youthful world swirling inside.

She had listened without speaking as her sister consulted with their mother about the course of her life ahead, a life she would admittedly have to accept. After hearing of the job opening, their mother took over the discussion. In the morning both Katherine and Maggie would call in late to work, stating a family emergency. They would go to the travel agency and make application before returning to their jobs. If and when the resort jobs were offered, they would immediately accept. They would pack and leave as soon as the travel arrangements were required.

Katherine's mother continued. The girls were to tell absolutely no one of their plans or destination. Absolutely, no one! At the time of their departure, Molly Flynn would visit their employers, telling them that a further family emergency had occurred, that her girls had been forced to leave without notice. Their mother would make up whatever excuse or story that needed to be told. Even their father would be told nothing more than his daughters had received a great job opportunity to make money for the family. The same would be told to their older brother and sister, who would only be given the truth when the time was appropriate. Whenever their father was to be released from the Veteran's Hospital, Molly and her husband would be immediately returning home to Massachusetts. For now, New York City would be left behind.

Staring down at her youngest daughter, Molly Flynn further directed that there be no contact with Jimmy Kane or his family at any time. All that this boy and his family must ever need to know would be that Katherine had run away from a marriage, nothing more. Once the girls arrived in Georgia and got settled, they would call her in either New York or Riverton on a Sunday evening at a specific time, to let her know they were safe.

Molly Flynn wasn't done. As soon as they were able, Maggie and Katherine would go to the nearest parish church and ask to meet with the priest. Katherine would tell him of her problem and ask for his help. Only after finding out what might be done, would other options be discussed. In addition, Katherine would take an assumed name. She would act as if she was married, that her husband was in Europe fighting the war. Since her middle name was Patricia, it would be easiest to remember 'Patrick', Katherine 'Patrick', this would be best. At some point Katherine should find a cheap wedding band at a local pawn shop and slip it onto her finger.

All during these instructions from her mother, Katherine remained silent, her eyes focused downward, nodding her head slowly to each of her mother's dictates. Maggie Flynn stood nearby, listening intently, her mouth slightly ajar. For both young women, their lives were now being delivered a much more certain reality of their course ahead, a course that only weeks before neither could have ever envisioned.

Finally, Molly Flynn softened her words of parental directive. She reminded her two beautiful girls that they were young and strong, and full of life. She reminded them that the current circumstances for many other Americans were very much harder, during this terrible time of war and sacrifice. And whatever the future might be before them, they would both be together, and poised for an adventure that each of them would likely never forget. And with those decisive last words, a worried mother began to cry.

Several days later, an early-morning train called the 'Silver Meteor' numbly jolted forward on its wheels, before picking up speed and leaving Pennsylvania Station behind. Breaking into the light of day, the passenger cars were busy with people making their way toward cities and destinations south of New York. The Silver Meteor's route would take Katherine and Maggie Flynn toward places in America they had only heard about, yet never seen. There would first be Philadelphia, then Baltimore and Washington D.C. Onward to Richmond in Virginia, Raleigh in North Carolina, Columbia in South Carolina, and then

Savannah, Georgia. Somewhere south of Savannah, they would disembark at a town call Thallmann. From there, the Silver Meteor train would continue on to Jacksonville, Florida, whereupon it would reach its terminus, before heading back the way it had come.

The woman at the travel agency had told the sisters that their trip would take approximately twenty hours, reaching their destination very early the following morning. At the station, a car would be waiting to take them to a place called 'The Castle', a resort-hotel with lovely gardens and beautiful white beaches on the shores of the Atlantic Ocean.

For both girls, the rush and excitement of their hurried escape occupied the early hours of their journey. They gazed out the windows of the train, viewing the new countryside passing before them, seeing all the people in their midst. There were traveling businessmen, couples with children, black porters working the aisles, as well as the many young men in uniform, casually casting furtive glances their way.

But as the enduring hours passed, they each silently felt the difficult and empty fear of leaving their mother and father behind, of forsaking their jobs and friendships, the daily lives they had come to know and expect. Two lives that in only a matter of weeks had so suddenly changed. Mixtures of emotion pursued them as they wondered what lay ahead.

As the railroad stations of unknown places came and went, the daylight hours turned from afternoon to night. The steady somnolent rocking of the wheels closed their eyes to a restless sleep, the journey rolling on and on. But upon their arrival in Savannah, they awakened with expectation, knowing they were now in Georgia, and that soon a new and elusive chapter in their unknown journey was about to begin.

A short time later, the porter approached their seats, announcing their requested destination. The Silver Meteor slowed to a stop. Outside, in the darkness of an early morning, only a solitary light shone on the deserted platform. The two sisters rustled with their baggage before descending from the train. Almost as soon as the porter helped them to debark, he leapt back aboard. Signaling with his arm, the passenger cars began to move, the warming lights of the train pulling away. They stood on the platform, very much alone.

Dragging their suitcases toward a bench by the vacant station building, the sisters huddled together, gripped with uncertainty. Not a person or vehicle had appeared in sight. Across the tracks, they could hear the strange rustling of something unknown in the darkness beyond. The minutes passed ever so slowly before them. But finally, headlights appeared in the distance motoring in their direction. As the car pulled up to the station house, they rose together hoping for safety. A young man jumped out of the car, a flashlight in hand. Their rescue from worry had come.

Riding in the car, the bluish light of a coming day began to grow. A soft mist hovered above flattened fields of grayish green, the grass knee-high in length. For most of an hour they passed over bumpy roads, through dark woods of tall thin trees, and by swampy ponds of water appearing black as night. Along the way, they witnessed small and rickety wooden shacks scattered in the open clearings, broken down cars and other rusted metal scattered beside.

Nearing their destination, they crossed over a narrow bridge flanked by wider bodies of water on both sides of the car. Straight ahead the dawning sun had begun to rise before them, almost blinding in its sight. The sides of the road were now bordered with whitish-yellow sand. Eventually, beach dunes came into view, topped by thick rugged bushes and bunches of grass. As the car rumbled slowly toward another small bridge ahead, suddenly to their right a vast and endless view of the Atlantic Ocean rose before their eyes, its surface glittering in the early morning light.

Moments later, the car turned onto a narrow drive. Giant overhanging trees with wide limbs spread above the car, as if going through a tunnel. Then, appearing through the front window of the car there stood a majestic two-storied building. Bordered by deep green palm trees and landscaped gardens, the structure could easily have been something the two young women might have seen only in picture books, a palatial image of wealth and status. Although they had witnessed such palaces of privilege in both New York City and Boston, this was like traveling to a tropical paradise. The car rolled slowly around a circle, before gently coming to a stop. Stepping outside, a warm ocean breeze rustled against their skins, the smell of salt in the air. Within a silent moment of hesitation, the girls stared in disbelief.

But with the slam of a car door, the real world returned. The shutter of its closing seemed to announce that one long journey had come to an end. Upon the shores of this mysterious seacoast, another was about to begin.

Most of two weeks went by as Katherine and Maggie Flynn settled into their new location far away from home. Katherine began her switchboard operator job, being placed with the other office personnel at the resort. Maggie joined the service workers, training as a waitress. Katherine got her own room in a large house on the grounds, while Maggie had to bunk with her new roommates in a separate dormitory-style building. Still, the sisters spent much of their personal time together while learning the ropes.

The Castle had been built by a wealthy auto magnate some sixteen years before, catering to other well-to-do northerners traveling south in the winters for the warming sun and sand. The exclusivity of the resort was abundantly clear. Its visitors were dressed in the latest of expensive fashions, well-groomed in appearance, and sometimes demanding in their tone and expectation. All of the staff who were engaged in any direct way with the vacationing patrons of the hotel were white in skin color. If some of the local colored people were hired in any way, they were always kept hidden, well-away from the hotel grounds. Many of the employees were seasonal workers from the Northeast. They often worked resorts like The Castle during the winter, before heading back in the summers to work vacation spots in the Adirondacks, the Catskills, or other locations where only the rich came to play. The two sisters also quietly learned that Jewish people were absolutely not welcome to visit such a place. Well-aware of their own family history, Katherine and Maggie understood implicitly between themselves, that as Irish Catholics not so very long ago, they too would have once been barred acceptance into such a socially superior domain.

Despite these unspoken boundaries of race and heritage, the current employees of the resort were gracious and kind, especially towards two young women whose beauty and personality fit the requirements desired. Nevertheless, Katherine and Maggie understood the necessity of their employment, both for themselves and their family back home. It would demand their courteous presence and singular perseverance, for they had no other place to go. And so, they both felt the pressure to show their ability, as well as their deference toward their superiors and guests.

Meanwhile, the true purpose of their mission had to remain a secret only they could share. During the first week of their arrival, they cautiously inquired about their religious necessity, uncertain about what to expect. To their muted surprise, yes, there were other practicing Catholics about. And each Sunday the resort provided transportation that would take both patrons and personnel to a small chapel on the adjoining island of St Simons. It was there that they could practice their faith. On the following Sabbath ahead, they would take the next step.

On an early Sunday afternoon in mid-October, 1944, Father Leo Zeller stood in the warm sunshine outside St Williams Chapel on St Simons Island. 'Father Z', as he was known by his local parishioners, had just completed his second mass of the day. As an associate pastor residing in the city of Brunswick, it was Father Zeller's position to administer to the small rural Catholic missions within the parish of St Francis Xavier. Each Sunday, he would travel to nearby Darien, before driving over to St Simons to perform Sunday mass on the island. As Zeller exchanged conciliatory greetings with various familiar parishioners, he was approached by two young women who asked to speak with him in private. Nodding his assent, the priest pointed them to a small rectory door at the rear of the chapel, explaining that he would be with them shortly.

Sometime later, the story that Father Leo Zeller received was not necessarily surprising. Over the two decades since his ordainment into the priesthood, including pastoral appointments in Washington D.C., West Virginia, and most recently Atlanta, Zeller was experienced in providing both advice and assistance regarding the particular problem that now confronted him. Also familiar would be the possible solution that he could help to undertake. Despite the problem's recurring frequency, it remained a delicate matter of which the Church rarely spoke or acknowledged. As Zeller motored his car along the narrow country roads back to the city of Brunswick, he was generally confident that he could provide both a medical and personal outcome that would best serve all concerned.

Katherine and Maggie returned to The Castle. They slipped out of their church clothing and into the only summer-like dresses they had been able to carry along. The October afternoon remained warm and full with sun. The sisters walked along a flattened stretch of island beach that spread into the distance. Beside them, the dark blue waters of the Atlantic Ocean reached far to the horizon, before meeting the brilliant azure sky. A soft and welcome breeze pressed against their skin, keeping the bugs and flies away. Seabirds glided along the cusps of the waves. And yet high above, they watched as a giant blimp moved silently over the coastline. Its hulky presence provoked a worried reminder that enemy submarines might be lurking somewhere unseen. It seemed the terrible war was never far away, causing silent internal fears, fears that all Americans shared.

Otherwise, Maggie Flynn was in general good spirits, another step in her familial responsibility having been met. The local priest had been kind, understanding, and willing to help. Upon their next free day from work, she and Katherine would travel together to Brunswick to meet with him, whereupon other matters would be discussed. Despite her feeling of accomplishment, Maggie understood that Katherine would not feel the same. Instead, each moment of this unwanted process continued to be something she wished might go away. But there was nothing else that either of them could do to change this current course in their lives. So Maggie would not beat her drum today, knowing it would have little effect.

Maggie was also quite aware that Katherine was different now. Her little sister was no longer the engaging and happy girl that she had once been before the 'problem'. That's how their mother had begun to refer to the situation from the outset, the 'problem'. Ever since the startling revelation of Katherine's unfortunate predicament, a quiet sense of sadness had prevailed upon her sister, accompanied by an almost fated resignation as to what lay ahead in her life. Maggie knew the unspoken shame that Katherine had to be feeling inside, the deep sense of guilt this mistake had cast upon both herself and the family. Maggie needed to be careful not to make matters worse, while forging ahead with all the things that needed to be done to bring this trouble to an end.

As Katherine herself walked with her older sister along the ocean shore, she silently felt better about her circumstance. The time spent with the priest had been somewhat comforting. By the end of their earlier meeting that afternoon, all of the worries that had been swirling within her, all the unknown uncertainties of the months ahead and what might happen, had quietly eased just a bit. Still, nothing could be done about the strange and mysterious feelings within her body, nor the unimaginable reality that one day soon she would give birth to a child.

Nevertheless, Katherine would try to take heed of what the priest had gently assured her. Be strong he had said, take care of yourself, and everything will be okay. Have faith and the Lord would look after her. But even though the priest's words had calmed her some, they could not answer the other questions that troubled her at night. They had been questions she was too afraid to ask, questions that wouldn't go away. Why did she have to continue to lie about her problem? Why would this child inside her be considered a child of sin? Didn't God have mercy on those who had sinned against his Will, but who had asked forgiveness for the error of their ways? She hadn't meant to hurt anyone on that night when she had made her mistake. She had given in to Jimmy Kane only because he said he loved her. Why now, was everyone so afraid and angry at what had come to pass?

At seven o'clock that evening, Maggie made a phone call to home. Katherine stood close by, her mixed feelings always within. The girls were required to speak only in the code they had rehearsed. It was the code their mother had directed upon their leaving, just in case the local operator in Riverton might be listening. Katherine did as she was told. Still, these ever-present questions remained unanswered. It was as if these questions had no time nor place in this world in which she lived.

Willa King was a woman of the South, born and raised in the state of Georgia. At the age of twenty, she had met and married her husband, Buddy. Buddy King was also a native Georgian whose current employment was as an engineer for the J.A. Jones Construction Company. The Kings' had a daughter whose name was Cassandra. In October of 1944, 'Cassie', as she was called by her family and friends, was eight years old.

Buddy King was a hard working man, and something of a mechanical genius. Although often a rough and tumble man in his younger years, Buddy had settled down when tasked with the support of a wife and child. Willa was a quieter soul, a devoutly religious woman who had been raised in the Catholic faith. Willa spent much of her personal time away from caring for her child by engaging in volunteer activities for her parish in the city of Brunswick. For Buddy King, religion was not necessarily his forte, but he tried to support his wife and daughter at every turn. In 1941, shortly before Pearl Harbor and the start of the war, Buddy had bought a spacious house in Brunswick that had become the family home. Buddy and Willa had wanted a second child, but for reasons unknown Willa had been unable to conceive.

Brunswick, Georgia was a small port city on the Atlantic Ocean. That changed with the beginning of the war. The community suddenly became a major naval shipbuilding site for Liberty ships. And the J.A. Jones Construction Company had equally transformed, becoming the largest local contractor for the Navy's effort. As a result, Brunswick had begun to grow by leaps and bounds, as people from throughout the north and south came for the work. In addition, the small city had been chosen as a US Naval training headquarters, as well as the home base for aerial blimps searching the nation's eastern coast for German U-boats seeking to destroy American ships at sea. As the Liberty boat construction efforts soared into a higher gear, the Brunswick facility was remarkably delivering a finished ship every sixty days to the country's defense. And just as quickly, the Navy would fill them with young seaman prepared to fight for their homeland's safety and freedom.

Under such critical circumstances, Buddy King was working long hours at the shipyard, six days a week. And Willa was
beginning to see that the stress of his grinding efforts had begun
to take their toll. There was little time for his wife and daughter.
Sunday was the only day there was to rest, and Buddy King
had begun a greater use of alcohol to try and relax. Willa quietly accepted this reality, as most of America was facing even
greater obstacles and fears. She could only put her faith in God
that some form of normalcy would one day return to their lives,
whenever this fearful conflict might come to an end.

Meanwhile, Willa continued her work for the church while
raising her child. When Cassie had come of school age, she had
begun to attend the St Joseph's Catholic school administered
by the church. Willa, herself, primarily worked hand-in-hand
with the associate priest, Father Leo Zeller. And over time,
along with their working relationship, a personal friendship
had developed as well. Through that friendship, Father Z had
learned of Willa's attempts at having a second child. However,
there had never been any mention of Willa's concern for her
husband or marriage.

So it came as some surprise that on a week-day afternoon
Father Z had called Willa King into his office, presenting a
proposition she had never thought to consider. Sitting in her
chair, she listened intently to the priest's recounting of a circumstance of which he had recently become aware. Two young
women had come to him after his mass at St. Williams Chapel
the previous Sunday. They had just arrived from New York City
to work at The Castle resort on Sea Island. The younger of
the two women was only eighteen, and unfortunately she was
pregnant with child.

They were two Irish girls, Father Z explained. They were
attractive, well-mannered, and of the Catholic faith. However,
the younger girl was in need of help. She was currently about
four months to term. And due to her age and other life circumstances, she felt the necessity to give up the baby. The two

sisters would be coming to meet with him again in a week or so, and likely some final decisions would have to be made. But Father Z felt confident that the choice would be to give up the child, as there appeared to be no other options.

If so, then the girl would need some place to reside in the months before the birth, while the Church considered certain preparations regarding adoption of the child. Would this be something that Willa's family might consider, to host and shelter the girl until the baby was born? But also, Father Z then presented a second option, the one that turned Willa's heart inside out. If perhaps she and her husband might also be willing to adopt the child, he would not be adverse to such a placement.

Willa unconsciously put a hand to her mouth, looking down at the floor, her mind whirling upon the proposition at hand. She sat silent for some time before responding. "I will have to give it some thought," she answered. "Of course I would need to talk it over with Buddy and Cassie. I guess I don't know what else to say."

"That would be fine," Father Z responded. The girls will not be coming to Brunswick until they can get free to make the trip. Just think about things for now. Then please let me know."

A short time later, as Willa King began her walk home from the church, her mind was conflicted as to the question before her. Yet within her heart, she felt a certainty she could not ignore.

Two weeks passed before Katherine and Maggie could make the trip to Brunswick. They met with Father Zeller at the rectory before going to the Brunswick hospital to meet with the doctor.

Dr. Howard Coburn was both professional and caring with Katherine. Not having seen this patient before, he inquired of her history. Katherine began her story. After beginning to have nausea and some cramping in Riverton, she had gone to New

York to see her father and mother. Her sister had been working part-time for a doctor in the city, who agreed to see her. The doctor had confirmed the pregnancy. She had not seen any other doctor since that day.

Dr. Coburn began his observations. The young woman appeared to be in good health and holding her weight. He checked her blood pressure, then her breasts and pelvic area. There was no doubt she was beginning to show. Coburn further inquired about her morning sickness. Katherine said the recent train trip had been hard, and although her nausea had become less frequent, she could feel things were happening inside. Finally, the doctor asked Katherine when she believed she might have become pregnant. She answered that it was likely sometime during the month of June.

It all made sense to Coburn. He explained that Katherine was very likely nearing the end of her fourth month. She would begin to grow larger now. And sometime in the near future she would feel the baby more frequently. He directed that Katherine continue to eat well, to get her rest, and refrain from any undue physical exertion. She would be expected to see him again in three weeks time.

Knowing that the girls were unfamiliar with Brunswick, Dr Coburn directed them to a department store where expectant mothers could purchase the clothing Katherine would need in the months ahead. In the meantime, they should stay in touch with Father Zeller as to any other necessities. But for the moment, Katherine was fine and there appeared to be no complications.

When Maggie asked about any payment for his services, Dr Coburn turned to Katherine, speaking with caution. "I've spoken with Father Zeller. He tells me that your husband is overseas in Europe. I won't ask you whether or not that is the truth. Instead, I will tell you that there is a program for military families in these situations, one that will cover the cost. Father Zeller and I will make the arrangements." Katherine and Maggie nodded quietly, their eyes glancing towards the floor. With the appointment complete, they gave their thanks to the doctor, before returning to the street.

Finding the department store and pooling their money, Katherine was able to purchase two loose smocks and other maternity clothing. They hurried to the transit stop, catching the late afternoon bus back to the island.

Sue Ellen Dampeer was the office manager at The Castle resort at Sea Island. A native of Georgia, she had grown up on nearby St Simons Island, having worked for the business since its opening in 1928. Over those sixteen years she had risen within company management to her current position. Working hard and learning all the various administrative duties of operating a hotel, Sue Ellen had seen The Castle survive and prosper, despite both the Depression and the current wartime troubles.

During that time, Sue Ellen had married her husband Earl Dampeer. Earl owned and operated his own shrimp boat, as well as engaging in the crabbing and oyster industry. Over time, he had become the main provider of daily fresh seafood for the resort. The survival and successful operation of the hotel had become the couple's life work and economic support. And during these years, as they toiled in their daily labor, they had come to see quite clearly how the other half lived.

Despite their critical importance to The Castle's operation, Sue Ellen and Earl, as well as many of the other local employees, they often worked behind the scenes. For ever since its initial inception, The Castle had sought to cater to the rich and fa-mous. They were mostly to well-to-do Yankees who came south each winter to enjoy the luxurious comforts and warmth the Georgia barrier islands could provide. And with winter being the busiest time of year, it was The Castle's desire was to make them feel at home.

The owner of this island retreat had therefore designed something of an unspoken but strictly held intent regarding resort personnel. Young white workers would be recruited from the north, then placed into positions that personally engaged with the vacationing residents. Caucasian locals like Sue Ellen and Earl, so marked by their deep Southern accents, were generally placed in positions of support rather than direct service to The Castle's wealthy clientele. And obviously without question, any of the Negro help that might be necessary to the resort's operation were strictly not to be seen. Gentile sophistication and refinement were the calling cards necessary for the continued success of The Castle's enterprise. There would be little or no exceptions.

As a result, all administrative personnel, including Sue Ellen's switchboard operators, were white Yankee girls from locations throughout the Northeast, hired on either six-month or one-year contracts. The shorter contract durations allowed for some of these workers to return north to work other mountain and ocean-side summer retreats that came with the change of seasons. This was the world of the rich and the well-to-do that Sue Ellen Dampeer had come to serve, knowing it would always be a world in which she would never be a part.

Sue Ellen was pleased with her newest arrival to the switchboard crew. She was a beautiful young girl with rich blonde hair, courteous and helpful whenever on the line. She had easily learned the standard routine and information quicker than most. Although this girl seemed unusually quiet for her age, and seemingly distant as if distracted in thought, she did her job well without complaint. She had come with her sister from New York, although they were really from Massachusetts. That had made more sense to Sue Ellen, for the young girl's accent was similar to the many girls from Boston that she had hired over the years.

Sue Ellen would have preferred to have had the two girls live together, but that was not her call. All administrative personnel were to be housed in separate quarters, each with their own room. The kitchen and restaurant personnel were housed separately in dormitory-style quarters elsewhere on the grounds. But Sue Ellen could easily see that the two sisters were very close, always together whenever their time was free. They seemed particularly innocent in regard to the somewhat vagabond lifestyle that many of the more veteran employees had come to know and engage. Sue Ellen figured that it would take some time for the girls to become comfortable with the ways of The Castle's world.

Having completed his daily morning mass at St Francis Xavier, Father Zeller returned to his office at the rectory, sipping his coffee while reading the daily Brunswick News. Each day at mass he would pray for the men overseas, honoring those who had been killed, as well as those still fighting to stay alive and perhaps one day return home. Unfortunately, the war continued to drag on ever so slowly. In the last week, a US ship had been sunk at sea in the Pacific Ocean. It was believed that all aboard the vessel had been lost. In Europe, the Italian front was at a standstill, with the hardships of winter soon to come. It was sometimes challenging for Father Z to keep his faith, despite this life-long calling he had been chosen to answer. Still, it was his duty to maintain the similar faith of others each and every day, while continuing to pray for peace on earth.

The ringing of the telephone interrupted the priest's morning reading. Picking up the phone, it was Willa King on the end of the line, a tinge of anxious excitement in her voice. Willa relayed that she had now spoken with her husband and daughter about the prospect of taking the child. Yes, she affirmed, they would be happy to have the baby. Zeller could feel an undercurrent of joy in the woman's voice. While Willa particularly expressed the excitement that was felt by her daughter, Cassie, it was obvious to the priest that the jubilation was shared by her mother as well.

Upon this welcome news, Father Z and Willa began to discuss the plans that would now be necessary regarding both Katherine and the coming birth of the child. They agreed that whenever it was time for the girl to leave The Castle, then Willa and the family would take her into their home. Dr Coburn would oversee the pregnancy and birth. At Father Z's request, there existed a government program available that Dr Coburn could access for little or no cost. And although it didn't need to be discussed, undoubtedly the child would be baptized in the Catholic faith. According to Dr Coburn, short of anything unforeseen, it was likely the due date would be sometime in the middle of March, give or take a couple of weeks.

As expected, there was no disagreement or concerns from Willa King, only a sincere dedication for what lay ahead. Father Z would now speak with the girl and her sister, delivering them the news. After hanging up the phone, Zeller rested back in his chair, a lightened breath of accomplishment exuding from his chest. Gratefully, God's will had spoken, becoming a good day within this dominion of His unfathomable creation.

Another month passed in the calendar year of 1944. Father Zeller continued his pastoral duties for St Francis Xavier in Brunswick, as well as his Sunday duties for the small Catholic chapels in Darien and St Simons. Like many other Americans, Zeller also continued his daily newspaper reading on the progress of the war. In the European theater, the Soviet army was pushing closer from the west, advancing toward Auschwitz. Heinrich Himmler, commander of the nefarious German SS, had ordered the remaining Jewish captives exterminated, followed by the total destruction of the camp. The effort would be an attempt to wipe clean the human atrocities that had occurred under the murderous Nazi regime. While in London, innocent civilians continued to suffer the haunting fear and destruction from bombing raids and rocket fire. In the Pacific, the Allies were pressing ahead, with bombing raids now reaching the city of Tokyo. In their defense, the Japanese Air Force had begun 'kamikaze' raids on US ships at sea. Although perhaps a corner was being turned in this dreadful conflict, the death and destruction of the war continued to rage.

Dr Coburn remained busy with his work at the Brunswick City Hospital, providing daily care for its local residents. Additionally, he performed weekly surgeries upon both civilians being injured at the shipbuilding complex, as well as the naval bases nearby.

At her home in Brunswick, Willa King made ready for an unlikely and unexpected visitor, preparing a vacant bedroom in the house for the young woman's arrival. However, Willa's anticipation was challenged by the worried signs of her husband's increasing stress, including his continued use of alcohol whenever he was home. Although she kept these concerns only to herself, she brooded daily about what they might foretell, and whether or not they might one day be overcome.

At The Castle resort, Katherine and Maggie Flynn had settled into their regular working routines. Each day, Maggie served the guests at the dining facilities, while Katherine worked the phones and assisted with reservations. However, it had now become almost impossible for Katherine to secretly hide the inevitable reality of her pregnancy. Although she had not yet been questioned by anyone in authority, her new friends and co-workers at the residence were silently in the know. But Katherine feared that at any particular moment, her boss, Mrs. Dampeer, would be inquiring of her condition.

Unbeknownst to Katherine, Sue Ellen Dampeer was already well-aware of the current situation. Only that Sue Ellen hadn't yet confronted this reality. As far as Sue Ellen was concerned,

Katherine Flynn was good at her job. She was a beautiful and kind young girl, one that Sue Ellen had come to observe and enjoy in her employ. For a week or more, Sue Ellen had been putting off addressing the inevitable. But once the busy the Thanksgiving week-end had passed, Sue Ellen figured it was time to face the circumstance. Still, whatever might be the outcome, she wasn't worried to decide.

On the Tuesday after the holiday, Katherine was called to Mrs. Dampeer's office in the early afternoon. For Katherine, sometimes Mrs. Dampeer's way of talking was hard to understand. All the people from Georgia seemed to speak long and slow, almost like they were whining about something. And often they would so shorten up their words that Katherine couldn't be sure what was said. But on this particular day, Mrs. Dampeer's accent was not so difficult that Katherine would mistake the content of her inquiry. And with that recognition, she knew that now had come the time to tell the truth. Maybe not the whole truth, but something like the truth, Katherine wasn't sure.

After admitting her obvious pregnancy to Mrs. Dampeer, Katherine continued to tell the lie about the baby's father, the lie that her mother and even Dr Coburn had inferred it was best to tell. The father was in the war, somewhere in Europe, but Katherine didn't know exactly where. Although she had told everyone she was married, Katherine confessed that this was not the case. The father of the child was really just a boyfriend, and she had made a terrible mistake. When her sister had seen the job offer, they had decided to come. Their mother had told them to go see the priest immediately after they arrived, to see if he could help. And only recently, a family had been found in Brunswick who was willing to adopt the child. And finally, Katherine admitted she would have to leave her work soon, to go live with the family until the child was born.

Sue Ellen Dampeer could easily see the obvious fear that crossed the young woman's face. A fear marked by a dreadful lonesomeness that Sue Ellen easily understood. Here was a young girl with a terrible problem in her life, and so very far from home. Katherine then pleaded that she didn't want to quit her job, but that the doctor and priest had said she must. She begged Sue Ellen that Maggie be allowed to stay, that it was not her sister's fault. Apologizing for her deception, Katherine could only admit that she just didn't know what to do.

Letting a short breath of emotion release, Sue Ellen Dampeer began to calm the girl's distress. Katherine was still so very much a child. And yet, this girl had never lost her composure, had never shed a tear. In calming response, Sue Ellen delivered her counsel. Everything would be okay. Situations like this were not uncommon. Katherine was not the first to be faced with such a circumstance. And no, Maggie was not going to lose her job. She would remain and finish her contract. As for Katherine, she would stay until the doctor and priest said she must go. But in the meantime, it was best that nothing more be said about her dilemma.

Sue Ellen watched as Katherine dutifully expressed her gratitude. She then asked when the child might be due. Katherine's answer was likely the middle of March.

"All right," Sue Ellen responded, "but when this is all over, when you are better and have recovered, I want you to return and finish your employment as you initially agreed. Can you promise that you will do that for me?"

Katherine lifted her head, silently nodding with further appreciation and relief. "Okay, let's get back to work. And remember, except for your sister, no one is to know. We'll keep this just between us." Thanking Sue Ellen once again, Katherine rose wearily before leaving the office.

Sue Ellen Dampeer smiled to herself, gently shaking her head. There was no doubt that everyone would surely know of this delicate circumstance, if they didn't know already. It would just be a matter of time. For the island world of The Castle resort was indeed a very small world. Luckily, it was also a place where almost everyone here was from somewhere else, whether it might be the vacationing tourists or the seasonal employees. And as for local island residents like Sue Ellen and others, there had never been as much as a wart or pimple on these isles that ever remained uncovered. Silence and looking the other way were often the island rule, unless a police matter might choose to intervene.

Over her years at The Castle, Sue Ellen Dampeer had certainly witnessed her share of private rendezvous'. She had witnessed both the mighty and the fallen come and go. For it was not just the people who came and went, but also the secrets of their lives they sought to carry inside. And in this Southern world, even though such secrets might remain unspoken, they were rarely ever kept.

Nevertheless, perhaps even more compelling to Sue Ellen, was the quiet courage that this young girl continued to display.

By mid-December, Katherine Flynn had packed her two bags and quietly slipped away from The Castle resort and the island life. Meeting Father Zeller at the church in Brunswick, she was introduced to Mrs. King and taken to her home. The house in Brunswick was big and comfortable, and she was given her own room. As she unpacked her things, a young girl suddenly appeared shuffling in the doorway, watching her intently. Katherine smiled and beckoned her inside, happy and willing to perhaps to have a new little friend, to gently help avoid the loneliness of not having her sister nearby.

"Are you a Yankee?" the young girl questioned.

Katherine had to laugh. The child's southern accent was obviously familiar by now, but still funny all the same. "Well, yes," Katherine answered, "I think I am a Yankee .... a Yankee from Massachusetts. Have you ever been to Massachusetts?"

"No," the child answered. "I've never met a Yankee before. But I've been to Savannah to be with my grandmother."

"Well, you know, I came through Savannah when I traveled to Georgia on the train," Katherine began. "But it was nighttime, and I didn't get to see the city. Is it pretty in Savannah?" Katherine patted the bedside, motioning the child to sit. The little girl entered the room and hopped beside her.

"Yes, it's very pretty, especially the houses and the trees. Mama and I would walk to the park."

Katherine smiled. "Uh huh. It's always fun to go the park. Well now, do you know that maybe I can guess your name in just one try. I'm really good with names. Do you think I can?"

"Okay, guess," the young girl responded. Katherine rubbed her hand under chin, pretending to think of a name. "Okay, I'm sure this is it. Are you ready? Is it Maaaay......belle," she asked with a fake drawl?

The little girl jumped right off the bed. "No........," the child answered, half-screaming with delight!

"Maybelle? Not Maybelle! You lose. You didn't get it in only one try."

"Well, let me try one more time," Katherine asked, before going through the motions of once again thinking of a name. "I know now," Katherine followed. "And this time I know I'm right. It's Cassie, isn't it?"

The little girl thrust her hands on her hips. "You cheated, didn't you? Mama told you, didn't she? Didn't she?"

Katherine laughed long and deep. She couldn't even remember the last time she had laughed with such unburdened joy, it had been so long. It was like a special salve in her so recently troubled life. Maybe in the months ahead she would have this little friend, one she could talk and play with, short of fear or worry.

But the moment of hopeful anticipation was suddenly brief. For quickly the real world once again returned. And little Cassie King had no idea what her childhood innocence might cause with the next words out of her mouth.

"Do you know what my Mama says, I bet you can't guess?"

"What, little one, what does your mama say?"

"Mama says......, she says that pretty soon, that pretty soon I am going to have a little baby sister or brother, that's what she says.............."

Katherine Flynn made every effort to keep the smile on her face. But inside her heart, an unwanted blade struck home.

The Christmas holidays of 1944 came and went, followed by a new year ahead. Maggie Flynn continued to work her waitress job for The Castle resort, serving its wealthy clientele in this ocean-side world known as the Golden Isles. Meanwhile, Katherine lived quietly in a stranger's home in nearby Brunswick, spending her lonesome days with Willa King and her daughter, Cassie, who had become her only friends.

As she neared her seventh month, Katherine could feel the child within her growing larger, beginning to move ever more frequently. Still, the time passed ever so slowly day after day. Willa's husband was mostly never around the family, coming home late at night, before leaving early the very next morning. Except for Sunday afternoons after going to church with Willa and Cassie, Katherine was rarely in the presence of Mr. King. He always seemed to have a glass of liquor in his hands whenever he was home. Although Mr. King did not seem angry or troublesome around the family, Katherine could feel a sense of worried concern and uncertainty in Willa's face, a feeling that something might be wrong. Nevertheless, over the past months there had been little Katherine could do about any situation, for she had nowhere else to go.

Mondays were always the best day of the week, for that was usually Maggie's day off from work. Maggie would either catch the transit or a ride from the island, arriving in late morning to the house in Brunswick. The two sisters would walk together for lunch at a nearby corner restaurant, often pausing to window shop along their route. And if the winter afternoons were sometimes warm, they would visit a nearby park to sit and share some time outside. These weekly visits with Maggie were Katherine's only link to her life before the troubled events that she continued to endure, the only time to hear news from home and possibly forget for a moment the necessity before her. The good news was that their father and mother were safe at home, their older sister and brother remaining okay and not overseas. Still, it seemed like her previous life hung suspended in a faraway place she could no longer see or touch, awakening each day to this continuing strange reality. It was an unknown world that had no past, poised with a future with nothing in sight. It was impossible to tell which place might be a dream and which was not.

The evenings that followed Maggie's visit were always the hardest. Alone again with her ever-present fears, her sister once again gone from her, Katherine would find herself speaking to this unseen little being hidden inside her body, this little someone who was ever so close within her. She prayed that the child did not share the dreadful angst that Katherine continued to feel. And so she spoke to this little someone with affection and care, creating for the child a future of happiness and love, of riches and hope, in a world always safe from danger. Then, saying a little prayer for each of them, Katherine Flynn would once again forcefully hold back her tears.

More weeks passed. In the middle of February, Katherine made her bi-weekly visit with Willa to the office of Dr. Coburn. Somehow, her health remained good, her pregnancy progressing normally. According to the doctor, the expected due date continued to be the middle of March, once again give or take. According to Doctor Coburn, although the increasing heaviness of her legs, the soreness of her back, the feelings of fatigue, the lack of sleep and frequent urination were difficult, they were normal signs of her condition. Dr Coburn went on to describe what Katherine needed to watch for in regards to the impending signs of labor and eventual birth. She continued to listen with her apparent stoic quietude, yet ever thankful that Willa was by her side.

But if Willa King appeared helpful and positive on the outside, on the inside she secretly worried about circumstances that the young girl beside her remained totally unaware. And while Dr. Coburn was both professional and direct in his assessment of Katherine's medical fitness, he too had secretly become advised of a potential development that this young woman, and even Willa King herself, need not know for now.

What went unspoken was a situation that Father Leo Zeller felt was necessary to deliberate and thus contend. On a late Sunday afternoon several weeks prior, following his travels to perform mass in Darien and St Simons, Willa King had invited the priest over to her home for a dinner with her family. And although her husband might have understood the importance of his conduct at such an event, certain indices had now become a reality that Buddy King could no longer control. The resulting consequence of certain occurrences that revealed themselves on this particular Sunday afternoon, had given Father Leo Zeller no choice but perhaps reconsider his previous decision regarding the planned adoption of an unborn child.

For most of a week, Father Zeller agonized over his concerns, before seeking the advice of several confidantes, including Dr. Howard Coburn. Although the counsel of these others could only sympathize with the priest's worried deliberation, as for Coburn himself, he sadly had some inside information regarding the situation. For as the attending physician for the J.A. Jones Construction firm down at the shipyards, there had been rumors circulating about the recent behavior of Buddy King.

According to Coburn, apparently the inebriation that Zeller had witnessed on the previous Sunday was not an aberration.

Over the prior several months, management at the company had witnessed similar instances of unusual behavior, although not necessarily direct evidence of drunkenness on the job. Rather, they were occurrences of behavior that suggested issues of mental instability or stress, including incidents of sudden volatility, as well as loss of memory or thought during the day. The fact that Buddy King had always been one of the best troubleshooters the Jones' company had on staff, as well as one of the more evenhanded and jovial men in regards to those who worked under his command, these recent instances of noted instability had certainly not gone unnoticed. From what Dr. Coburn had been told, the company remained watchful of the situation.

And yet, due to the incessant demands of the war effort, as well as Buddy King's incredible expertise, for the moment, all the company felt they could do was monitor the behavior in order to protect workplace safety. And in the days since the previous outbreaks, any further instances of unreliability had not been reported.

Father Zeller could only thank his physician friend for this current information. But both men generally agreed that the prospect of another child in the King family at this time was likely not the best of circumstances. Yet, Coburn advised that he could not be the one to make such a decision. Undoubtedly, the doctor would continue to do all he could to make sure the mother and her child got the adequate care they needed, but only Zeller could make any call in regard to the future of any adoption arrangements.

Throughout that day and evening, the Father Z struggled with his conundrum. Yes, Buddy King had been noticeably intoxicated during his Sunday visit, but he had not been antagonistic or threatening in any manner. In fact, it was just the opposite. Buddy King had been excessively jovial, and yet foolishly embarrassing to a fault, all of which had been disquieting enough to raise Zeller's concern. But now, Howard Coburn's related information had raised another level of genuine discontent.

And if not for the priest's deep and genuine affection for Willa King and her daughter, any reversal of the Church's adoptive placement might have been more easily reached. Instead, Willa and Cassie's hopeful expectations and desires for wanting this child only further challenged his thinking. And certainly on their behalf, he shared similar heartfelt wishes of his own.

But in the end, the future of the child must come first. In the end, that must be the only prerogative. Zeller would have to sit down with Willa King, to discuss and measure the consequences of whatever decision he would have to make. And although his final determination would have its effect, there remained a more constant unknown which the priest hoped he would not be forced to engage. It was an unknown that Zeller honestly hoped would not occur, but it also was one that surely could not be presumed. And that particular unknown was the confused emotions of a mother with child. For in the depths of any mother's heart, as well as the instinctual love and protection for her own, there remained a decisive event that the priest knew well would always be in play.

On the last day of February of 1945, in the rectory office of Father Leo Zeller, Willa King sat numbly in a leather chair facing her parish priest. An empty sense of loss had left her vacant inside. Across the desk between them, Zeller, his head bowed in prayer, petitioned for assistance and solace from their shared creator above. And yet, despite his words of heavenly request, the inevitable sorrow of Willa's heart could not be stilled. The prayerful words seemed to fade from the room as breathlessly as a whispering breeze. For Willa, the following silence was long, as if watching a loved one as they disappeared from sight. She was left with only her enduring faith, her belief that God's will had spoken, and that one wishful day she might come to understand.

But in Willa's more secular and practical mind, she knew. Tragically, this would not be the time. Her hopes for the newborn child would have to be forsaken. Somewhere along her path in this world, she had come to know that life on this earth was often full of challenges, challenges marked with events that must be overcome. They were setbacks needing to be dutifully met with perseverance, setbacks that must be shorn of selfish anger or recrimination, including the avarice of a covetous heart. As a faithful servant of her lord and savior, Jesus Christ, Willa King knew what was best. And yet, while burdened with such an understanding, the depth of her pain could find no relief.

And even though Father Zeller had led her to this place, it was true, she had considered coming of her own accord. Her husband was suffering, in ways she could not describe or help to intersect. She had prayed that another child might awaken him from the depths of his distractions, perhaps give them both something to grasp hold of, something to bind them together until better days might come.

But sadly, it had been only her wishful thinking. Buddy seemed unable to swim to shore. And Willa knew it was more than just the alcohol, more than the strain of an occupation he had always enjoyed and loved. It was something more serious, an unknown disorder no one else could see. But whatever might have been the cause, right now Buddy King was not the man she married, not the man she had come to love so many years ago. There was no way to explain away these intuitions she had felt in her mind, nor the visible reality she had sought to deny. For some time she had tried to suffer this secret alone, hoping it might reverse. But her fears had been undeniable, and now they were coming to pass.

And so, it was best that the child be placed elsewhere, whenever it might arrive. Although her husband had agreed to the adoption and the housing of the mother, he had rarely spoken of the circumstance, nor taken the slightest interest from the very beginning. That alone had only furthered the depth of Willa's solitary concerns. But for now, it was her precious daughter for whom she worried most, the terrible hurt and loss of a little brother or sister that would not be coming home.

During these last several months, Willa had been able to shelter Cassie from any distress about her father, and what the future might bring. That reality, Willa feared, might be coming soon enough. But now, with the impending loss of having Katherine soon to be going away, and without leaving behind a baby child to love and share, thoughts of her daughter's response were excruciating to imagine. Father Zeller broke Willa King's silent anguished reverie.

"And so, Willa, we need to talk about Katherine and the child in regard to the coming weeks ahead. As we have both agreed, Katherine will remain with you and the family until her labor begins. And as we both well know, she is under the impression that the child, once born, will be remaining with your family. From all my discussions with her, she has stated a happiness and relief that the baby will have a safe and comforting home. So it is best for now, in fact it is extremely critical that she continue to believe this is true. So, I beg you, Katherine must not be made aware of these new circumstances in any possible way. The same must go for Cassie, and I strongly advise even for your husband as well. I know that this is a very difficult request, but this matter has now become an exceedingly delicate situation, and must remain so until after the child has been placed."

"Also, I have made it very clear to Katherine, as well as her sister, that once the child is born, they are not to come near the home, or try to contact your family in any way. For as you are aware, Katherine will likely be returning to The Castle for a number of months after the birth. I've made this prohibition to her in the strongest way possible.

Zeller paused for a moment, shifting restlessly in his chair."Now, I believe that Father Bertram and I have found a young couple who wish to adopt. They are of the faith and have a good home. Of course nothing is for certain, but I can assure you that the Church will find the optimum location for the child. That's all I can tell you for today, but you can rest assured the child will be taken care of in the best possible way. I need you to believe that's going to be the outcome. And finally, we all wish and pray that things might have been different, but I think you would agree, under the circumstances this is the best result for all concerned."

Again, an uneasy silence hung within the room. Willa King let her gaze fall unconsciously toward the floor, while quietly nodding her assent. Then, she steeled herself and spoke. "Yes, Father, it's for the best. It's the best for the child. And thank you, Father, for all that you have done." But Willa King's words sounded hollow as soon as they left her lips, knowing deep within her shallow heart, the result of her words would never go away.

On March 11th, 1945, Katherine Flynn went into labor at the home of Buddy and Willa King. She was quickly transported to the Brunswick City Hospital. Dr. Coburn arrived at the hospital and advised that the patient be sedated. In the hours that followed, the mother's labor and childbirth went without complication. The child was born in the early morning hours of March 12th.

Immediately after the birth, the newborn was quickly moved to the hospital nursery. Father Zeller contacted The Castle resort to inform Katherine's sister. After working the day, Sue Ellen Dampeer drove Maggie to Brunswick for a visit at the hospital. Due to the agreements regarding the child's welfare, neither the birth mother nor any family member would be allowed to see the baby. However, an unsuspecting nurse at the facility did admit to Maggie and Sue Ellen that the baby's gender was a boy.

Katherine's post-partum recovery progressed quickly, and three days later she was released from the hospital.

Willa King had collected Katherine's clothes and other belongings, driving them out to The Castle; whereupon Sue Ellen made ready for Katherine's return. Later that evening, Willa King sat with her young daughter on the bed of a now empty room within their Brunswick home. Willa tried hard to explain the agonizing news. A baby brother would not be coming home. That night, both mother and child held each other close, crying themselves to sleep. Buddy King, who had been recently informed of the changing circumstances, did not come home until very late.

On a Monday morning in the latter days of March, Father Leo Zeller sat at his desk in the rectory of St Francis Xavier reading his morning paper. The day before, a baby boy recently birthed by a young woman named Katherine Flynn, had been quietly baptized in the Catholic faith. The young couple who had received the child currently lived in Brunswick, where they had come for employment during the war. However, it was their intention to return home to northern Florida upon the ending of the conflict.

Gratefully, the war in both the European and Pacific theaters was beginning to turn. Large-scale bombing campaigns upon cities in both Germany and Japan were beginning to cripple the enemy. Allied forces under General Montgomery were pushing to cross the Rhine. In response, Adolf Hitler had ordered the destruction of all German infrastructure and hardware that lay in the path of the Allied advance. Although American naval forces were still suffering significant casualties from the Japanese 'kamikaze' raids on their ships at sea, these tactics appeared to be last-ditch suicidal efforts by the Imperial Family to thwart an impending surrender. Along with the rest of his nation, Father Zeller continued to hope and pray for a world that might soon be at peace.

On the previous Sunday, after his service of mass at the chapel on St Simons, Zeller had met with Katherine and Maggie Flynn. He assured them both that the child was now in the good hands of the King family, with everyone appearing happy and well. But silently within, he petitioned for God's forgiveness in regard to his deliberate mendacity. While Maggie Flynn seemed pleased to hear the news, Katherine's response appeared quietly resigned. Zeller understood the girl's presumed mixture of emotions. It would take some time for Katherine to begin to forget the months of tribulation she had been forced to withstand. He recalled a strange remark that Dr Coburn had once made upon a previous but similar occasion. "It's like a person who has lost a leg. They are alive and their life will go on. But the missing shall always remain."

Zeller quickly turned the conversation to reminding the sisters that their difficult but brave task had been courageously accomplished. It was best now for them to move forward with their lives. They had done the right thing for all concerned, and they could also be certain that the Holy Father had given them his blessing. But also aware from past experience the distinct possibility of a reversal of intent, the priest once again reminded them that no visitation or contact could be allowed. Nevertheless, while making his drive back to Brunswick on this Sunday afternoon, Zeller couldn't help but ruminate with a measure of sorrow the circumstances of a world that must separate a mother from her child. He could only rely on his faith that the Holy Father and his Church knew better than he.

And so Katherine and Maggie Flynn returned to their current obligations at The Castle resort. They would have to complete the contract of their employment for another six months. Maggie would continue in her waitress position, while Sue Ellen Dampeer welcomed Katherine's return to her job in the office. Only their mother back home in Massachusetts had been given the news of what had transpired. 'Daddy Jim' Flynn would never be told, nor would their older sister or brother until more time had passed. The secret must always remain forever in the family.

Time passed. The warm spring of the South began to bloom. And the world at-large continued to turn. The white flowers of the early magnolia trees began to show, their lemony fragrance filling the morning air. The spreading branches of the live oak trees were filled with dark green leaves, the Spanish moss hanging languidly between. On the grounds of The Castle, multi-colored carnations bordered the walkways, the gardenias soon to come. And within the swampy lowlands beyond the resort, fields of saw grass spread with new life. While on much more firmer ground, the longleaf pine forests reached tall to the sky, with fresh verdant wire grass cushioning their base.

On April 12, 1945 America's cautioned belief that the war and its victory might soon be near was shaken by the sudden death of its remarkable leader, Franklin Delano Roosevelt. While the entire country grieved in sorrow and uncertainty, Katherine and Maggie were moved by the desperate anguish of the Negro people on the island, whose wails of loss and mourning spread throughout The Castle's domain. Despite the loss, hopeful news from both the European and the Pacific fronts continued to arrive.

With each passing day, the sisters' dreams of home continued to grow. And with her past burdens physically lifted, Katherine's youthful beauty and personality began to restore. Her caring boss, Sue Ellen Dampeer, remarked that Katherine should consider a career in modeling upon her return to New York. And Maggie, hearing of Sue Ellen's recommendation, echoed the possibility that Katherine should give it a try. Upon these urgings, Katherine began to hope that modeling school might become the next chapter in her life. Her spirit became alive with a future she now could begin to imagine, something she had been unable to consider for so long a time. As for Maggie, returning to a career in nursing remained her personal goal. As these wishful prospects grew closer with each daylight hour, the girls became more confident in what might be their lives before them.

And yet, for Katherine, these daylight possibilities always gave way to the night. And there, alone with herself and her thoughts, sometimes a hidden sense of pain and guilt remained. Whenever the busy activity of her working life was shorn for a time, a desirous wanting for her missing little child would arrive. What did he look like? Did he look more like her or his father? What name had they given him? Were Mr. and Mrs. King taking good care of him? And was Cassie happy playing with her new little brother? As Katherine tried to drift into sleep, she continued to make herself believe that God would take care of him, that everything would always be okay, that he would be happy in his life. But such hopeful intentions never seemed to fill the vacant hole in her heart. She prayed that as time went by this missing might begin to pass, and with such passing her own happiness might continue to grow.

Sadly, there remained a similar emptiness of which Katherine was completely unaware. Willa King's lonely nights were equally as difficult, her own vacant loss keeping her from sleep. Upon the anguished telling to her daughter, Cassie had cried for most of two days, heartbroken at the news of a little baby brother who would no longer come. And Katherine's sudden disappearance from Cassie's life only added to this sorrow. As for herself, Willa's deep heartbreak could not be shown. For she needed to salve her daughter's distress as soon as it might be reached. This would have to be her course. She had prayed daily that her child's memory would be short. And thankfully, in recent weeks things were slowly getting better for Cassie. But in Willa's own quiet moments alone, this loss would forever be remembered.

Spring turned to summer on the barrier islands of Southeast Georgia. At The Castle, the beautiful month of May was noticeably quiet with activity. Many of the resort's annual patrons from the Northeast had now found their way home for the season. Along with their leaving, many of the employees of the hotel headed north as well. Soon, with schools beginning to close for summer, other wealthy visitors from the South would begin their own annual sojourns to these island beach towns along the Atlantic Ocean.

Earlier in May, the war in Europe had come to an end with Germany's final surrender. The joy of a nation could be felt across the land. As the summer worn on, Katherine and Maggie plodded onward, their eventual release coming closer every day. In their free time, they sunbathed at the beach, swimming in the warming ocean waves. They made occasional trips to Brunswick for lunch and shopping in the town. And each Sunday morning they rode to St Simons, attending Sunday mass at Saint Williams Chapel. Occasionally, they would approach and say hello to Father Z, the priest always assuring them that the King family was happy and well.

In the second week of August, the war with Japan came to a sudden and horrific end. The joyful celebration that rang throughout the country was noticeably tempered by the awe and bewilderment of a bomb that could create such incredible death and destruction. At his weekly mass the following Sunday, Father Zeller asked his parishioners to pray for the innocent Japanese people, particularly the women and children for whom no sufficient blame could ever be assessed. Still, with the war at its ending, many thousands of American soldiers would gratefully be returning home.

Soon, the month of September arrived, filled with even greater anticipation at the prospect of going home. Each day crawled ever so slowly to its end. On their final trip to Brunswick, Katherine implored to Maggie that she needed to walk surreptitiously by the King family home to say good-bye. It would surely be innocent enough. Without a question, Maggie understood. But as they walked furtively past the house, the home appeared silent and hollow in the afternoon sun. There was no Cassie King or other children playing outside, no baby toys strewn throughout the small front yard. Even though the curtains remained in the windows, and nothing seemed particularly out of order, an unexpected anxiety surged through Katherine's body, an unwanted concern that something might be wrong.

Maggie, however, felt no particular unease. It was just that nobody was home, like so many other daytime residences on the quiet neighborhood street. Nevertheless, later that night, as Katherine lay alone in her bed, the impression of that moment continued to haunt her thoughts.

On Sunday morning September 30th 1945 Katherine and Maggie Flynn woke up in their separate quarters and dressed for church. Following mass at St Williams Chapel, they found Father Leo Zeller to say their farewell. Father Z gave each young woman a hug and blessing for their safe trip home. Still, Katherine could not help but ask once again for any of news of the King family and her baby child. And as was the necessary imperative, the priest continued to maintain his guiltful deception, although he hoped for the final time. In fact, Father Leo Zeller knew more than he could ever relate. With the demilitarization of the war effort now underway, the young couple who had received the child had recently returned to their hometown somewhere north of Jacksonville. The baby child was now miles away from the home that Katherine Flynn might always recall within her reflections and memory. Despite his own conflictions over his lack of fidelity to the truth, Zeller held firm to the precepts of his Church's mandate in these matters, that such a deliberate obstruction would always be best for both the mother and child.

The two sisters returned to The Castle, beginning to pack their belongings for their early departure the following morning. Sue Ellen Dampeer stopped by with her husband to say her good-bye. She brought along a package of homemade brownies as a snack for the long train trip ahead. Over the past months Sue Ellen and Katherine had grown very close. Sue Ellen reminded the two girls that should they ever seek to return to The Castle, a job would surely be waiting. In the late afternoon, Katherine and Maggie took one last beach walk along the ocean's shore, saying farewell to this strange and beautiful isle that they likely might never see again. In the evening at seven p.m. they made their last call home, their mother sharing in the excited happiness of their imminent return.

Arising in the darkness of the following day, a car and driver waited as they packed their things aboard. Leaving the Castle behind, memories of their distant arrival a year before roamed amongst the hushed pine forests of this Southern world. Reaching the tiny railroad station at Thallman, this time they would not be alone. The morning sun had risen above the trees, and several other travelers stood along the worn wooden platform, their suitcases resting below. Not long after, the Silver Meteor could be heard in the distance, making its northern return.

For a Monday in October, the passenger cars were now spare and roomy, the morning train so early in its run. The two sisters easily packed their things and settled in for the trip. But minutes later, the porter came strolling down the aisle, proclaiming a short delay.

With a pause in this journey before her, Katherine Flynn fell into moments of silent reflection. And once again, a familiar recurring emptiness beset her. A surge of recollections forced their way into her thoughts. Her earlier morning excitement was now replaced by the weight of a lingering sense of loss she

could not avoid. In all these months gone by, Katherine had endured her fate without a tear, having been forced to tread ever
forward toward a duty that she had been directed to commit.
But now, this long unwanted responsibility was giving way to a
deep and undeniable sense of shame, and worse, burdened by
a fearful guilt that she was leaving something precious behind.

Just then the passenger cars jolted on the track, beginning
to roll slowly forward. Katherine turned her head, peering out
the window. The open fields of this place called Georgia began
to pass beside her, the train gradually picking up speed. With
each desolate moment, Katherine Flynn slipped further and
further away. It was only then that her tears began to flow,
falling toward a broken heart whose scar would never heal.

WESTERN
SWING

WESTERN SWING

"You'll feel better once you cross the Mississippi." Paul had told his sister by phone the night before. Now, on this early afternoon in May, Erin began to pass over the wide expanse of river below. The swollen Mississippi appeared to be pressing at its banks, full with winter runoff, perhaps threatening to flood. Erin's eyes darted quickly to take in the view. But the interstate traffic was intense, a roaring tractor-trailer barreling beside her, blocking any further chance to look away.

Paul was wrong. She didn't have that better feeling until hours later upon crossing the Missouri. Approaching this second river bridge, the bluffs of western Iowa rose beside her. Crossing the water below, she fought through the rush hour traffic of Omaha, Nebraska. Only then did that better feeling come over her. In the distance, a forever sky seemed to reach down and touch the flattened landscape of the plains. As the setting sun began its descent, the spare lonesomeness of western America stretched out towards the horizon. Erin could feel it now. She was finally leaving her life in the east behind, finally heading her way back home.

Tired from the third day of her drive, Erin turned off the exit for Lincoln, a college town that felt safe within her mind. She found a motel near the highway that looked like it was cheap, before getting a good night's rest. Early the next morning, she showered and dressed. She rearranged her belongings in the camper. Checking out of the motel, she stopped for gas and coffee before returning to the road.

With the dawning sun rising behind her, Erin pointed further west. Through the windshield, the green of spring mixed with the black earth of cornfields tilled and planted for future harvest. Sipping her coffee, she settled in for another long trip, hoping to reach Boulder by nightfall. There, her brother would be waiting to join her.

Until then, it would be a long day alone, accompanied by thoughts and reflections of her past. Yet, they would be mixed with anticipant notions of a future ahead. The past year or so had been hard. Erin had known for some time that things might never be right. Nevertheless, she had forced herself to believe that she might be wrong, that maybe something could change. But in the end, she couldn't reverse the necessities she felt about herself. She continued to care for Justin, just not in the same ways she had before.

It took some time to render that truth. There had been no determination of right or wrong, no tragic mistake or hurtful events that precipitated her decision. It was just the changes that often come with time. But how do you tell someone that your life wants to be somewhere else, with no persuasive reasons to explain, no purposeful intent or action that may have caused such a recognition. One can only admit that something has been lost, and would likely never come back again.

It hadn't always been that way, not in the beginning, nor for a very long time. When Justin had said, "let's go to New York City", she shared in that adventure. They had met at college in Portland, Oregon, enjoying their time together. Upon certain intimate moments Justin said he loved her, and she had answered the same. For the both of them, the security of their words and affections never really wavered.

But as the shared experiences of the big-city life went on and on, Erin began to grow tired, her sense of adventure beginning to fade. She missed the west coast of America. She missed the places she had grown to know. Something was changed in her, a strange feeling that time was beginning to run.

With her thirty-second birthday recently passed, she began to verbalize her desire to return. And despite being plagued with a measure of guilt, she hoped that Justin would offer no resistance, which he honestly confirmed. Thus, a final wedge had been driven. And so here she was today, alone with herself, living the decision she had made.

Erin understood she could not push these memories aside, knowing they would chase her for a time. Perhaps one day soon they would begin to slip away. It was odd to think about, the pull of the human psyche for distant places unknown, only to be followed by consistent yearnings for what might have been left behind.

Her mother and father had grown up in the east, before meeting and traveling together to the Great Northwest. They were hippies looking for a new place to be, a new life to live. Eventually, they found the little town of Port Swan, resting on the shores of the Puget Sound in Washington State. Both she and her older brother were born there. But when Erin was five and Paul was eight, their mother and father were separated, their father leaving for Seattle and a different life. Things were strange and painful for a time. Fortunately, she and Paul weren't the only kids in Port Swan whose parents had failed to stay together. For a lot of the kids, it wasn't unusual to be going to see your father in some other place.

But growing up on the edge of a continent had its own barriers of intent. Unless you were sailing to Hawaii, or heading for Alaska, there was only one way to go when your own youthful wanderlust began. And for many like Erin and her brother, Paul, Seattle wasn't far enough away. As for Paul, it had been Utah and the Rocky Mountains in Colorado. For herself and Justin it became the drama and busy excitement of New York City. And yet, over time, Erin's earlier desires to roam began to temper. She started to miss the west. She never begrudged Justin for wanting to stay. New York had always seemed to suit him better than her. Despite her current uncertainties, the wide open spaces that surrounded her this morning were filled with new intent.

Several hours passed. Erin left Interstate 80, heading southwest towards Denver. Across the flattened rangeland of eastern Colorado, she thought about the stories she'd read by the author, Kent Haruf, his books about people and life amidst these desperate plains. She could sense the strange and difficult realities of his characters as she drove so near his fictional world.

Not long after, the Rocky Mountains began to appear far into the distance, their jutting peaks capped in white, telling her she was close. Knuckling down, she entered the metropolis of Denver, battling the traffic, turning north towards Boulder. As the evening sky darkened again toward night, she called her brother to receive his guidance. She found him waiting on the street in front of his home, each of them holding a cell phone to their ear. The sight of Paul's presence in the headlights provided a renewed sense of comfort. She was happy to feel safe, despite her weary fatigue.

For the last number of years, Paul had lived and worked in both Utah and Colorado. In Moab, he learned to raft the river. In between the job, he hiked and rode mountain bikes, even taken up photography. At some point, he and his girlfriend moved to Boulder, where he worked seasonably for the Park Service, then doing construction or other odd jobs in town. Sadly, about a year ago their relationship had failed. Nevertheless, Paul had remained in Boulder, planning to work another season in Rocky Mountain National Park. His job would not begin until sometime later in May.

With weeks to go before the beginning of his contract, Erin was pleased that Paul would be joining her for the rest of the drive back to Washington. Together, they were planning to spend some time with their father in Seattle, before crossing over the Puget Sound to see their mother in Port Swan. It would only be a quick trip for Paul. As for her, Port Swan would be the time and place to figure out what was next.

Brother and sister spent a couple of days in Boulder, driving up to Nederland and Ward on their second afternoon. The following morning, after packing the camper with her brother's gear, they headed south to Denver and were back on the road. Upon reaching Interstate 70, they began their ascent through the Rockies, headed for Moab.

Later that afternoon, they descended from the high-country, down toward the rugged canyon-lands below. Picking up some supplies and several straps of firewood in Grand Junction, Paul drove further west to a deserted campground surrounded by dusty brush and stunted trees. It was a place that Paul had camped before, carved with miles of mountain-bike trails throughout the sand-washed terrain. With the fall of a darkened evening, they sat beside a campfire under a cold and starlit sky. Wrapped in their winter coats, beanie caps and gloves, Paul sipped from a pint bottle of whiskey, while Erin drank from a metal thermos cup filled with wine. By the fire, they talked about many things.

"You know," Paul began to admit, "lately, for some odd reason, I've begun to feel like time is getting short. I'd never thought about it much before, but now I'm not so sure. After the break-up, it was pretty tough for awhile. It was kind of like being lost in the woods, wondering which way to go. But now, even though I feel okay with things, I've begun to think about the clock. All of a sudden I'm halfway to forty and wondering where the time has gone. That maybe I better get serious about something, you know, like choosing what I really want to do with my life. Anyway, crazy stuff like that. Of course, right now, I don't have a clue what that something might be."

Erin sat silently, watching between the flames as her brother took another shot of whiskey from the bottle. She leaned back in her lawn chair, sipping from her wine.

"Well, misery loves company," she remarked half-heartedly. "Anyway, thanks a lot for bearing your soul."

Her brother was quick to respond, softening his words with worry. "Now wait a minute, I didn't mean to go to a bad place or anything. Not if this stuff is particularly hard for you. I know that you're probably going through the same kind of stuff right now. Sorry if I hit a nerve."

Erin easily shook her head. "No, no. It's not that," she countered. "Okay, well maybe it is, in a way. But not to worry. It just feels like I've got a big start on you already. A two-thousand mile start the last few days. That's all I meant.

In the firelight, Paul silently acknowledged her response.

"I'm just glad to be out here tonight," Erin continued. "Out here with you and the stars, this camp fire, and finally away from New York. It's been something I've been missing for a long time. And now it's finally coming to pass. It's not like there hasn't been any second thoughts, or even a sense of regret about certain things. But I suppose those concerns sort of come with the whole situation. Anyway, there's no need to be alarmed. I'm really okay with everything. In fact, I'm in total agreement with you on the question of what the future might bring. It's just that those particular thoughts have been going on for quite awhile now."

"And it sucks doesn't it," Paul responded. He suddenly stood up. Stick in hand, he began to stoke the fire.

"So tell me, sis," he asked jokingly, "is this what some people call a mid-life crisis? I've always heard about that so-called condition, I just never thought that I might be having one."

Erin let her gaze fall toward the sparks rising from the fire, mulling the question. "So, do think that's maybe what Mom and Dad had way back when," she asked. "A mid-life crisis?"

Paul remained standing in the fire light, his head turning slightly askew.

"Huh, I never really thought about it that way. Maybe it was. Well, that's something to think about."

Erin got up from her chair. "I need more wine. And we need to change the subject. But you know, I guess we both made it okay through Mom and Dad's mid-life crisis, or whatever one might call it. So there's no reason to think we can't make it through our own."

Paul remained standing by the fire as his sister made her way back toward the camper. "Yeah, I guess you're right," he agreed. Paul drew another sip of whiskey from the bottle.

"But hey, it sure is one beautiful night."

The following morning, sister and brother lazily awoke to a chilled blue sky. Paul started a small fire, burning up the last of the wood they had purchased the day before. Erin heated water for coffee on the camp stove. Sitting at their picnic table, the temperature warmed quickly under the gaze of an unobstructed sun. As they began to pack for the road, Erin removed her sweats, putting on a gray skirt and white top. Today, they would only be driving further down to Moab, to meet and stay overnight with some of Paul's old friends. She wanted to at least look presentable.

Back on the interstate, Paul took an exit onto a secondary road, a two-lane highway that would follow the Colorado River down to Moab. The road stretched empty and straight, far into the distant horizon. For a number of miles they passed only a single car. After pulling the truck over to relieve himself, Paul reached into the camper, pulling out his camera. Erin stood nearby, taking in the view.

"Hey, will you do me a favor? I want you to lie down in the middle of the road."

Turning her head, Erin gave her brother a disdainful look. "You're kidding me, right?"

"No. It will be cool. Hurry now, before a car might come."

Erin looked both ways down the highway, before smiling and quickly heading onto the pavement. She gently laid herself down across the center-line. Leaning on her elbow and striking a pose, Paul clicked several quick shots.

"Okay, I got it."

Erin stood up, brushing herself clean. As they both took a look through the viewfinder, Paul was all smiles.

"Yep, I got it. This will be great. Mom will love it."

Erin shook her head. "You're a trip. You know that don't you?"

Paul grinned in return, heading toward the truck. As they opened the doors to climb inside, Paul could see a vehicle coming their way.

"All right", he cheered. "Just in time."

Driving into Moab, Paul pointed out familiar places during his years living and working in the town. After eating lunch by the river, he suggested driving out to the Arches National Park. But they both agreed that being a tourist was not necessarily an appealing desire. Later in the afternoon, they met with several of his friends, before staying the night. Early the next morning, saying their good-byes, they got back on the road. Seattle and Port Swan were still a long ways to go.

Erin sat beside her brother at the rest stop, watching as Paul peered at the road atlas. "Utah is a really weird state," he began. "And Southeastern Idaho isn't much better. What do you say we stay on the interstate and head for Montana before turning west? Taking I-84 would shorten the trip, but, I'd rather head for Interstate 90 in Montana."

"I don't really care," Erin responded, "whatever you'd like to do."

"Well, I say we should keep on going, unless we find a nice place to camp somewhere. Or maybe just get a motel. There won't be much to see for awhile now."

"Sure," Erin agreed. "We got coffee, we got trail mix, and your music has been pretty good. You could turn it back on if you like."

Paul started the truck, accelerating back onto the interstate, settling in behind the wheel. He turned on the music, keeping it low.

Erin was enjoying the music that Paul had brought along for the trip. The songs kind of fit with their journey, the type of landscapes they had been passing along the way. Although not a musician, Paul had a keen sense of what he liked. It was different from the music that Erin normally listened to back east. There was the Brian Setzer Orchestra, Asleep At The Wheel, as well as more notable country and western artists like Willie Nelson and Dwight Yoakum. But he also had some Neil Young and Little Feat, musicians that their dad had always liked. Erin hadn't packed any music along. She had thought it best not to rock the boat with Justin over the division of too many things. It felt good to be hearing something new.

"So what did you mean when you said that Utah was a weird state," Erin inquired. "I mean you lived here for like five years, didn't you?"

"More like four, I think. Hell, I don't know. I just happened to be thinking about the goddamn Mormon influence in this state. Sort of feeling glad I wasn't around it anymore. Utah always reminds me of that whole institutional religion crap. You know, how religion has pretty much caused more death and misery in the world's history than any single deal."

Erin turned her head toward her brother. "I guess I've never thought about it that way. I usually think about the good things that churches do for people. You know, like worshipping together, providing food and shelter in times of need, doing all kinds of good works, those sorts of things."

"Yeah, but I'm not talking about those kinds of things, those good community things," Paul responded. "I'm talking about religion's history of power and control over people.

It seems like every religion sooner or later starts making all these rules. And pretty soon, they immediately start demanding strict obedience to those rules. And then, if you don't happen to submit to those rules, they go about destroying you. And believe me, the Mormons are particularly good at that little exercise, they're almost like a cult. You either buy into their view of the world, or you're out. You're either a robot to their mandates or you are an enemy of the church and destined for hell. It's kind of hard to explain to people, but you can feel that robotic response if you choose to live outside their insular domain. Of course these days it isn't as bad as it used to be. Times have changed some in Utah. But you can still feel that strange almost lock-step reality for the hardcore folks, and their so-called tablets and all that shit."

Erin spoke quietly. "I guess I don't really understand."

"I know," Paul agreed. "You really have to experience it for yourself. It can be very subtle. But believe me, it still exists under the surface here in this state. It's like some kind of strange brainwashed behavior. And you know it when you encounter it. But I'm not just talking about the Mormons, as weird as they are. I'm talking about all those other cults of faith, the ones who use their power and punishment to maintain their control, and quickly create enemies of others just to keep that control. I mean, as far as history goes, it could just as easily be the Catholics, the Muslims, or all those other crazy sects. You know, the ones that Dad used to mention, the Moonies, or those Rajneesh knuckleheads back in Oregon, not to mention the People's Temple and the Jim Jones' catastrophe."

There was a momentary pause in the cab of the truck. But Paul went on. "Now, I'm not talking about spirituality, at least not in relation to the existence of good and evil in this world. I mean, most people understand the obvious necessity to a have a moral code for humanity. Rather, I'm just talking about how organized religion can often become another form of human corruption and greed. Spirituality and belief are great if you just keep it to yourself. But whenever some so-called preacher starts to build some grand house of worship, look the fuck out!"

Erin was surprised by her brother's apparent strong opinion. It wasn't an opinion she had ever heard from him before.

"But don't you think people need something to believe in, something to give their life a goodness of purpose and intent? Don't you think most of the Mormons just want to do what's right?"

"Well, that's exactly my point," Paul answered. "Why then all this other crap? Like it's either heaven or hell, either my way or the highway, that kind of thing. I mean even the Amish people kick out their own kids for wearing regular clothes, and maybe wanting to be like the other kids their age. It's all bullshit. Freedom of religion is okay, it's good, believe whatever you want to believe. But don't start making rules about how everyone else is supposed to live, then burning them at the stake if they choose to think differently." There was another pause before Paul continued.

"Religion should really be like you and Mom. You both have your magic stuff and your belief in karma. You guys got your incense, and you got your lucky trinkets. But you don't go around telling everybody else they better do the same. You don't go around tar and feathering your neighbors until they start believing like you do. That's all I'm trying to say."

Erin broke into a laugh at her brother's description of the things around their mother's home.

"Now, wait a minute", she shot back, a hint of sarcasm in her tone. "I'm not as bad as Mom, you know that. She just believes in the spirit and the eternal goodness of everyone. And she just likes her little symbols to remind her of those things. Lucky trinkets? Is that what you call them? When we see her, I'm going to tell her what you called them."

Erin's response managed to break her brother's serious frame of mind. He chuckled at her retort.

"Yeah, that's what Dad used to call them from time to time, her lucky trinkets. Of course, they were already living apart by then. But he really was just picking on her, that's all. Just making a little fun."

"Yeah, and now you've grown up to be just like him, is that what you're telling me? Men.........., good-god almighty! Would someone please tell me, why in the world God thought that 'men' were such a good idea? In fact, it was goddamn men who started all this trouble in the first place. All this trouble that you now think is so terrible and unfair. So please tell me, why in the heck did God make that mistake?"

Paul just smiled at the windshield in response, while considering an answer. He loved these moments when he could just tease and get his sister's goat. "Football," he advised. "God just needed some guys to play football."

Erin turned and stared at her brother with a menacing grimace. "Yes, that must be it," she sharply replied. "Football, just another kind of war, that's all."

It wasn't much longer and the drive north crossed over the Utah state line, leaving religion behind.

"Hey, would you mind putting on that CD we listened to yesterday?"

Erin and her brother had ended their drive the evening before, stopping overnight at a motel near Idaho Falls. The current morning plan would be to get through Montana, perhaps reaching Spokane by evening. If so, it would be another long day's drive. Erin started behind the wheel.

"Which one," Paul asked?

"The thousand miles from nowhere one," Erin answered.

"Oh, Dwight Yoakam. Yeah, sure. It's good isn't it?"

Paul shuffled through the small cardboard box of music he had brought along for the trip.

"Thank you," Erin said. "That song is kind of what it feels like out here, like a lot of wide-open nothing. There's just so much range and sky, and the mountains in the distance."

"You got that right," Paul returned. He slipped the CD into the player on the dashboard of the truck, punching up the song Erin requested, the music beginning to play. Erin mutely mouthed the lyrics to the song as she drove along the highway. When the song finished play, Paul turned the music down a bit.

"Yeah, I first heard that song at the end of a movie I was watching. But damn, I can't seem to remember the title today. It was a dark thriller film and full of suspense. It had Nicholas Cage and Dennis Hopper. And Hopper, geez louise. He played this really creepy hired-killer dude, which he was obviously great at. Damn, I hate it when I can't remember certain things. But actually, even Dwight Yoakam was in the movie. He had a bit part as a truck driver. Anyway, it's kind of funny you should ask for that song, because it takes place in Wyoming, in western country like this."

"Would I like it," Erin asked?

"Are you kidding? No way! It's definitely not a 'chick flick'."

"Well, here you go again. Always defining what we women might like or not like. And you don't even realize it, do you?" Unable to help himself, Paul answered the question.

"Hey, but you know it's true. That movie has guns and murder and a whole bunch of creepy assholes. Even the leading actress in the film is a bad person. You'd be scared and want to walk out. You're just like Mom when it comes to that stuff, holy smoke. You two always prefer some kind of romantic love story, blessed with a beautiful happy ending. I can't tell you how many times I had to endure those films way back when."

"We do not," Erin was quick to respond. "But even if we did, that doesn't mean other women might not like your movie. It might not be a 'chick flick' for them. Do you get my point?"

Paul leaned back against his seat, his eyes turned up to the sky, which happened to be the top of the cab. "All right, already," he admitted with a sigh. "It could be a 'chick flick', yes, as well as a 'guy flick'. Is that what you want me to say? But whenever I remember that damn title, I'm going to send it to you. And you've got to promise to watch it all the way through, okay? Right to the bloody end. Mother of mercy ....!"

Erin turned her head toward her brother, giving him a smirk, then quickly shifted her eyes back to the highway. "We'll see," was all she would say.

Outside, the landscape was little more than barren range-land, its dry and rugged beauty tinged with the green of spring. Shadowed mountains lay in the distance, their peaks topped with the white of retreating winter snows. The interstate traffic was light, the drive gradually rising in elevation toward the Continental Divide. Shortly after, the truck crossed the Montana state line, another marker in their journey having been reached. Soon the road began a gradual descent. The speed limit was now seventy-five miles an hour, the surrounding horizon remaining far into the distance.

Now silent with her own thoughts, Erin's recent life in New York felt so ridiculously remote. A thousand miles from nowhere seemed much more than the title to a song. Rather, it was imbued with a sense of openness and freedom, a freedom she continued to both welcome and fear.

Near the city of Butte, Interstate 15 met its connection with Interstate 90, the journey once again turning for the west. At a rest stop, she and Paul exchanged positions, Paul taking over the wheel. They were making good time. Her brother felt certain they could reach Spokane by early evening. For Erin, it was somewhat hard to believe that by the end of the day she might be back in the state of Washington. She would soon be closing in on her old home, facing the next chapter in her life. It would be a mystery waiting to be solved.

The American road of Montana and the West. Highway signs and mile markers, entrance and exit ramps, light stanchions and guard rails. Overpasses and median strips, worn pavements and passing lanes, with freeway shoulders scattered with abandoned vehicles or road kill. Telephone poles and fence posts strung with wire. Cut banks and pointed hills dotted with trees. In the distance, mountain peaks pocked in white, framed by cumulus thunderheads casting blackened shadows across rock and field, with rays of splintered sunlight streaming between. Rest stops with cheap coffee and the sound of flushing toilets. Parking lots serviced by weathered panhandlers, all seeking ragged cardboard redemption, while mumbling 'god bless you' words of careless gratitude, as fossil-born motors crank again to a start.

Once again back on the asphalt strip. Tractor trailers and tandems, motor homes and fifth wheels, silvery sedans racing ahead, dodging lackadaisical drivers on speed control. Insects make funeral homes on windshields and grills. Cops hide behind rocky outcroppings, beaming electronic devices across the road, before spitting gravel and flashing lights as they begin to hunt their prey. The spacious breadth of a fast and furious country under a wild forever sky. All the while, a Stray Cat's tune rocks on the juke. With windows down, it sings loud against the violent air.

Paul and his Erin push further toward a falling afternoon sun. A jacked-up rig with oversized tires goes rocketing past, rifles hanging in the rear window of the cab, leaving them far behind.

Erin shifts in her seat, the sight of the guns prompting her unease. She turns toward her brother, his eyes focused ahead.

"Why is it that so many men feel the need to have a gun in their lives," she quietly asks.

Interrupted from his own thoughts, Paul let the question hang in the air. "You mean those guys? I guess I'm not really sure. I certainly have my opinions. But are you sure you want to hear them?"

"Well, I certainly have mine," Erin responded firmly, "but they obviously don't make any difference in this stupid country."

"Well, it happens to be a lot of things, sis. Maybe our history for one thing. Like the Revolution and the settling of the West. The need to hunt in order to put food on the table, or protect the family home. I guess those would be good for starters. But mostly in these days and times, that's all a crock of shit. These days it's all about money to my mind. It's the gun manufacturers, and their lobby arm the NRA. As well as those anti-government talk-radio assholes, railing on stations you can hear every night on the AM dial. Not to mention their corporate advertisers, who allow all this conspiracy crap to be sold for the money it will bring. Unfortunately, the emotion of fear still sells in this damn world. Anger and hate still sells. The divisions of 'us' versus 'them' still sells. Anyway, that's my two cents for what it's worth."

"But what about those murderous weapons of war that can kill dozens of innocent people all at one time," Erin questioned. "Don't those guys in that truck have children and families too? Why can't they understand the danger? Don't they want to be safe as well?"

"Yeah, you'd think so. But it's so ingrained, what can you do? They've been sold that big government is coming to get them. Or maybe it's the commies, or the gangs, the Islamic terrorists, take your pick. As a result, in recent years, even some of my ranger buddies in the national park have to carry a gun. Guns in the very places we have put aside and protected to afford children and families some simple peace and solitude. I recently read somewhere that the United States has more guns per person than anywhere else on the planet." Paul tried to make a joke.

"So, are you angry and need a gun? Hey, just raise your hand. Thinking about killing yourself? Hell, just go ask your neighbor."

"But then again, murder and mayhem isn't just an American problem. There are much higher rates of killing and death across this world. But I doubt whether that little piece of knowledge would be much consolation, particularly when someone is aiming at you with a semi-automatic weapon. And all you were doing that day was making a simple trip to the grocery store. Anyway, it certainly gives some pretty absurd meaning to the concept of a peaceful democracy, that's for sure."

Erin remained coldly silent in her seat, a pained expression upon her face. Paul quickly realized he had gone too far, that this was not the time or place to be cracking wise, especially to his one and only sister in the world.

"Hey, sorry to talk like that," he tried to apologize. "Those guys in that truck were probably pretty good guys. They likely have brothers and sisters, maybe girlfriends or wives they love very much. And maybe they have kids they would do anything to protect. It's just not that easy, Erin. Sometimes, it just happens to be the goddamn ways of this world. And hell, we're in Montana of all places. People here just have a different way of getting along."

"I understand," Erin answered, appearing to wipe something clear of her eye. "I was just thinking about something else in my life. But I don't want to talk about it now. Let's just change the subject, could we? I didn't mean to bring it up. It's just thinking about all those innocent families who lose a loved one forever and ever, and their little boy or girl was just going off to school."

"You want to hear some tunes for awhile. Maybe some more western swing tunes," Paul asked. The discussion surely didn't need to go any further.

"Yes, please, I'd like that," she answered.

"We'll be in Missoula soon," Paul calmly advised. "We'll stop and get a good meal. Then we'll head for Spokane and get another room. I've got an idea for tomorrow's drive that I think you will like."

"What's that?"

"I'll tell you later. We'll make it a surprise."

After dinner in Missoula, Paul kept control of the wheel, letting Erin ride by his side. With the music turned off, they rode along in both discussion and silence toward the northern neck of Idaho and Spokane. Eventually, the landscape gave way to darkness, their headlights piercing through the night. With a cup of coffee and his second wind now in gear, Paul dodged around the big rigs, pushing their journey further west.

He and Erin talked about all kinds of things; about home, about dreams and parallel realities, about the state of the planet, of over-population and climate change, of the hirsute speed of life, and finally about love and regret.

Erin reflected on how she and Justin had slowly grown apart. First there had been the loss of passion, followed by an unspoken coldness they each had begun to feel inside. Slowly, it became as if they were living as roommates under the same roof. Yet, each was too conflicted by the situation to confront their current reality. And thus, silently, each within themselves, they began to imagine separate plans, until Erin had finally forced the break.

But as soon as Justin had quickly agreed, Erin suddenly felt terribly alone, wondering if she had made a mistake. At that point she became troubled by regret. There would now be no happy marriage, no future and family joined together. What remained was a weakened emptiness inside, coupled with those fears about what would be next in her life.

"I felt like a bird on a wire," Erin tried to explain, "my little head turning this way and that, as if looking for a caring friend."

It took all her perseverance to break the spell. But once it came, she began to look ahead, the faith in her decision restored. Driven to succeed with her task, she bought the truck and camper, gave notice to her job. And with each practical step in the process her anticipation grew, finally feeling excited about a new life and future ahead. She would return home to Washington and figure things out.

Paul listened with understanding. His sister's recent situation obviously felt familiar, but in a somewhat different way. His own failures had been far less mutual in their realization, for he had been the one suddenly left behind. Although his own estrangement had likely been present for awhile, he hadn't paid it much attention. And for one guilty of such a sin, they often become the last to know.

His own circumstances were not as recent as his sister's, and would never be as honest in their telling. Maybe it wasn't in a man's DNA to share those kinds of emotions, to be able to speak to their effects. Instead, it was best to share as little as possible. That had been his own predictable response, to simply let the agony of time slowly carry the past away. For in the end, Paul figured the real reasons were often little more than irreconcilable differences. Differences that no plaintive words or actions could ever hope to change. But Erin was his closest companion. He needed to give his feelings a more measured response.

"You know," he began, "even if you and Justin had gotten married, it could have turned out the same. Maybe if you and he would have had a child or two, things might have been different. There would have been a shared responsibility, a lot more reason to make things work. But as we both know, even for Mom and Dad that was not the case. When it occurred for us, it really hurt a lot. But Dad stayed close and we got over it. And eventually we came to understand. It's sort of like that bumper sticker you see around, 'Shit Happens'. It just does sometimes.

And mostly people get over it, before finding a way to move on."

"I suppose you're right," Erin agreed. "I guess you and I were like that bird on the wire. But it did hurt, and I felt so scared and lost."

"Hey, but we survived. And mom and dad survived. And they both did their best for us. In fact, we were pretty lucky compared to some of our other friends. We were spared any violence or hate. And nobody should beat themselves up too much. It is what it is, just a part of life. And we still have time. But we have to stay open to it, try to be happy and let it come."

Erin shifted in her seat. "I think I am going to close my eyes for awhile. Are you going to be okay?"

"Sure, I'm good. I'm going to get us to Spokane."

"I love you big brother," Erin said gently. "Thank you so much for coming along."

"Piece of cake, sis. I love you, too. Now get some rest."

When Erin awoke, the truck was slowing to a stop. Rubbing her eyes, she stared at an overhead red light through the windshield. "So where are we now? Are we in Spokane?"

"Yep, we made it. We're back home in Washington."

"Are we going to stay here for the night?"

"Well, not exactly. Do you remember that surprise I mentioned earlier? I'm thinking of changing things up a bit. At least if you think it's okay?"

"So, what's up," Erin asked?

Paul continued driving onto a busy thoroughfare, the evening lights of the city surrounding them.

"Well first, we got to get some gas. But I've been thinking of getting off the interstate and taking Highway 20 the rest of the way to Port Swan. So instead of stopping to see Dad in Seattle, we would drive first to see Mom at home. We can take Highway

20 all the way, head over the North Cascades, then take the ferry into town. But only if you agree. The route will be a little slower of course, but definitely a more beautiful trip. What do you think?"

"No, that sounds great to me," Erin answered. "And we haven't told Dad yet when we would arrive, so it's not like he is waiting for us, right?"

"Yeah, that's what I thought. Let's do it. I'm not in any hurry to deal with Seattle right now."

"But what about tonight," Erin inquired?

"Okay, so we're going to drive north for about another hour or so. Do you happen to remember that summer when I worked as a crew leader for the Youth Corps? I think you were just getting out of high school that year."

"Oh, that summer when you were in Eastern Washington? I do remember."

"Well, my crew did a lot of work north of here, north of Spokane. I'd really enjoy driving back through that area again. So for tonight, we'll drive up to a town called Newport. I know a good motel there. And Newport is where Highway 20 begins."

"Well, the motel part sure sounds good. I sure don't want to have to set up camp tonight."

"Yeah, we'll camp tomorrow night along the way. I know a good spot in the Methow Valley. And the next day we can make it easily into town."

Sometime later, they arrived in Newport for the night. The next morning greeted them with sunny warm skies. Heading north out of town, they followed a wide and deep river called the Pend Oreille for fifty miles.

At a junction nearing the Canadian border, Highway 20 took a hard turn to the west. Climbing up Tiger Pass, the road seemed enclosed by a thick forest of trees, and later pocketed with a chain of pristine mountain lakes.

Paul described the landscape as the 'north country', saying the locals often referred to the area as the 'forgotten corner' of the state. Although the landscape was not exactly the same, Erin mentioned how the current terrain vaguely reminded her of their home on the Olympic Peninsula.

Paul agreed. "This region easily gets more rain than most of Eastern Washington," Paul remarked. "Still, it's pretty damn cold in winter, and much hotter and drier in summer. It's mostly pine country, but there are even pockets of western red cedar over here, which tells you something about the rain they get. But more unique to this country are the larch trees, what the local folks call 'tamaracks'. In the fall, their needles turn a yellow-orange in color. Along with the brighter yellow leaves of the birch trees, this area is an awesome sight in the fall. But for now, it's just the regular green of springtime, along with the white-water run of the rivers and creeks."

As the drive fell in elevation toward the town of Colville, Paul continued with memories of his travels in the area. "In a way, a lot of people don't know this country very well. Sometimes, I think it's because they believe this place to be the land of the Nazi sympathizers, or so they've been told. But I have found that opinion to be an obvious misconception. The people here can be especially friendly and down-to-earth. Sure, they're conservative in their outlook and politics, just like a lot of places in America. And over the last decade or so they have struggled financially due to a dying timber economy. But despite their troubles, they are the kind of people who would not waste a moment to help you out in a jam, or even think twice about waving hello to you on the road. Especially when it comes to the tribal folks over here. Heck, they pretty much wave at everybody they pass on the road."

Paul continued. "I sort of miss being in this part of the country at times. It just feels more real to me. Boulder is so full of a liberal arrogance these days. And according to Mom, Port Swan has become similar in that very same way. It's kind of that smug attitude of privilege that some people exude toward the world. They think that just because they have money in their wallet their shit doesn't stink, that only they know the right way to live in this world."

"But what I like so much around these parts, is that what you see is what you get. There is a base honesty with the folks here, at least the ones who have lived here all their lives. For some reason I really appreciate that."

"But aren't they angry about what's happened to them," Erin asked, "I mean like the loss of jobs and opportunity and things?"

"Yeah, I think deep down they are. Like they feel like certain things have been taken from them. Their children have to move away for work. And the mom and pop stores can hardly make it anymore. The overhead is just too high. Most of the timber mills are closed and not coming back. And because of the changes in technology and the global economy, the few jobs that do remain here don't need as many people. So the future for them is dim. But on the outside, they really don't let it show. They stay close to their own, and just grind it out day after day."

"But why do we see so much intolerance in this country," Erin asked? "Aren't we all in this together in some way?"

"Yeah, I think that's where some people have gotten off track. They have been sold that it's because of immigration, or big government entities like the Forest Service. They've been told that's the reason they're in this fix. Then the hate mongers come along and tell them they're getting a raw deal. They tell them that it's all those other people who are the ones to blame, people of a different color or religion. But really, it's just the American oligarchs that are stoking these fears. They know that creating divisions will always be good for business. They try to sell them gold or guns and all that shit. Well, you can't eat gold and guns as far as I can tell. And these folks would only have to talk to their Native American neighbors to know how this story goes."

"Anyway, in my view, the bottom line is that the super-rich will always find ways to divide and conquer. They create divisions of hate amongst the ones most marginalized. They use flags and steeples and other symbols in order to distract them. They urge them to go to church and pray for their eternal salvation, while getting them to donate their very last dime as their going out the door. That way the status quo is never shaken. And that's just fine for those cats living at the top." Paul turned toward his sister as if seeking some response.

"Geez, you sure go to some dark places sometimes," Erin complained. "All I really wish is that people could be happy and well, to just love their neighbor and enjoy the beauty and spirit of life together. And whenever they can, to try and help others in need. All this other stuff you talk about just gets in the way."

Paul looked ahead down the road, speaking toward the windshield. "I understand. I suppose that's what I want too. But I guess until it comes, I will remain someone arguing for true democracy and change."

Erin smiled to herself, realizing an opportunity. "Well, don't you worry, big brother, my feelings are probably just a 'chick thing' anyway. But one day, you'll see. One day the women of the world won't really need your help. One day we will fix it all, and make things right." Paul laughed in response, raising a finger to the sky.

"Okay, you win. That's two big points for the little sister. I guess she wins the kewpie doll, today. So step right up and take your pick."

Leaving Colville, the drive passed through the town of Kettle Falls, before crossing over a narrow steel bridge, traversing Lake Roosevelt and the Columbia River. The lake appeared low with water. There were wide swaths of sandy bottom, with high exposed banks on either side. Paul explained that many miles to the south, the Coulee Dam lay forged deep into a desert canyon. And with the springtime runoff, the strictly-managed river system would soon be filling with huge amounts of water. Most of the seasonal melt coming from snow packs in Canada, as well as the western side of the Rockies in Montana.

Up and away from the Columbia, Highway 20 began a climb over the Kettle Range and Sherman Pass, before curving its way down to the town of Republic. At Republic, Paul gave up the wheel, trading places with his sister. Erin continued the drive, heading further west. Soon the terrain broke out into the wide expanse of the Okanogan Highlands, a spreading openness of elevated rangeland, surrounded by roughened crests of timbered hills topped with Ponderosa pines.

Descending down into another canyon, the route turned due south along the Okanogan River. Close to the river, the northern reaches of Washington's apple country began to appear, with thousands of acres of orchards resting along water's edge. With the advent of spring, this normally dry interior lay blessed with verdant green, the white apple blossoms giving way to budding spheres of tiny fruit. All the while a warm and brilliant sun shined within a magnificent sky of cumulus blue.

Erin was filled with the beauty of the domain before her eyes. She felt a lightness of being within her, a strange sensation of desire she hadn't felt in so long a time. With Kd Lang's "Absolute Torch and Twang" playing in the cab, with the windows rolled down, her elbow resting against the rushing air of the road, she could feel a sense of being happy again, free with a spirit she couldn't describe. Angling further over another crest of narrow timbered hills, the highway poured down into the Methow River Valley, its whitewater fury reflecting the sunlight as it tore over broken logs and rock. And then, stretching before them in the distance, she could see the high mountain barrier of the North Cascades. Further beyond, the evergreen and salted water of the Pacific coast lay hidden over its divide.

In the mid-afternoon, they made camp by a lake just outside the town Winthrop, letting the solar heat warm their winter skins. Later, after catching some dinner and drinks at a cowboy bar in town, they slept outside under chilling western stars. Tomorrow they would finally be reaching home.

The following morning they made coffee and breakfast, casually starting their final day. It would only be a five or six hour trip to go. As they packed up their gear, Erin called their mom, surprising her with news of their imminent arrival. Back on the road, the Methow Valley began to narrow as they approached the jagged mountains above. After a harsh winter of snow and ice, the pass through the North Cascades had opened for traffic only a week before.

Soon enough, they began their sharp ascent. The truck climbed quickly in elevation as the roadside boundaries grew heavy with white. Behind them, the morning sun rose further in the sky. Ever higher, the pavement seemed to narrow in width, its shoulders disappearing. Mounds of snow reached as high as basketball rims, the truck tunneling between them as they crested Washington Pass.

Paul stayed silent, his hands gripped tight to the wheel, steering close as he passed the oncoming traffic. Erin kept her eyes steady ahead, also remaining speechless as they drove. Dipping lower for a time, the highway climbed again toward another pass, before finally beginning a gentle descent, the road widening a bit to their grateful relief.

"Sure glad I didn't get stoned this morning," Paul joked as he began to relax, his tension easing behind the wheel.

Exhaling a sigh, Erin returned a response. "Wow. That sure was scary for awhile. How do they ever get those piles of snow so high and straight?"

"I don't know," Paul answered. "Some pretty big equipment plows, I guess. But these mountains sure got some snow this year, I'll tell you that."

As the elevation continued to drop, the snow-pack began to ease further away from the road, allowing brother and sister to marvel and enjoy the magic of a whitened landscape, pressing against trees and sky. With the sun heating above, humps of snow fell from the branches of towering firs, plopping down toward the earth below. Steady rushes of water emptied off the steep cut banks to their left, disappearing into hidden culverts below the road.

"It's all so beautiful," Erin expressed. "I'm really glad we chose to come this way. It's just so cool to be back in this world, and now to be so close to home. Sometimes it's hard to believe I ever went away."

"I've been sort of thinking the same thing," Paul followed, "at least for the last couple of days. I suppose every place has its own sense of adventure and beauty, whether it's the city, the mountains, or some faraway places over the seas. I guess people have always desired to find something new in their lives, to see what's around that next bend, or over the next hill. I guess that's what brought Mom and Dad out here way back in the day. And as for us, I guess we both needed to do the same, just in a different way."

"You probably won't believe this," Erin began, "but I met people in New York who had never once been beyond the five boroughs of the city. That really blew my mind."

"Huh, that is really hard to imagine," Paul replied, before pausing with the thought. "I guess you could say they must have found their comfort zone," he stated sarcastically. "Either that or they couldn't find a way out. But what can one really say," he questioned? "To each his own I suppose."

"Yeah," Erin confirmed, "but pretty sad as well."

Highway 20 wound further down its timbered slope, slowly falling toward the west coast of America. Along its descent, Erin and Paul could look below the road, catching a short glimpse of the Diablo Lake Reservoir, the water's fabulous turquoise-green color sparkling brilliant in the midday sun. Eventually, their journey gave way to the forested foothills of Western Washington, before landing on the flatland plain of the Skagit River Valley. Upon this arrival, the populated busyness and pace of the United States made its return. After fighting through the congested corridor of Interstate 5, they passed over a river bridge to Whidbey Island, before steering south within the island's interior to the ferry landing near Coupeville. Paying the fare, they would have to wait for most of an hour before making the final crossing to their childhood home in Port Swan.

Having parked in the loading area, brother and sister climbed out of the truck, walking to the beach to stretch their legs. Returning to the camper, they rolled down the windows, waiting for the boat to come. Erin called their mother on her cell phone, saying they were close. Then, resting back in her seat, she breathed a sigh and spoke.

"Well, here we are, back where we both began."

"Yep, six days on the road and we're gonna be home tonight," Paul half-sang a lyric from the song. "So, are you excited to be back here for awhile, back in the Great Northwest?"

"Oh yeah," his sister replied." I can hardly wait to see Mom and be back at the house. But you know, at the same time I've been doing a lot of wondering about whatever could be next."

"Well, that's to be expected," Paul agreed. "But hey, don't worry, things will work out. Spend some time with Mom for awhile. I know that will be good for the both of you. You'll figure things out. Something new will come up. It always does."

"And you," Erin asked?

Paul stretched in his seat. "Well, I've got the park season to do. So I don't have to think about things for awhile. But Boulder doesn't necessarily hold me anymore, if that's what you mean. Just like you, I guess I'll see what's happening in the fall."

Erin slightly nodded her head. "After we go over to see Dad, and then you go back on the plane, I've been thinking of going down to Portland to see Jessie, maybe check things out down there."

"Oh, yeah? She's got that little restaurant going down there, right?"

"She does. She says it's really doing well."

"But you're not thinking about waitressing again or anything, are you? You're an accomplished paralegal now. You can go anywhere with that experience."

"No, I'm not thinking about that, but I do need to get back working pretty soon. And maybe Portland would be good again. I mean I've got a lot of old friends down there."

"Well, they say Portland's the place to be these days, from what I hear," Paul returned. "A pretty young city, so it might be a good place to start."

For a time, there was an extended silence between them. Out in the water, they could see the ferry boat approaching.

"I don't know," Erin mused. "Have you ever thought about having children? Perhaps having a family and that sort of thing?"

Paul turned his head toward his sister. "Well, that's a big question, sis?" They both watched as the boat slid into the dock. "Well yeah, it wasn't so long ago where I actually thought it might be coming sooner rather than later. But then we both know what happened. So I guess for now it will fall down the 'to do' list for awhile."

"Me, too, I suppose," Erin whispered quietly. "I guess I need to do the same. Put it down the list."

The ferry emptied of cars before loading for its return. Sister and brother ascended up the stairs, taking a booth in the cabin. Through the wide windows of the boat, they could see the afternoon sun as it began its predictable fall over the Straits of Juan de Fuca, and further towards the Pacific horizon.

Gazing out across the dark green water, they once again fell silent with their thoughts. But then, Paul shifted suddenly in his seat. His eyes grew wide, a happy smile crossing his face.

"I got it. It just came to me." He stared at his sister, a dumb-ass expression bearing down upon her.

"What, you nut ball," she questioned, staring back!

"The movie," Paul answered! "That crazy movie that you just have to see. It was called 'Red Rock West'. I've been trying to remember the title for three freaking days. It finally came to me."

Letting her brother's words sink in, Erin's expression began to take on a devilish appearance, before delivering a mocking response.

"Okay. Okay," she spoke with firm interrogation. "I say we rent it tonight. Yes, tonight. That way, Mom and I will have a chance to test your little so-called chauvinistic theory. And maybe, just maybe, put you in your place."

Paul stared back at her. "You're on, sister," he declared, answering as if accepting the challenge.

But deeper inside, Paul knew he was screwed. There would be no turning back. If he could ever be certain about anything in his life these days, he could be certain about this. His little sister was going to watch every last second of that damn film, every last second till the television went black. And yet nevertheless, he would love her all the same.

As the ferry began turning through its course, the town of Port Swan appeared in the distance, the old brick buildings of its waterfront district rising to meet the bluffs of historic homes above. Beyond, the blue sky of spring raised high toward the heavens. And somewhere within that ultimate void, the reluctant hopes of two unknown futures would eventually find their way.

THE GREEN
AND
THE BLONDE

AN AMERICAN JOURNEY

John Thomas Baker

THE GREEN AND THE BLONDE

Seen through the prism of historical context and geography,
The *Green and the Blonde* explores a unique and slowly
forgotten time in America. John Thomas Baker presents
and honest portrait of a post-war generation
that answered a siren's call.

thegreenandtheblonde.com
Available for preview and purchase on Amazon (Kindle and POD)
visit our facebook page

Lost Wages Publishing LLC, John Thomas Baker
lostwagespub@olympus.net
PO Box 1051, Port Townsend, WA 98368
360-385-6564

John Thomas Baker has lived and traveled
in the Northwest for almost forty years.
He currently resides with family and friends
in Port Townsend, Washington,
on the Olympic Peninsula.

ACKNOWLEDGEMENTS

I would like thank the following for their assistance in regard to the publication of this work. Marsha Slomowitz for her competent book design skills, as well as her thoughtful understanding regarding the appearance I was hoping to create. Michael Hale, well-known Port Townsend artist and friend, whose cover art once again reflects my personal intents. Bill Mawhinney, promoter of local writers and their work, for his editorial suggestions regarding the text. Also, to Charlotte Wedin, whose intimate knowledge and experience regarding the care of the aged and infirm in our society was of significant assistance. As well, several dear friends whose emotional support never fails during the long hours of literary gestation. Rob and Anne Sears, Julie Knott, and writers Gary Lemons and Bill Ransom. As well, to the 'Breakfast Boys', who sometimes have to lend me an occasional ear. To all, I am lucky to be within the orbit of your lives.

As a side note, the external design of 'Western Swing' hopes to pay a sense of homage to the illustrative genre of western novels within the literary pantheon of American writing. A simple gesture to the freedom and feelings evoked by a wide and lonesome western sky.

~JTB